05/15

# INNOCENT
# DAMAGE

## ALSO BY ROBERT K. LEWIS

*Untold Damage*
*Critical Damage*

# INNOCENT DAMAGE

A MARK MALLEN NOVEL

## ROBERT K. LEWIS

MIDNIGHT INK
WOODBURY, MINNESOTA

First Edition
First Printing, 2015

Cover art: iStockphoto.com/5457540/terex,
iStockphoto.com/19016042/Photo_HamsterMan,
iStockphoto.com/8297743/Manuela Krause
Cover design by Kevin R. Brown

Midnight Ink, an imprint of Llewellyn Worldwide Ltd.

This is a work of fiction. Names, characters, places, and incidents are either the product of the author's imagination or are used fictitiously, and any resemblance to actual persons, living or dead, business establishments, events, or locales is entirely coincidental.

**Library of Congress Cataloging-in-Publication Data**
Lewis, Robert K.
    Innocent damage / Robert K. Lewis.— First edition.
        pages ; cm — (A Mark Mallen novel ; 3)
    ISBN 978-0-7387-4110-9 (softcover)
1. Ex-police officers—Fiction. 2. Missing children—California—San Francisco—Fiction. 3. Kidnapping—Fiction. I. Title.
    PS3612.E979I56 2015
    813'.6—dc23

                                        2014045140

Midnight Ink
Llewellyn Worldwide Ltd.
2143 Wooddale Drive
Woodbury, MN 55125-2989
www.midnightinkbooks.com

Printed in the United States of America

## DEDICATION

*Dawn, thank you for all that you have done for me, all these long and complex years.*

# ACKNOWLEDGMENTS

What a journey. Once again, my heart swells with gratitude toward all the people that have made this road possible yet one more time:

My agent, Barbara Poelle. She'll throw a barstool through a window just to hear the music of the shattering glass—then pay the repair bill with a grin as she asks for another round.

The entire staff at Midnight Ink: my editor Terri Bischoff, the ever-patient Kathy Schneider, Beth Hanson, Rosie Wallner, and of course Katie Mickschl, too. Thank you for working so hard to bring Mallen out of the darkness and into the light.

To my family: Sandy, Ed, Janet, Ron, Sherri, Jim, Garrett, Jamie, and Siobhan. Thank you so much for sticking in there and cheering me to the finish line. Xoxo

To my parents: I only wish they could've been here to see their youngest do some good for a change.

And finally, most importantly, to Dawn: I owe my life to this person, and hands down, she's the best person to owe a life to.

# ONE

THE WINDOW WAS UNLOCKED, just like Yates had been told. The bedroom beyond was dark and quiet. Again, just like he'd been told it would be this time of night. He crouched on the fire escape as he slid the window up only an inch or two at a time, counting to ten between each push of the lower sash. It was a precaution he really didn't think he had to take, not with the noise of the city all around; a metal blanket many residents willingly folded around them. But this was how he'd been instructed, and so that's the way he'd fuckin' do it.

He crawled into the small room. On a thin futon by the far wall he saw what he'd come for. A three-year-old girl lay under the covers, sleeping on her stomach. He approached quietly, moving slowly on the balls of his naked feet. He'd been told she was potty trained so that wasn't something to be concerned with. He'd explained back that it better fuckin' not be a concern. He wasn't somebody's goddamned mother, for Christ's sake.

Yates reached into his coat pocket and brought out the rag he'd taken from the painting class. Doused it with the chloroform. Was it really okay to chloroform a little kid like this? Karachi had assured him it was, but he didn't like or trust that asshole. Yeah, Karachi had hired him, but the guy'd been acting like one of those go-betweens you see in a movie or something. This wasn't some Tarantino film. This was real life. Yates reassured himself that all he had to do was get the little shit and bring her safely to the meeting place.

*Whatever…*

Stalked toward the futon. Money was money, and he sure as Hell needed some. The kid was curled up under the worn blanket, her right thumb in her mouth. He bent closer, looming over her. Tensed as he got ready to strike. She moved a little. Whimpered like she was having a bad dream. Well, he figured as he loomed over her, sh'll have more than that in a little while. His right hand moved with the speed of a cobra, the rag slapping down on the little nose and mouth as his other arm scooped her off the bed, blanket included. She went out instantly and he used the blanket to work a makeshift bag of sorts. Slung it heavily over his shoulder. He laughed silently, feeling sorta like a demented Santa. *"Ho! Ho! Fucking Ho!"*

Crept back across to the window and through. Closed it silently, his gloved hands never making a print. The entire operation had taken less than five minutes.

As he climbed back down the fire escape, he couldn't help

but feel he'd earned his money. The first part was over, and it'd gone off without a hitch.

Now it was Miller Time.

# TWO

MARK MALLEN JOGGED UP to the dock mailboxes and leaned against them, breathing hard. Shook sweat from his head like a dog does after running through sprinklers. Checked his watch. Still had a few hours before picking up Anna for their day at the park. Now was the time to finally see if that Sode kite would fly. He'd found some very lightweight nylon strips and worked them together in a dizzying geometric pattern tail that would look great up there in the sky.

Or so he hoped.

Got his breathing under control as he limped down the dock to his floating hovel. It was the top of the month, and that meant time to send the rent to Oberon. The deal had been Mallen would pay the rent and Oberon would let him stay, *if* he kept up the place and made the necessary repairs. Well, he'd been staying, but quickly learned he wasn't the fixer-upper handyman he'd thought he could be.

The morning newspaper lay next to the front door. He picked it up as he passed inside, tossing it on the kitchen counter as he went toward the bathroom. Stripped down. In what had become a sort of ritual, he checked the crook of his right arm. The needle holes there had healed, but had left behind some faint, blue/black marks. He was okay with their calligraphy. A reminder of what had been. That thought made him gaze down at the still healing cuts and bruises all over his body. A history of his work since getting clean of the needle. Those cuts and bruises looked like some demented form of graffiti. He'd certainly seen a shitload of action the last few months or so. The ribs still hurt, even weeks later. The nail holes in his right hand had healed, but man ... would that hand ever *not* be stiff again? Maybe it would be like one of those old war wounds that acted up before it rained. *Such was the life of a recovering junkie ex-cop.* He got into the shower and took a long, hot one. Came out of the bathroom twenty minutes later in jeans, drying his hair with a clean towel. The last clean towel he could find. Time for laundry again. Had to wonder if he even would've had money to do laundry if it weren't for the severance package the police had given him when they'd told him to take a hike off into his city of needles.

Wondered if he should call Chris and confirm, but thought better of it. Ever since he'd brought her back from that night at the Palace of Fine Arts, and the men who'd taken her hostage, he knew she needed space and time to heal. He also knew he'd never forgive himself for putting her through what those men had done to her, scarring her like they did, emotionally and physically. It didn't matter what she'd said about not holding him responsible: it was his fault, pure and simple. She'd also told him that once she was feeling a little better, she was going to go and talk to someone. Maybe a therapist who specialized in PTS. He'd answered that it was a great idea. He'd also apologized again for putting her through it… putting her through everything.

He had some time before driving into the city, so sat down on the couch and opened his paper. It was on the last page, in the local news section titled "Crime Alerts," that he read something that made him sit up. A three-year-old girl had been abducted right out of her bedroom sometime the night before or very early that morning. The mother's name was Trina Marston.

He knew her.

Read the short article again, just to make sure it was the same person. Yes, it mentioned she lived in the Tenderloin. That's where he knew her from. During his days when he'd been wasting his life away in the Loin, shooting smack into his arm like it was going out of style. They'd even shot together a couple times. She'd lived in his building for a bit. Her little girl was only about two years old the last time he'd seen Trina. It was about that time that she'd moved to a building a couple blocks away. But in that hood? A couple blocks could sometimes be like moving across the ocean. He reread the article a third time. The daughter, Jessie, had been taken sometime after 8 p.m. The article for some reason mentioned Trina's arrest record. That she'd been found with some heroin on her once. Also once with some pharmaceuticals that didn't belong to her. She'd been given probation. Told to get into a rehab program, a program that the article seemed happy to point out she was not participating in. They quoted Trina's response when asked about why she hadn't followed through with the rehab program. "I'm not like those rich people you see on TV who go into rehab. They have families, or maids, to look after their kids. I have nobody to watch my child, except me. That's why I haven't gone, yet." The article then wrapped up with a thinly disguised line almost insinuating that if Trina had been a better mother and not an addict that maybe she could've somehow prevented the abduction.

"Such fucking bullshit," Mallen mumbled to himself as he tossed the paper onto the coffee table. Thought about Trina as he sat there. So, Trina had never made it clean. A couple times they'd been together, she'd sounded like she really wanted to try and get out from under the needle. He especially remembered this one time, right before they were going to shoot up in his apartment. There was this faraway look in her dark eyes. They even watered up a little. At that moment, she looked like she wanted to be anywhere but where she was, anyone but who she was. But then the needle went in, the plunger slowly down, and the eyes changed into veiled mirrors, turned inward.

The longer he sat there, the heavier his heart became. *Her daughter, little Jess, gone? Shit.*

In that part of town, chances were it was a molester. He hated the sick feeling the thought left in him. He knew from his cop days that the Tenderloin was home to more registered sex offenders than any other hood. He also knew the stats: that a lot of the children who go missing were never seen again. Never. Or, if by some stroke of luck they were found, they ended up being so emotionally and physically wounded they could never get themselves back to normal. Even with all the help in the world.

Mallen checked his watch. He could do it. Make it down to the Loin to see Trina, if only for a moment. Let her know she wasn't alone. Maybe he could find out if she really felt like she'd had enough with the drugs. Maybe he could help her get clean. Just like Gato had done for him.

The least he could do was to go see her. Jesus… it could've been Anna that had been taken. Had almost *been* Anna when the Darkstar men had come for her and Chris. He got dressed. Shrugged into his leather jacket, snatched up the car keys, and went to the door. Remembered the kite at the last minute and ran back upstairs to his office for it. Picked it up, but stood there for a moment as he looked over at the file cabinet. He always had this argument with himself now: to go out armed, or not. It felt like he'd never be able to move his life forward if he kept going around with a gun in his pocket. But it seemed that ever since he'd gotten clean, he'd seen some very dark things. Sick, dark things that showed him the world was indeed a deep well of nightmares. Sure there was good stuff. The kite in his hand. Anna. But in the end, he always figured that to protect the good stuff he would just have to go around with a gun in his pocket. Maybe one day it was an argument he'd actually fucking win, and leave the weapon home. Who knew? He went to the cabinet drawer. Pulled out the Glock, stashing it in his left coat pocket. Grabbed up the kite and left.

At least kite flying was a safe endeavor.

# THREE

THE BRIDGE TRAFFIC WAS heavy, but he still made good time back to the hood he'd spent fours years in, all of it with a needle sticking out of his arm. Parked the Land Cruiser, wondering if Mr. Gregor would take him up on his offer to somehow buy it from him. Hopefully the man would say yes. Hopefully the man would let him make payments.

Mallen got out of the truck and walked down to the location given in the article. Near the corner of Turk and Jones it said. He cruised up and down the block, checking the mailboxes for names, when he could get close enough to spy the names through the heavy iron safety gates. Found the building Trina lived in only because the black, rusty gate had been propped open, allowing him to walk into the lobby and check the bank of mailboxes. Made his way to the elevator, sidestepping a fresh stain that he couldn't figure out whether it came from the front, or back, of a human being. There was evidence aplenty that a lot of people didn't give a fuck either way, as they had just moved right on through it, tracking it everywhere. He smirked then; he seemed to be in danger of becoming almost bourgeois the longer he lived across in the North Bay. It was important for him never to forget his world before that home. The world of the Tenderloin. The world of needles and copping drugs. He always needed to remember what had happened to him. What it had taken to get his life back. Without that knowledge, he would be lost. Would get over confident, sliding right back into what he'd once been: a guy that woke up one day with the needle still in him.

He found Trina's door, which wasn't really difficult. The hallway bore the recent appearance of the SFPD Shreds of yellow tape littered the thin and worn carpet. Print dust was still all over the door and doorknob. Hell, he thought as he walked up, she probably wouldn't even be home. Was probably staying with friends. Maybe family, if she had any in the area. He didn't know if she did or didn't. Knocked, trying not to use his cop knock.

"Yes?" The voice was so soft he thought he hadn't heard it.

"Trina? It's Mallen? Remember? Mark Mallen?"

A moment of silence, followed by the sound of the chain sliding back. The turning of the deadbolt. The sad, oh-so-sad eyes were the first things he noticed. Then it was how incredibly thin she looked. Reminded him of a Holocaust survivor. The needle was eating her now. She pushed some lank, dirty brown hair out of her face as she looked up at him.

"Wow. You did get clean. I'd heard, but I ... " she let it trail off.

"Yeah, why would you, right?" he said with a smile. Like it was a gag now that everyone just played along with.

She stepped back, hesitating as she glanced over her shoulder at her living room. "It's a mess, Mallen. The cops, you know, they…" Gave it up. Just stood by to let him in.

It wasn't like he was expecting anything other than what the room turned out to be. Goodwill, or street-found, furniture. A TV about a decade old. Blankets thrown over the couch and chair to hide the fact that the stuffing was escaping. There were also signs of Jessie here and there: clothes and pajamas, coloring books. A few toys probably from the same Goodwill the furniture came from. Trina offered him the overstuffed chair hidden under a bunch of faded Mexican blankets.

He sat down. Watched as she limped over to the couch and let herself down onto the cushions. "What happened to your leg?" he said.

"It's nothing. Just some guy in the street. Tried to steal my stuff. I kicked him in the nuts. He kicked me in the hip, threw me down and took off."

"With your drugs?"

"You been gone a long time."

"Yeah, guess so." Shifted in the chair. "When I read about Jessie, I wanted to come and see you."

Tears started in her eyes. "They'll never find her," came the quiet response.

"I'm sure they will, Trina. Jessie will come home—"

"Safe and sound," she mocked. Shook her head. "That's the same bullshit the cops told me. Was nice of them to try and jack me off about it."

"What makes you say that?"

A moment, then she said, "The laughter while they looked over Jess's room. The shakes of their heads as they looked around my place. *Our* place." She went sad again. Glanced down at her hands resting in her lap. He thought he heard her say her daughter's name, but couldn't be sure.

Mallen looked around at the living room. The room mirrored the lives of its inhabitants: desperate and sad. It tore at him. "Trina," he said, "I have a good contact downtown. Maybe I can get you some better news on Jess's disappearance, yeah? Maybe my contact can help get some better people on the job." Could he really make good on his words? Oberon was busy, as usual. Was it possible the detective could really get better cops on the case? It was possible, sure, but it was a real long shot. Maybe Gato could help by keeping an ear out for anything on the streets about a kidnapped little girl?

But what could he do *now?*

"I … I read about the conditions of your probation," he said quietly. "Read your response to it. If I—"

"Bullshit!" she flared. "If you what? If you looked after my daughter so I could go to a rehab program? If you helped get me into a *good* rehab program? Bullshit, Mallen! Bullshit! You can't do anything for me. I need my girl back, I.…" She started to cry. Put her face in her hands. Shoulders wracked with sobs.

"Trina," he told her, "I'm not sure what I can do. What I'm saying is that I want to do *something* to help you."

She looked up then. Glared at him. "You want to help me, Mister Clean? Really help me? Then let me suck your cock for ten bucks so I can get some smack. *That* will help me!"

"Trina …"

She got up then and came over to him. A moving, breathing rail of a human. "You want to fuck me in my ass?" she screamed.

12

"You can. Twenty dollars, man. Even *more* smack! Come on, mister Mallen! Come the fuck on! Beat me! Cum on me! Just give me my money! That's what everyone here thought of me anyway, so just fucking do it, you prick! Just fucking do it!" The following silence was a huge, sudden void of quiet. She stood there, shaking with every fiber of her being. Like she only now realized what she'd been saying.

Mallen got to his feet. Put his hand gently on her shoulder. Gave it a squeeze. "Trina," he said quietly, "no. I won't do any of those things, and you know it. What I will do is try and help you, any way I can. If it's getting you into a program, that's what I'll do. If it's going with you to that program every day, that's what I'll do, too." He pulled out a piece of paper from his jacket, along with his pen. Scribbled his phone number down on it. Put the scrap of paper on her open palm, closing her fingers around it. Some tears dripped down onto his hand, soft and warm.

"Anytime you need to, you call that number. I'll do what I can for you." He turned and went to the door. His hand was on the knob and turning it when she spoke. It was like listening to the last sound before a ship sank beneath the water.

"Will you help find my daughter?"

He stopped. Looked back at her. She quivered as she stood there. Because of the weather, or expectation, he couldn't tell. Her dark, wet eyes went unblinking as she stared at him, waiting.

"Yes," he said, then left, quietly closing the door behind him.

# FOUR

MALLEN HEADED BACK TO his truck after leaving Trina's. On the way, he looked at the neighborhood. The grime. The crime. Amazing to him the will to survive, and what people were forced to endure. The more he thought about that though, he realized that statement wasn't really accurate. Some out here weren't forced to endure, they welcomed the opportunity. Sometimes maybe it seemed like a test, a test to see how much they *could* endure. Still, now that he'd been clean for some time, he could see with better eyes the need that some of these people had. Like the woman who begged for change on the street corner. If he remembered correctly, her name was Beatrice. Older. Obese. In a broken-down wheelchair, her body covered under a stained, threadbare blanket. Skin tanned the color of dark leather. She'd been begging on that corner for over five years. She'd disappear for a few weeks, then reappear with a new wheelchair and some clean clothes. Looked like she'd had some days where she could bathe, or be bathed. Eyes were brighter. But then, over time, she wore away again. Eyes turned off. Wheelchair went rusty and rickety. Her voice lost its temporary vibrancy. And then there she was: back to being what she was before the respite she got Lord knows where. Some women's shelter, maybe.

———

Mallen managed to pick up Anna a few minutes early. That had been a lucky break, given the usual San Francisco traffic. He never again wanted to be late for *anything* involving his daughter. Wanted to show her that she meant everything to him. He needed to show Anna, and Chris, that he was here to stay. No more going back to the needle. Not ever.

Anna rushed out of the house as soon as he'd pulled up. Sure, she'd be excited, but he could sense there was something more to her coming out so fast and on her own. Glanced up at the window, half-expecting to see a man's shadow in the living room window. There was of course no one. Still, it was strange. He got out and went down on one knee, his arms spread wide. She fell into them, nuzzling against his unshaven neck.

"Good to see you, A," he said, whispering it into her ear.

"Daddy," she replied, "you're on time."

He laughed as he put her in the backseat, passenger side, then buckled her in. Couldn't help it: took one last glance up at the door. No Chris. Could he really expect more, after everything that had happened? Should he really wonder if she wanted no part of him and his world? And would that be the way it was going to be from now on? He hoped not, but however it played out, that's how he'd play it.

He drove them over to the Marina Green, that huge swath of greenery by the blue waters of the San Francisco Bay where people came to play soccer, have a picnic, or just sit in their cars, smoke dope, and talk.

"Daddy!" Anna said as she ran with the kite he'd brought, "w

"Okay, A." He let her lead him over to the middle of the area she'd chosen. Looked ahead as he planned his run. The wind was good today. Not too heavy. Almost just right. His daughter waited impatiently, wanting him to get the kite up in the air so she could take over. It was too big for her now, but one day she'd be the one bringing the kite up from the world, up into the deep blue. He wondered then if she'd still want to do this, when that time came.

He brought the kite string tight in his hand. Looked ahead again, checking the wind. It was strong from the west. No fog. Took off running, not being able to remember the last fucking time he'd felt so good. The string went taunt, and he felt it twist a little in his hand and he knew without looking the kite was in the air. But then he did look over his shoulder and had to admit to himself that he'd done well. Fuck yeah, he had. It was a beautiful kite. The kite soared upward, a swipe of color across the sky.

"Give it to me, Daddy!" she insisted as she came running to him.

"Here you go, A," he replied. Gave her the reins, stepping back to let her work the line and thus work the kite. He watched with pride at how capable and into it she was. Watched as she pulled and released the string, making the kite go higher and higher. He was with his little girl, and that meant he was at peace. Something rare. He watched her as she looked up at the kite, and it reminded him so strongly of Chris when they'd go out to the beach and she'd look up with wonder at a squadron of pelicans as they flew by.

They'd been at it for about an hour when Mallen's attention was caught by an unmarked cop car pulling into the parking lot. He knew it was a cop car by the fact it was too clean, too normal, and too big. The car pulled into the slot nearest to where he and his daughter were. A woman got out from behind the wheel. She was short. Mallen judged her as just above regulation. Dressed just like a detective in the police force. Another detective, a man, exited the car. He was built big and heavy. The woman detective motioned for her partner to hang back by their vehicle.

As she walked toward Mallen, he thought he recognized her, but couldn't be sure. The faint memory he had was of her in uniform. Could swear he'd worked with her at some point. As she got closer, a name came to him: Gwen Saunders. And then he knew that they *had* worked together. On a drug case, back before he'd gone undercover.

How the fuck had she found him? And why was she looking for him? He didn't want this type of shit fucking up the world he had with his daughter. She'd already been through a lot. She didn't need any more bullshit.

"Saunders," he said as she got closer. "Didn't know you were into kite flying."

She looked up into the sky. At the kite sailing around. Watched as it soared and ducked and seemed as free as a child without a care in the world. "I'm not, Mallen," Saunders said.

17

Anna picked up on the vibe in the air now. The tension. Moved a little closer to her father.

"How did you know where to find me? Freaks me out, ya know?"

"Figured it would." Saunders kept her eyes on the kite. Watched as Anna lost control and the kite dove down toward the grass, his daughter yanking just enough on the string to keep it from taking a total nosedive. Instead, it hit the grass and rolled. Anna ran over to it immediately. Scanned it for damage as she walked back to Mallen and Saunders.

"It'll survive, Daddy," she smiled.

"Oh yeah it will," he replied. "Takes a lot to kill a kite made by me."

Anna smiled at him again. "Watch me. I'm going to launch it this time!" She ran off and readied the kite for another run. Mallen watched her get out of ear range before he said to Saunders, "Why are you here, Gwen? Been a long time. I'm out of that world. You know that."

"Since you got booted off the force for your fashion sense about street drugs?"

"That part of my life is over, too. You must've heard about that." He bent down and picked up the spool of unused string he'd brought. "What do you want?"

"Daddy," Anna yelled, "watch me launch it!"

"Go for it, A," he yelled back. She was going to learn everything on her own as she went through life. He could see that. Made him proud. He and Saunders watched her run across the grass, picking up speed, the string going tight and the kite lifting off into the air. And only a minute ago he'd been thinking she wasn't ready. *That's my girl.*

Saunders watched her for a moment longer before she said, "You heard about the kidnapped little Marston girl?"

"Yeah. I heard."

"Well," Saunders told him, "I've been assigned to the case."

"Lucky you, I guess."

"I thought maybe you could help me, Mallen."

"Yeah?" Kept his eyes on Anna. Watched as she sailed the kite higher and higher. "How could I help you?"

"You know that part of town. Thought you might've heard something. Or, maybe will hear something."

He looked at her then. "Told you I was out of the game."

"And like I said, I'd heard something to that effect. But you still know people there and don't try to tell me otherwise. People that could help you find out things." Pulled out her notebook. Opened it. "Eduardo Calderon, maybe? Gato, right? That's his street name, right?"

"Gwen," he replied, a smile working to appear, "you want to turn me into your snitch? You gotta be fucking kidding me."

She told him, "Mallen, you know this is probably a sex crime." Glanced down at the grass, then again over at Anna. "I just want to find her. Wouldn't you, if our places were reversed?"

He watched Anna flying the kite that he'd made for her. The one he'd sweated over. Sweated over because it had to be just right for her. Nothing less than perfection for his little girl. Even back when he was shooting dope, he'd always made the kites perfect. The greatest thing to happen to him, outside of Chris, had been Anna. And again, he was struck by what he'd lost. How much he'd lost.

What if it had been *his* daughter?

He weighed the angles on helping Gwen. If he were to help Trina, then he *would* need someone on the inside of the department. Someone who could check arrest records for him. Run license plates. He couldn't go to Oberon all the time. Not with all the help Obie had given him in the recent past. He would need information at some point. Gwen could be a big help in finding Trina's daughter.

Finally, he nodded. Told her, "Okay, but it's gonna work my way, yeah?"

She seemed relieved by his agreeing to help. "What way is that?"

"I give over what I find, but you give me what I need."

She didn't even need to think it over. "Agreed."

"Good. You have any leads at all?"

Gwen consulted her notes again. "Maybe. A man named Hendrix. Tommy Hendrix. He's an addict. Was seen very early that day hanging around Trina Marston's building."

"Wait a minute. Drug addicts are *not* kidnappers. You know this. So he was hanging around? So what? There must've been at least twenty other addicts hanging around that street, too."

"Because he was seen later that day, flush with money. And junk." When Mallen shook his head, she added, "Look, I'm not saying he did it. But what I am saying is that he could be connected in some way. It's a strange coincidence."

Anna began pulling the kite back down to Earth. He checked his watch. It was time for lunch. He thought about what Gwen had told him. Hendrix seemed like a real long shot. The guy could've just robbed some house or apartment. Still, he figured, he had to start somewhere. "I'll follow up on it," he told Gwen.

She pulled out her card. Turned it over and scribbled something down on it. "Here," she said holding it out to him, "here's the number to my cell. Call anytime you think you have something."

He took the card. "Got it, Chief," he replied as he dug into his coat pockets. Came up with a crumpled receipt for some pizza he'd bought last week. Scribbled his cell phone number down. Handed it over to Gwen.

"And when I say anytime, I mean it, okay?" Gwen replied as she took the piece of paper he offered her. She then put her notebook back in her jacket. "And I mean *anytime* you have anything. Don't leave me in the dark."

"Got it, Chief."

# FIVE

MALLEN HAD PLANNED TO take Anna to her favorite place in Fisherman's Wharf, but she insisted he take her home and let her make him grilled cheese sandwiches. She would not be denied, so he agreed and drove her home. He made sure to call ahead.

"Hey," he said when Chris answered, "Anna's insisting that she make me grilled cheese for lunch. Just wanted to give you the head's up, see if it was okay."

The pause was a little longer than he would've liked, but she said it was fine, adding, "This is good timing, anyway. You'll be able to meet Daniel."

"Ah. Well, you're sure it's okay, yeah?" He glanced over at Anna as he said this.

"Of course it's okay, Mark. Your daughter wants to cook you lunch. I think that's sweet." She was forcing it, he could tell.

"All right. We'll be there in a few."

He turned onto the street where Chris and Anna lived. Was going to pull into the driveway but there was another car there. One he didn't recognize. Must be this guy Daniel's car. In a fit of "I don't give a shit" or maybe it was more a fit of "I pissed here before you did, motherfucker" he pulled up behind the car and parked. Didn't care if he was hanging ass-half out into the street. He'd eat the fucking ticket.

Smiled at Anna as they got out of the car. She led him by the hand up the stairs and into the house. His daughter took him right to the kitchen and sat him at the table. Just like her mother had done countless times in the long-ago past when he'd come home after shift, back in his uniform days.

"I'll start cooking," she said. Like she was about to perform a magic trick of some sort.

"Okay, A," he replied, adding, "but Daddy's got to leave soon, honey. Got some errands to run."

That was when Chris entered the room, and not alone. Daniel. Good-looking guy, Mallen had to give him that. Older than he would've expected. Graying at the temples. Definitely kept in shape. Dressed like right out of a Lands' End catalog. This must be the guy she'd been taking calls from ever since he'd gotten back into their lives. She handled the meeting well, but Mallen wasn't surprised by that. Even having gone through what she'd gone through, she was still Chris: strong, both inside and out. Somehow this little scene made him realize that she'd make it. She'd eventually be okay. There was still a long road, sure, but she'd keep moving forward. Anna was blessed with such a strong mother.

Chris smiled at him. Daniel stood there, behind her right

shoulder. "You want me to make you and Danny a sandwich, too?" Anna asked.

"No, honey. We're fine. Thank you."

Daniel came over to Mallen. Put out his hand. "Pleased to meet you, Mark. I'm Daniel." He had a good grip. Good sign.

"Nice to meet you, too." Mallen said. Looked over at Anna, saying, "A? I'm gonna have to pass on lunch actually. I'm running later than I thought."

"Oh no you don't," Chris said, "you're going to sit right down and let your daughter do for you. Daniel and I were on our way to the back yard. He's really into horticulture. Has some great ideas for the back yard and garden."

*My garden*, Mallen thought. *Hell, that's what you get for fucking off in the Tenderloin with a needle in your arm, asshole. When you shoulda been here doing for your family.* Jealousy reared its legendarily ugly head then but he shoved it back into the cave it came from. The room filled with the smell of cooking cheese and toasting bread. He watched as Daniel gave Chris's shoulder a squeeze as he went to the back door. "I'll start looking at those rose bushes," he said as he left.

"I'll be right out," she replied.

"Take your time, babe."

After Daniel had left, Chris said, "I wondered a long time whether to send him out before you got here."

"Glad you didn't," he replied as Anna came over and put a grilled cheese sandwich down in front of him. He kissed her on the forehead. "Thank you, waitress."

"Just leave the tip, sir," she replied with a giggle.

"Glad I didn't?" Chris said.

He shrugged as he bit into the sandwich. To stall for time, maybe? Finally said, "It's like what I told you before. I don't have a right to say anything, Chris. I only hope that you end up happy." Quickly changed the subject. "How are you doing?"

She put her hand over her stomach... over the shirt that hid the scars. Scars of the symbol carved there. "It's healing," she said quietly. "But I have nightmares all the time. Wake up screaming. I can't be here in the house at night by myself. If I am, I don't sleep. Can't take pills to sleep because then I won't wake up when someone comes after me."

"Yeah... you definitely need to feel safe. I'm sure." Mallen replied, not knowing what else to say. Gazed out the garden window. Gotta hand it to Daniel, he thought; dude is just out there tending flowers and not paying us any attention at all. Good work there. Smart man. "He been staying with you? If so, I'm glad you have someone who makes you feel secure."

"Daddy!" Anna cut in, "You're not eating your sandwich! You have to keep up your strength!"

"Sorry, babe," he said, then took another bite.

"It's not that he makes me feel secure," Chris said, "it's just that I need another body here in the house with me right now." She seemed to be debating something with herself for a moment, then added quietly. "I... he sleeps on the couch, Mark."

Nodded his head as he chewed. "I appreciate you telling me that. You didn't have to, I know. Hope I didn't do anything to make you feel that you had to tell me."

"No," she replied, "you didn't. I just wanted you to know. I... I can't have that kind of contact yet, with any man."

"I hope that changes for you at some point, if you want it to."
He finished his sandwich and got to his feet. "I better be going."

Went and scooped up his daughter in a big hug. "Thanks for lunch, Chef Anna. Sorry I got to eat and run."

As he put her back on her feet she shrugged, saying, "Men. Always eat and run, eat and run!"

He and Chris had a good laugh over that one. Chris walked him to the door, where he told her goodbye and left quickly. Being physical or not, he couldn't shake the feeling of jealousy toward the man who was now sleeping on his couch. He'd bought that couch.

———

Back in the truck, Mallen headed east over to the Tenderloin. To the Cornerstone. If anyone knew where to find an addict like this Hendrix was supposed to be, it would be Dreamo his ex-dealer. Dreamo knew everybody, especially if they were addicted to a substance. Amazing how the man had gone from helping him get high to helping him get information on all sorts of pieces of shit assholes looking to hurt people and take their money, or their life.

The bar was average, crowd-wise, even though it was Saturday afternoon and there was a Niners game on the TV. A couple dudes huddled together at the end of the bar looked up when he walked in, then quickly began whispering to each other. As Mallen approached the bar those two men got up and left. That got his radar humming. Had to wonder now which fucker he'd once known while undercover they'd go singing to. Couldn't place them, but then again, he hadn't paid them too much mind in the first place. Maybe he'd only leant them money one time back when he was in a golden-induced haze. Maybe they'd been afraid he'd come asking for his dough. A part of him thought that was all bullshit though. Trouble was now brewing, fire set on "high."

That was when Bill came over. A scotch, neat, in his hand. Put it down in front of Mallen with a smile, saying, "Mal, how's tricks?"

"Okay, B. You?"

"Doin' alright." Glanced around the bar before saying. "You on the thing with Trina Marston's daughter goin' missing?"

"Jesus, Bill. What'd you do? Put a tracking device in my shit?"

Bill chuckled, his large body bobbing. "Not in this life, motherfucker. No, a plainclothes was in here earlier today, looking for you. Some woman cop I've never seen before. Said she was investigating the Marston kidnapping. I told her I didn't know or hear anything about that. Then she, right out of left field, asks about if I seen you recently. Then, later that same day, you show up. Right outta the blue. Doesn't take a detective to guess it's all connected.

"We'll make a detective out of you yet, B," he said as he took a drag from his glass. "Dreamo?"

Bill chuckled. "He's in." Indicated the hall that led to the bathroom. "I'm countin' to twenty, Mal, okay?"

"I'd be disappointed if you didn't, Bill." Made his way down the graffiti-covered hall to the bathroom. To the room where Dreamo dealt out dreams and madness and escape. He noticed some new graffiti on the walls. Someone had done a pretty good rendering of a Hieronymus Bosch painting. A large view of a field in Hell. He passed by and entered the men's room. There was the familiar crunch of glass under his boots. Had to wonder if it was Dreamo's early warning system. A way to wake him up when anyone came into the room should he be asleep.

"Dream?" he asked as he walked to the stall.

"Ex-customer," came the thready reply.

Mallen pushed on the stall door. And there was Dreamo, just like every time he'd come in here to buy smack. Sitting back, leaning on the toilet tank. The burning candles that were always there in the stall had been moved around, their owner maybe looking for a fresh outlook, as someone would do with moving the furniture in their apartment. Three now sat on the plastic toilet paper rack, along with the rest now being arranged on the floor around Dreamo's feet. The scent of something that reminded Mallen of henna filled the air. Just underneath that smell was the faint odor of burned smack. Made the hairs on the back of Mallen's neck stand up. Antenna searching for a wavelength. Would it ever be different for him? And as always, the answer came back strong: *probably fucking not.*

Dreamo pushed his sagging Mohawk out of his eyes. It was longer now, dyed a raging purple. "Well," he rasped, "what does my ex-customer want?"

"Just some talk," Mallen said, leaning against the wall and lighting a cigarette.

"Those will kill you, ex-customer," Dreamo said, indicating the cigarette.

"If not this, then something else."

"Good point, philosophy professor Mallen."

"You hear about Trina's daughter?"

"Yeah," Dreamo replied. "That's some fucked-up shit, man. Taking someone's kid."

"That's right. It's *very* fucked up. Who knows what the fuck is happening to her as we speak, yeah?"

Dreamo regarded him for a moment. Faint smile there now. "Mallen, you're gonna try and help Trina, aren't you?"

"If I can, yeah."

"Right the fuck on, man. If you were still a customer, I might even give you a small freebie. To show my support for your very just cause."

"I appreciate that, Dream. What I need though is a lead on a hypo hound. Tommy. Tommy Hendrix. He a customer?"

A shake of his head, then Dreamo said, "No. Not one of mine."

"Would you tell me if he was?"

"Fuck yeah I would, man. Jesus, ex-customer ... you think I'm down with people snatching kids? If I had a customer involved in that shit, you fucking know I'd fucking tell you about the mother-fucker."

"You know where I can find this guy?"

The dealer considered a moment before saying, "Yeah, I think so. I think he shoots over behind this one building on Harriet Street south of Market."

"Guy shoots out of doors?" Someone had to be really at the end of luck to have to shoot out on the plains.

But Dreamo told him, "Naw, man. There's an old car there. An old station wagon. Like something your parents would've owned back in the day. Fake wood on its sides. You know what I mean? Anyway, this guy shoots in that car. I'd heard, anyway. If it's the same dude, I'd also heard he sorta lives in it."

"How does he manage that?" Mallen said. "Why doesn't it get towed?"

"Jesus, Mallen, how the fuck should I know? Maybe he's got a fuckin' guardian angel. I dunno."

"I hear ya. So he *does* have a guardian angel? That what you're saying?"

A nod. "But you did not hear that from me, ex-customer."

"Why? He got a bigger, older brother?" Sighed then. Last thing he needed was another Teddy Mac/Carpy thing.

Thankfully, Dreamo shook his head. "He's got some free pass. Heard it was from your old employers. But that's *all* I heard, you hear me?"

"I hear ya, man. Thanks."

"For what? I didn't do shit, Mr. ex-customer."

"Right."

# SIX

MALLEN DROVE DOWN TO Market Street, near where Dreamo had told him Hendrix "lived." Parking was a bear, and why wouldn't it be? Daytime, during the week? It would be easier to find a working bathroom at Burning Man. Had to find a spot blocks away, over near a guitar repair place on Lafayette. The parking gods couldn't be with you all the time, yeah? Hoofed it back to Harriet Street.

There was the station wagon. An old Ford Country Squire. Dark blue in color, complete with luggage rack and the fake wood sides Dreamo had told him about. The windows had makeshift curtains in them, blocking out the sun and the people who walked up and down the sidewalk. The car sat heavily on its wheels. Must be packed with crap; all the shit a person needed to survive on the streets. Maybe the fucker *did* have a guardian angel, Mallen thought as he stood at the corner, gazing at the vehicle. There were no parking tickets on the windshield. No bright chalk marks on the street-side tires. No nothing. So even the meter maids were keeping away from this particular car. Again, all that tied in with what Dreamo had said. Must be someone in the police watching over this vehicle. Mallen wondered why that might be so, and what it might mean. No matter how much he thought about it as he stood there, the answer that always came back was the question: was Hendrix a snitch?

He walked up to the wagon to get a closer look. Walked all the way around it. The curtain job was a good one; no way could anyone see inside. Mallen glanced up and down the street. There was nobody around, though he knew enough about this part of town to know that nobody would care about what he was about to do. Just another guy who forgot his car keys. He put his ear up against the curbside back passenger window. Listened for a long time. No, there was nothing going on inside. Wished he had a Slim Jim. Would've made this a lot easier. He was about to go look for something to help him break the lock with when he stopped suddenly, his gaze caught by something on the ground.

A small pool of blood. Just under the back passenger door.

It'd seeped through the bottom crack of the curbside passenger door. He squatted down and touched it with his index finger. It was sticky, but not dry. Now he really wanted to get inside. Tried each door but of course they were all locked. Thought about calling Gwen first, but he wanted to get what he could from the car before the troops came and did what they had to. He went quickly to the driver's window. Glanced up and down the street. Took his elbow and smashed the glass. Shards rained down on the asphalt. He unlocked the door and opened it, leaning in to see what was inside. The body of a young man lay inside on its back in the rear seat, face frozen in a grimace of agony. A hypo stuck out from the crook of his left arm like a pin in a pincushion. Blood had flowed from his nose and mouth and dried on his face and clothes. A lot of blood. Mallen also noted a lot of blood under the body, telling him the man had bled from every possible hole. Blue-white skin had turned the man into a strange wax-works figure. He knew immediately this was an overdose. An OD ruptures blood vessels, is like an atom bomb going off in the internal organs. Man … he couldn't help but wonder at how many times he'd come that close. There were times, more than he wanted to count, that he'd known right as the shit went into his arm that he'd bought something bad. That had been back before Dreamo. Back in the early days of his Tenderloin life.

Mallen glanced around the car's interior. Found the registration. Yeah, Hendrix. Figured he had only moments before he would have to call it in. Made sure not to touch anything with his fingers. Used a pencil to poke around, or wrapped his hand in his shirt. Hendrix didn't have a lot of belongings. Most of the wagon was given over to blankets, books, and cans of food. Checked the glove box. Found an expired registration from three years ago, a flashlight, and some matches. Found a piece of paper, torn and crumpled. A name and number had been scribbled on it, but the torn part made it impossible to read. "Kara–" and "725-8–" was all he could make out. Maps of Idaho and Michigan were shoved under the front seat. Keys were in the ignition. He turned them to see if there was any juice in the battery. There was, and a faint beeping noise came on. He unlocked the rear door using the electric locks in the armrest. Turned the key back to off and then got out nonchalantly, moving to the rear of the vehicle. Opened the back door just enough to look in. Back here was where Hendrix had done his hoarding. Bags of clothes. Heaps. There was a sick feeling in the pit of his stomach when Mallen saw that they were women's clothes. What the hell did *that* mean? He'd heard nothing about a serial killer at work. And a guy living in a station wagon just didn't fit the bill. So, why all the women clothes? Maybe Hendrix had more secrets up his sleeve than shooting H. Mallen shook his head as he looked through the bags of old clothes and garbage. He was beginning to feel that this stuff wouldn't lead anywhere, but he continued to dig carefully through the piles anyway.

Then he found it.

It'd been carefully hidden, or so its owner hoped, inside a world atlas book that had had its insides cut out with a not so sharp knife.

A pile of child porn.

"Shit ... " he said under his breath. Glanced again over at the body. The OD hadn't happened long ago. He could tell that by the blood and condition of the body. Sighed again. He couldn't just leave now and call it in without checking Hendrix for clues.

"Don't worry, Henny," he said to the corpse as he climbed closer. "This won't hurt a bit."

He gently ran his hands over the body. Found a small bag of horse. Well, this wasn't a drug thing. Checked for a wallet. There it was. It'd fallen to the floor and was lying by one of Hendrix's feet. Mallen snatched it up. Inside was almost five hundred dollars. All in twenties. The horse Hendrix had on him was only about thirty-bucks worth. No junkie keeps this kind of money around for long. He checked the marks on Hendrix's arms. There was a recent track there. Just off center from another recent hole. So, he'd shot, then shot again soon after?

No way. A junkie looking to kill himself wouldn't have made such an effort to hit the *exact same hole in his arm.*

This was made to look like an OD. Someone had maybe been looking for Hendrix. Found him here in his car. Had maybe even found him high. Maybe they'd brought the skag, then waited. Came back, even? Came back after they knew that Hendrix had shot up with his own dope?

He sat there for a moment, wondering what to do. A car horn blasted in on his thoughts and he knew it was time to go. Checked the street. Only a few people on it, and those were at the end of the block. Walked quickly away from the vehicle as he pulled out his cell. He paused for a moment. Call Gwen? Or maybe call Oberon first? This wasn't about a kidnapping anymore. Now it was murder.

He had to call Obie. Tell him what he'd found. He'd call Gwen after. And hell, she never told him to call her first. Dialed Oberon's number and waited.

"Detective Kane," came the familiar voice that he had to admit he'd come to rely on.

"It's Mallen."

He was sure he heard a sigh on the other end of the phone before the detective said, "Mark? Why is it that you call me at the worst possible moments?"

"You caught another case, man? Sorry."

"No, not a case," Oberon replied, "I'm off duty, and don't have to report in for a few hours. I happen to be entertaining a friend."

"No shit. Really?"

"Of course, really. You believe that I only exist when you call?"

"Well..."

"I'm busy, Mark, as I said. Make it fast, please."

"Well, I hate to break in on your date, Obie, but I've found a body."

Another silence. He heard Oberon move somewhere else. The background sounds faded. Less echo. Oberon said quietly, "Please repeat that. You say you found a body?"

"Yeah. For my sins." He described what he'd found in Hendrix's car, and how he'd found him.

"And what, Mark," Oberon asked patiently, "were you doing there in the first place? In a car belonging to a junkie?"

That hadn't occurred to him. That people might think that he would be there to buy from, or shoot with, Hendrix. "No, man," he answered, "I'm just checking into something for a friend. That's all."

"Really?"

"Obie," he replied, "really."

There was relief in Oberon's voice when he spoke next. "Okay then." He paused. "This was over south of Market? An old station wagon?"

"Yeah, why?"

"I'd heard something about a stoolie that lived in an old station wagon. It was 'hands off' for that vehicle."

"That's what I thought when I saw it."

"Mark, why are you calling me and not 911?"

"It's the timing of it all."

"And? I'm not reading you on this."

Mallen hesitated. Knew that involving Oberon would mean answering questions like this. Wondered now if he should've just called Gwen. No, he'd been right to call his friend. "It's about the Marston kidnapping. You heard about that, yeah?"

"And what would you have to do with that?"

"I know the mother."

Another pause, then, "And you want to meet and talk, right?"

"Yeah. Can we meet after I call this in to 911?"

"No," Oberon said, "I'll call it in. Stay close to your phone. I'll be down there myself." And with that, Oberon ended the call.

Mallen stood there a moment. Wondered who Oberon's friend might be. Funny, he realized he'd never thought of Oberon having a life outside of being a homicide detective. That's how much being a cop could eat up your life, feast on you. He crossed the street, found a dark alcove to stand in, and hunkered down to wait for the troops to arrive. They weren't long in coming. A couple black and whites, followed by two unmarked cars. The detectives got out first. Went to the station wagon. One of them crawled inside, but backed out immediately, calling for the uniforms to cordon off the area. That was when Oberon arrived. His friend was dressed for a dinner party, not a murder party. He waited while Oberon looked over the scene. Talked with one of the detectives for a moment. Oberon then walked to the perimeter of the crime scene, pulling out his phone. Mallen moved out from the alcove. Got Oberon's attention. His friend saw him, came over as he put his phone back in his pocket.

"I agree with your assessment," Oberon told him. "That man did not shoot himself up that second time. The other detectives feel the same way. That man was murdered."

And there was that word again. Murder. And yet one more time, Mallen wondered why being sober was better. And the answer always came back the same: Anna.

"You have any leads on this, Mark?" Oberon asked. It was actually the first time that he could think of where the detective actually asked for his input on a case.

"No, man. I don't. But it's early days for me, you know?"

"Have you met with the Marsden woman? The mother?"

"Yeah. She's in pretty bad shape."

"Did you get anything from her? Other than what would be in the report?"

"No. Anything I got was from Gwen Saunders. She—"

"Saunders?" Oberon said. "She approached you on this?"

"Yeah. Why not? We'd met on a case once back when I was in uniform. She knew I'd lived in the Loin. Told me she figured I might be able to help."

Oberon looked dubious at what he'd just been told. "What?" Mallen said. "What is it?"

The detective considered for a moment, then replied, "Nothing really concrete. She's a fairly capable detective. Not great, but not bad. Very hungry to move up."

"Well, who isn't?"

"Very true. Some cops, though, look for *any way* to solve a case. Any way possible. Cops like that, Mark? You stay away from. They should be considered dangerous at best."

"Hey," Mallen said, "remember who you're talkin' to, yeah?"

Oberon smiled. Nodded. "Sorry." Added, "So how did you leave it with Saunders?"

"That I'd help her as much as I could. Who I really want to

help though, is Trina Marston. I want to help her get her kid back."

The detective eyed him for a moment, then said, "Well, I guess I better go and pay up my life insurance. We know what happens when you get one of those 'save the world' feelings."

# SEVEN

MALLEN LEFT THE SCENE of Hendrix's demise. The fucker had died the hard way. But then again, he was someone who got off on pictures of nude children. Did that make his death hard, or justified? Or was it just not that black and white? Maybe it also depended on the motive for him dying. Whoever had killed him probably, *most* probably hadn't done it because of Hendrix being a piece of shit. Not because he was a pedophile. No, it was probable that whoever had put Hendrix out of his misery did it because *they* needed him dead. Jesus, where did the black start, and white end?

He sighed. Pulled out a cigarette as he walked back to his... no, Gregor's truck. Again reminded himself that ownership of that metal creature would have to be fixed. He had to admit: he was falling in love with the damn thing. Reached the Land Cruiser. Hendrix. What happened? Did Gwen even know about it? Inside the truck, he yanked out his phone. Closed the door and dialed her number.

"Saunders," she answered.

"Mallen."

"You have bad news." No question there.

"So you know."

"Just heard. Been waiting for you to call … waiting and sad that you didn't call me first."

"Sure." He pulled out a cigarette. Lit it. Blew out some smoke, replying, "You never said anything about being hired exclusive. I do what's the right thing to do, when I can figure the fuck out what *that's* supposed to be."

"Okay," she replied, "don't let your moral compass stab you on the way out, okay? What did you find in shitbag's wagon?"

"Nothing much. He had bags of women's clothes, which is creepy on its own. Was a junkie. Had about $500 bucks in his pocket. Oh, and he had a stash of child porn, and had been murdered."

"Child porn? Shit. How do they know he was murdered? Maybe he just OD'd. Lots of junkies—" Stopped then for a moment before continuing. "Sorry, you probably know all this."

"Gwen," he said, "no need to apologize. I don't run from what I was."

"When I started to track you down, I heard a couple things that back that up." There was a silence on the line, then she said, "I need to know who in the force he was connected to. And also who on the street he hung with."

"Who on the force he was connected to? You're kidding,

right? That's way more your world, Gwen. I can try the other request, but no way on the first one."

"You have some friends still inside. Don't you? At least one."

And it bugged him that she knew that. "You know, I'm suddenly beginning to wonder if this is what I signed up for. Don't lose sight of the fact that this is me and you. Not you and me, all right? You don't tell me what to do. I follow my own threads, as I see them sewn."

"Look, I need you to work with me on this, Mallen. Come on … a child is in danger here and you're whining to me about which one of your friends to hit up for intel? Like I said: you can go places I can't. Come the fuck on."

He kept his gaze on the ground at his feet. Didn't like what she'd just said. He was feeling boxed in, very fast. But there was a little girl to consider. He would've burned down the world to get to Anna if she were missing. "Okay," he said, "alright. I'll try."

————

He'd only been driving a handful of minutes when his cell rang. Checked the number. It was Chris.

"Hey," he said. "Everything okay? What's up?" Didn't mean to sound so paranoid and nervous, but ever since her abduction he'd been on pins and needles about anything concerning her.

"I'm fine, Mark. But …." The hesitation there was enough to feed images of Anna in trouble. He'd just seen her a few hours ago. Still …. Then she said, "It's about your father."

He pulled into the parking lot of an old motel on Van Ness. The world receded. Dropped away faster than a block of concrete tossed in the ocean. She wouldn't have called if it wasn't something serious.

"Yeah? Pops?"

"The facility called here … they had no other number. They said to come, and come soon, if you wanted to see him … one last … well, you know."

"Got it. Thanks."

"I'm so sorry Mark, I know how—"

"I know. Thank you. Talk soon."

———

If there'd ever been a time when he'd felt he'd let Ol' "Monster" Mallen down, it was with the choice of the facility he placed him in. There just hadn't been the money to do better. God help him but he would've given his eyeteeth for more fuckin' money.

He'd always wondered how it would end. As he pulled into the parking lot of the Alzheimer's home, he couldn't really wrap his head around the idea that the end time was now. That his father would die here, in this way. A lion, if it doesn't get killed on the plains, finds some dark, dank cave to die in. Or maybe some muddy riverbank to die on. The lion doesn't die like this. Not in a place like this.

There was plenty of parking in the lot. Every time he'd been here, there had never been more than a few cars. But it wasn't like he'd been here a lot, either. Being a cop, then an undercover cop, then a junkie cop, then a junkie, then a recovering junkie meant a lot of time spent in those goddamned endeavors. Or, that's what he liked to tell himself, anyway.

Parked near the entrance. Opened the truck door, but stopped. Sparked up a cigarette and just sat there for a moment.

His father was dying. No, the two of them hadn't been close. Monster had never taken him fishing. Or taught him how to build a balsawood model airplane. But he was *still* "Dad." But was that really true? Wasn't he "Monster Mallen" first, *then* "Dad"? It sure as fuck seemed that way. It was "Monster Mallen" that had taught him how to swim. Had just thrown him in the doughboy pool and yelled, "Swim, Mark! Swim!" That was Ol' Monster. Not "Dad."

He dropped the half-smoked cigarette onto the asphalt. Ground it out with his left boot. An exclamation point to the conversation roiling in his head. Went over to the building door and inside.

The reception area still had that muted, geometric-patterned carpet. The fireplace over on the right, two wingback chairs facing it. Books on the shelves that looked like they hadn't been read in years. On his left was the reception desk. A nurse sat behind it, typing on a keyboard. She wore a soft blue smock. Hair up in a bun. Smiled at him as he approached. Same smile she probably used one hundred times a week.

"Can I help you?" she asked. Crisp voice.

"Yes. I received a message about my father. Last name Mallen."

Gone was the smile. "Yes, I spoke with your wife. Go on ahead. Room fifteen. I'll page his caregiver."

"Thank you." He turned and went down the hall. It was lined with chairs on which sat, or spilled, the elderly. People all in various stages of their illness. Some looked up at him as he went by. Others stared off into space. Maybe they were reliving what was left of their past. Maybe as far back as childhood. Seemed that the disease ate its way back through the life of a person. The last thing you were left with was childhood. Your parents. Your first bike. Who the fuck knew?

An elderly woman got out of her chair as he walked by. "Tommy!" she said, her voice quaking.

He stopped. She came up to him. Tears in her eyes. "Tommy... my Tommy..." A nurse came over. Gently took her by the shoulder to lead her back to her chair. "Tommy?"

He smiled at her. "I love you, Mom," he told her, then continued down the hall. Heard the woman say to the nurse, "My son came and saw me. He loves me."

Mallen stopped at the door to his father's room. Really needed another cigarette now. His hands were shaking. He took a breath, then pushed the door open. There was his dad. Wasted away. On a frame as big as his father's, that wasting seemed even more severe. Eyes closed, and he seemed to be barely breathing. He approached the bed. He knew Ol' Monster Mallen didn't exist inside this frame anymore. Knew that his father didn't, either. And those thoughts made him feel the years more keenly than he could ever remember.

The caregiver came in. Young woman, dressed as you'd expect. White pants, flowered smock. Danskos on her feet. He couldn't remember how many people had looked after Pops in all these years. "Mr. Mallen?" she said to him. Quietly. Trying to be respectful, and making it, too.

"Yeah. Thanks for looking after my father."

She went over to the bed. Checked the fluid bag that hung from the side of the bed. The bag that was tied via catheter to his father's insides. The fluid in that bag was murky. A burnt yellow.

There were no more IVs. No more machines. Ol' Monster was past all that now. At least there was no pain, Mallen told himself. He figured that this is what comes after the losing of all the memories: the body stops remembering how to breathe, the heart forgets how to pump. He sighed, and pulled up a chair. Watched his father's face. He realized then, at that moment, he envied Ol' Monster his loss of memories. There were a lot of them Mallen wished he could forget.

The caregiver finished arranging the blanket and tilting his head so he could breathe better, trying to make his father as comfortable as possible. Turned to Mallen then and told him, "I'm sure he's glad you got here when you did."

"Yeah."

With that she went out quietly, the door closing behind her with a soft, hushed hiss. He took his father's hand. "Sleep, Pops. Just let it go and … sleep."

Stayed that way for another hour. The afternoon ticked away. Hand in hand. In that time, Mallen watched so many memories play on the screen in his mind. Made him think of his mother, his memories of her now faded and spare. Everything faded, right? That was life, yeah?

He could barely hear his father's breathing now. He'd been watching Ol' Monster's chest rise … then fall … always wondering if this was it: the last time. Shook his head then. What a shitty way to go. Wouldn't Pops kick his ass for letting him go out this way? Right now, at this moment, Mallen wished with all his heart that he'd done it differently. He should've talked more with his father, found some other way for him to check out, even if that meant a bullet on a cold cliff above the ocean. That would've been so much fucking better than this. Ending up in some bullshit care facility with a hose stuck up your cock, your mind wiped empty of its past, its present, and its hope for a future.

*God fucking damn it . . . .*

And then what happened, Mallen never forgot. Ever. His father's breathing deepened with a shudder and his hand suddenly tightened on Mallen's. And there they were, two men, hands clasped in bonding. And his father opened his eyes. Stared right at him. Like he saw him, saw that it was his son. Like he remembered.

It was a whisper from across the room it was so soft. "Look after them."

And that was it. Mallen felt the hand relax, and that was it. And he cried. Couldn't help himself. Almost laughed then. Ol' Monster Mallen never brooked crying from his son.

# EIGHT

MALLEN LEFT THE CARE facility in the late afternoon, about an hour after his father died. He'd signed all the forms, what seemed like a mountain of them. One life equaled a lot of paper, and that was just fucking wrong. Monster's ashes ... his father's ... would be ready in three or four days. Once the coroner's office did their bit, he'd get the death certificate. Got back into the truck and lit a cigarette. He called Chris, to let her know what happened.

"I'm so sorry, Mark. I know what he meant to you."

"Yeah ... ." He paused then, before saying, "Hey, I won't be around too much for a bit, okay?"

And she answered his pause with one of her own. Finally told him, "If you need to talk though ... ."

"Thanks," he replied. He'd called to tell her Ol' Monster Mallen died. He felt numb now, but how would he feel later? He had no idea. Only time would fucking tell. But he hadn't only called about his father. No, it was also about Daniel. About Daniel and Chris. About Daniel and Anna. He needed to make sure he didn't pop off and punch the guy in the throat for moving in on the family he had no right to feel he would win back. It felt like the death of hope.

"I appreciate the offer," he continued, "and I just might take you up on it. For now just tell Anna I love her and we'll go kite flying again soon. Maybe even mix it up with a movie."

"Okay," she replied, "you take care of yourself, all right?"

"I will. See ya." Ended the call and started up the truck. Took a deep breath. Opened up a drawer deep down inside himself and put, no … stuffed, his father's death into that drawer, shutting it up tight. Put a lock on it. That was for later. For now? For now he needed to get back to the whole Marston thing. That would keep him afloat. Keep him moving forward. And that was what it was about.

Hendrix was dead. Gwen would have to find what she needed in the department herself. He would take to the street. Pulled out his phone and dialed Gato.

"*Vato,*" came his friend's voice. He could hear kitchen sounds.

"You busy, man? I can call back."

"Nah, I'm good. Hang on." Put his hand over the receiver. Could hear Gato speaking to someone in Spanish, then say, "What's up?"

"You at home?"

"Yeah. A friend of mine is going to help look after *Madre*. I'm still sort of *rigidez y dolor* from the bullet that *chingador* got me with." That night outside the mailing center at the beach had been one of the most intense firefights they had seen in a very long time. His friend had been lucky to get out with just the one bullet.

"You could've stayed in the hospital longer, G."

"Fuck that. I got shit to do," came the reply.

"Well, I'm glad you got someone to help you out. That's good."

Slight pause. "We hope it will be. I'd still rather have Lupe here." Lupe. His friend's sister, the sister he needed back in his life and who had disappeared as neatly as smoke in the air. A part of Mallen thought, and he didn't want to admit it, but after Gato's last foray down to L.A., he figured that Lupe was most probably dead. And he knew and understood that his friend wouldn't even consider that possibility. Just wouldn't, or couldn't go there.

"I know, man," Mallen told him. "There will be an answer to this. I know there will be. Have you thought about what your next move will be?"

"No. I can't even think about leaving again until I know my *madre* is being looked after."

"It's getting that bad?"

A pause, then, "Yeah, *vato*, it is." A silence, then "I don't, *do not* want to put her in one of those bullshit homes, you know? *No es possible.*"

"Yeah, I do."

"Can't let that happen to her, *Hombre*. Can't. *Yo amo a mi madre. Ella no puede terminar en uno de los orificios shit!*"

"I have no idea what the fuck you just said, but I get the gist of it, G. We'll look after your mother. We'll keep her safe and comfortable. You have my word on that."

"Like I've always said, Mallen: there's a good heart beatin' in that chest. Why the call, man? What's up? We back on duty?"

"Yeah, I think we are." Gave Gato the background on everything that had happened since he'd walked into Trina Marston's apartment. After he got to the part about what he'd found when he went to Hendrix's wagon, he said, "Can you check around a little bit? Find me a lead maybe on who Hendrix had been hanging with lately? Maybe someone NOT in his usual drug world?"

"Sure, *vato*, sure." He heard his friend put his hand over the receiver. Spoke to someone, then told Mallen. "But I can't do it tonight, Bro, *lo siento*. I gotta train this girl in how I want my *madre* looked after, you know?"

"I hear ya. Just give me whatever you get, whenever you get it. I got a couple things of my own I can follow up on. Call me whenever, even if it's at 2 a.m., okay?"

"Got it. Be safe, my brother."

That brought a smile to his face. "Same back at you, *hermano*."

Gato laughed as he broke off the call. Mallen stared at his phone for a moment. Today was really the day to find out his friends actually had lives of their own. Did he? Did he have his own life? Had his family, sure. Anna. Chris. But really... wasn't he just running around trying to keep the fuck busy? Sure, it was better than trying to keep the high, but what he had now didn't seem like much of a life. Whatever it was, it would have to do.

He sat in the truck, hand on the shifter. Watched a car pull into the lot and park. An older couple got out, the woman holding a bouquet of flowers. They looked a bit sad and apprehensive as they made their way to the lobby door of the facility. He didn't blame them for feeling that way. Not at all.

He'd asked Gato to try and find anyone Hendrix had been hanging with. But that didn't mean he would just go home and wait for Gato to call. No, he had to keep moving. How long could he rely on the fucking generosity of his friends, anyway?

But where to start?

Then it hit him. Yeah … that guy might help him. Been a long time, but still …

… this guy owed him his life.

———

Radley Pawnbrokers was located way down on Leavenworth. Near Eddy. Mallen had no fucking idea who Radley was. The guy who ran it now was Manny Blackmore. Maybe Manny had bought it from this guy Radley. Maybe Manny had the junk store handed down to him from his father. Who knew?

Mallen gazed in through the grime-encrusted window. Years of car exhaust and street dirt had worked the glass a dull yellow. There was a lot of jewelry in the windows, along with some musical instruments and some MP3 players. The jewelry was dusty, the MP3 players a few years old, and the sax sitting on its stand a now faded note. The window consisted of anything a junkie or regular addict might steal and then pawn immediately.

Because that's what Manny Blackmore did: he fenced. The store was legit, but he was still a fence. Took in stolen goods at a low price, then turned around and sold them at a slightly, if not much, higher rate. Mallen had to wonder as he pushed through the door, the tinny rusty bell above it ringing-out a warning, just how sweet a retirement plan had been socked away by Manny between this store and his other business.

Blackmore came out from the back. Short and round. More bald than the last time Mallen had seen him. More grey, too. Skin the color of a rainy day. Made Mallen think about Blackmore's legendary love of whiskey. "I'd heard you'd moved across the water, Mallen."

"True. And yeah … left a lot of things behind, in case you're wondering."

"I wasn't, but thank you for sharing just the same."

Mallen smiled at that. Walked over to the counter. "You lookin' for a radio, Mallen?" Blackmore asked. "Maybe a slightly used iPod?"

"Not in this life, man. I like my music on LP. For my sins."

"Ah, yes! Age shows itself in the strangest, most humbling ways." Blackmore came and stood on the other side of the counter. His manner said that this was obviously now a business transaction. Mallen got it.

"Hendrix. Tommy Hendrix. You know him?"

"And why would you, in the name of all that is fucking holy, care?"

"You don't know Trina Marston, do you?"

A brief passing of sadness clouded the man's eyes. "Yes, I know her. She's pawned things here before."

Well, that wasn't anything new. Junkies pawned stuff as fast as people changed their underwear. "You heard about her daughter?"

"Yeah," Blackmore said with a sigh. "Terrible." Regarded

Mallen a moment before saying, "And again I ask, what has it fuck all to do with you asking me about Tommy Hendrix?"

"Tommy got himself shuffled off from this mortal coil."

A shrug. "More room for the rest of us."

"Yeah," Mallen said. "But, he's still dead, yeah?"

"And?"

Mallen pulled out a cigarette. Lit it. Had to play it cool here. Too hard, and Blackmore would never talk to him again, about anything. The weather, ball scores … you name it. "I was just wondering, is all. Did someone have it out for Hendrix? It's not a big deal, but this Trina and her kid thing … I dunno … it's got me buggin', I guess."

Blackmore studied him for a moment. Chuckled. "That still don't explain crap about why you give a shit about Hendrix. The guy was a pair of eyes on the street for the cops. Everyone knows that."

"Well, I have to admit: I didn't."

"Yeah, but if the stories are true, this ain't your world anymore. Why the fuck would you know this crap, right?"

Mallen blew smoke out through his nostrils. "Right."

"Look, Hendrix was a piece of shit. Liked little children. Girl or boy didn't matter, as long as they were hairless, okay? He was a pile of crap. If he's dead, then I'm hoping you're finding the guy who killed him so you can pin a fucking medal on his chest. You read me?"

"I know he was a piece of slime, okay?" Mallen replied. "But this isn't about him, yeah? It's about Trina and her daughter, Jessie. That's why I'm trying to track down the shitbags that knew Hendrix."

Blackmore looked at Mallen for a moment. Shook his head slightly, then went behind the register. Came out with a book. Like a personal address book. Looked at Mallen again. "So … Trina? About her and Jessie?"

"Fuck yeah, man. Why do you think?"

"Well, hell … Mallen. In this hood? Please."

"It's about Trina and her missing daughter."

There was the faint sound of pages being turned. Blackmore sighed. Looked out the window for a moment as he said, "I could really be fucking myself, Mallen, if this shit got out."

"I know. It won't, trust me on that one. I know what you're putting on the table."

Another pause. Then Blackmore glanced at the page. "Shannon Waters. William Lucas."

Mallen patted his pockets. Found a pen. No paper. Blackmore sighed. Gave him an unused pawn ticket. Mallen wrote them down. "So they came in with Hendrix? Pawned something?"

"Yeah. Something. Can't remember what though."

Something stolen of course. "You got addresses then, right?"

Blackmore shook his head. Shut the book tight. "Addresses? I thought you were some sort of private detective now, right?"

"C'mon. Really?"

"Really. Sorry, but that's as far as I go." Stashed the book under the counter. "Good luck."

Mallen shoved the pawn ticket into his coat pocket. "Thanks."

He was at the door when Blackmore called out to him. "You won't tell anyone about this, right?"

Mallen opened the door. Looked over his shoulder at Blackmore. "Fuck no, man. We're good. Rest easy."

# NINE

YATES SAT ACROSS THE room from the little kid. She'd cried for a long fucking time. Wanting her mother. It unnerved the fuck out of him. In the end, he got her to shut the fuck up by giving her some food. Put a little crushed-up Valium in with it. Not a lot, but enough that he figured she'd shut the fuck up and relax. Jesus, even when they were little, bitches were a pain in the balls. She'd eaten up every last bit of the SpaghettiOs. Was about fifteen minutes later that she began to get groggy. Then as Sleepy Time landed, she lay back on the blanket and bummed off to sleep.

Now he could think. Finally. Looked again at the message from Karachi. *Meet. Now. On the beach, across from La Playa and Kirkham. You know.*

It was a simple thing to do: get the kid, bring it to the buyer. Now? Now it felt dangerous. Meeting out there at the beach. At night. And fuck no way did he trust Karachi. Yates realized that he needed Griffin. Griffin could be his backup. From the window, his eyes scanned the street and other cars. Fucking asshole Griffin. No longer feared, but still acting the part of enforcer. Then again, the fat bastard was better than nothing, and he knew no one else who would do it. Something inside told him that this could turn out bad. Well, at least he had *his* equalizer. Checked the shells again. Full mag. No way anyone was going to make a mausoleum for him. Fuck that shit. *Hell*, he laughed, *you can make a mausoleum out of burnt spoons and used clothing?*

The kid seemed almost comatose. Shit, had he given her too much of the blue boys? He scooped her up, the blanket wrapped around her like she was a babe swaddled in her father's arm. Went to his car, checking again the location of the meet. Put her in the passenger seat. Buckled her in for some reason he didn't really understand. Just told himself it was to keep the package safe. She muffled some sound. Like in the middle of a nightmare. He stared at her for a moment, feeling every bit the piece of shit work he was doing. Got strong. *Yeah, kid … sounds like it's a bad dream. Well, it certainly fucking is. For both of us.*

He drove over to Griffin's place. The fat fucker waddled out like he was not only the toughest asshole on the block, but the toughest asshole in the world. Maybe back in the day, Yates thought, but not now. Still, he was going to help, and you could count on him to keep his yap shut. And that fat ass had a gun. That was enough for Yates.

Griffin came up to the car, saw the child belted in. Pursed his lips at Yates. "Aw, daddy wanna bay shore baybee iz otay?"

"Fuck you and just follow me in your wheels. If the shit hits the wall, shoot at everything around me until I'm outta there."

Griffin nodded. Held out his hand. "You want the best, you pay the price."

Jesus … like this bowl of bloated shit was "the best." He wasn't anything to Yates, except a finger on a trigger. Yates handed him a fold of twenties. Griffin looked at it. Nodded like he just scored Fort Knox. Asshole. "I'll be right behind you. Just sprayed my ride matte black. Nobody will see my little stealth machine."

——

The trip to the beach took no time at all. No traffic this late at night. That was a two-edged sword. Yeah, less people hanging about, but you stand out more. What if a cop stopped him? What then? Throw the kid out the window and haul ass? Shoot the cop? Both are basically the final nail in your ever-rotting coffin.

He repositioned the gun. It was more accessible this way, shoved between the driver's seat and the center console. Fuck it, he thought: if you gotta go out, go out in a blaze of glory. Why the fuck waste away in prison? Fuck that shit. But he met no cops, or anyone else as he drove down to the beach. Got to the meeting point. Cars lined the street, and he wondered then if he could even find fucking parking. *Fuckin' San Fran* … He did find a spot, just up the street. Parked. Wondered where Griffin would park. Could that fat fuck be capable of actual wartime thought? Checked on his passenger. Still out. He could leave her here. Go to the meet. Have them come back and take what they paid for. Fuck 'em. What was he? A waiter?

Got out and walked to the corner. A dark shadow disengaged itself from the darker shadow cast by the entryway to a building.

Karachi. Wearing his usual black trench coat. So fucking *The Matrix*.

"Where is she?" Karachi asked.

"What the fuck, man? You want me to bring her over here in a stroller? She's asleep in the car." He lit a cigarette. "It's all good, man."

"All good," Karachi echoed. "Better fucking be."

"Where's my money?"

Karachi looked up and down the street. Typical Karachi. Like he's in some fucking gangster film. Brought out an envelope and quickly shoved it at him.

"Better all be here," Yates said. Quietly moved his other hand closer to the grip of the pistol shoved in his waistband.

But Karachi only shook his head with disgust. "You do your job? You get paid what was promised. You *don't* do your job? You get sent underground."

"Yeah yeah yeah … I hear ya." He put the envelope into his coat pocket for now. Would have to hide it in his car somewhere until he got home. "Well? You comin' to get her? Where are the buyers?"

"He's here," Karachi replied. "Waitin' for you to give her to me. That's what buffers are for, right? So you don't know him, and more importantly for you, that he don't know your fuckin' face, dude."

"Well, let's get this done then, man." He led Karachi back to his car. The two men glanced once up and down the street. No one around. He opened the door and released the safety belt.

"How precious," Karachi said. "You playing the concerned parent."

He ignored Karachi. Scooped up his little prisoner and handed her over. There. It was done now. Karachi handled her roughly as he positioned her better in his arms. She whimpered a little. Yates almost reached out to calm her. Caught himself just in time. "Don't wake her, man," he said quietly.

"Or you'll what?" Karachi answered.

"Nothing. Nothing."

Karachi, turned to walk away. Stopped. "You hear about Hendrix, man?"

"No, what?"

"He got wasted."

"Why is that any different than any other motherfucking day?"

Karachi turned back, this time a pistol in his hand, carefully balancing the girl's legs. "Because this time he got wasted all the motherfucking way."

Yates tried to go for his gun, knowing it was way too late, way too whatever. There was a shot that sliced the night like a quiet knife and he felt the bullet slam him in the lower stomach. As he fell there were other shots. *Griffin . . . .* Then he fell. Then it was black.

—————

Karachi didn't even wait for the body to land. Was already walking away into the shadows before the other shots went off. Concrete was torn up. Some hit him in the face. He felt a bullet slam into his forearm and he almost dropped the kid. Almost made it to the buyer's car but then there was another shot and he dodged out of reflex, dropping the package. He saw the buyer get out of the car, wanting the kid, but bullets erupted, one slamming into the car's fender. The buyer gave one last look at the child, then jumped back into his car and in a burning rubber cloud disappeared.

Whoever the fuck was out there wasn't very good, but they were very lucky. Like someone playing a good round of "Whack A Mole." He heard sirens now. Closing fast. He caught one last look at the kid, near the place where the buyer's car had been. "Motherfucking shitbag Christ!" he said under his breath. He was bleeding and had to get away. Fuck! Get away. That was all he could do, right? Get the fuck away?

Well, if that's all you can do, then you do it.

———

Griffin listened for a moment. Reloaded, just for the hell of it. Just like in the movies. Listened. There didn't seem to be anyone around. And that was when he heard it.

The sound of a crying kid. Sirens were happening and happening louder all the time. But above it, he could hear a kid's crying. *The package!*

He ran across the street as Karachi's car screeched around the far end of the block. Went to where Yates lay. There she was. Shivering, not knowing what the fuck was going on. As the sirens grew closer he scooped her up and bolted as fast as he could back to his car. Tossed her inside and took off, pedal to the metal. Grinned as the car roared away. Now he had something that somebody wanted, and badly. This little critter would pay gold. Dividends of gold.

# TEN

MALLEN CAME OUT OF another bar, this one in the Mission. *What a shithole.* The bartender wasn't like Bill that was for sure. What a dickhead. He wondered for a moment if word had gotten out onto the street that he was back. Not only from being a hypo hound, but also from being an undercover cop.

*Hell, that's all I need....*

He had to, *had* to find either Shannon Waters or this guy William Lucas. Both names were pretty singular. Went to the door-way of a store that hadn't been anything since a couple years ago. Stood there for a moment in the blackness of the store entrance, thinking about whether to call Gato again, or not. In the end, he pulled out his phone. He needed help. Street help. He checked his watch. It was late, but he needed to talk to his friend. Dialed Gato's number.

It was picked up right away. "*Vato,*" his friend answered, "it's like we're on the same wavelength or something. I was just going to call you."

"You found something?"

"Well, yeah … and no."

"Not about the kidnapping. It's Lupe, right? You found something about her?"

He could hear Gato let out a breath he'd probably been holding. "Yeah, man. I did."

"Where is she? Not L.A., right?"

"No, man. Vegas. A woman about her height and looks, with the street name Paloma, was seen around the casinos. One of the older ones. The Four Queens. I gotta go check it out, man."

"I know. Fuck yeah, of course you got to, G." Changed the subject, quickly and lightly. "How's the girl working out you hired?"

"Ah … it's okay. She's nice and seems to care."

"There's a lot of reservation in that voice, brother."

Gato laughed. "Mr. ex-cop. I should've known. No … it's cool. Just not into leaving my mother with strangers, you know?"

"Sure. Dude, I'll check in on her when I can, okay?"

"Thank you, bro. I know she would like that. She talks about you and your 'handsome face' all the time."

"You didn't tell me her eyesight was going, Gato."

A soft laugh on the other end of the line. Mallen pulled out a cigarette and lit it. Had the feeling he'd need a lot of the things in the near future. "So, you're off to Vegas, yeah?"

"I gotta go, bro. I'm sorry."

"Hey, don't fucking apologize to me over something like this,

63

okay? Not ever. You have a line on Lupe. Your sister. You have to go. Go."

"And you, *mi amigo*? What will you do?"

"I got lines of inquiry to follow up with. It's all good, like I said."

# ELEVEN

SHANNON WATERS SUCKED AND sucked on Tre's cock, her head slowly bobbing up and down, up and down. Oil derrick slow. They were at the back end of the parking lot next to the Pizza Hut on Geary, behind an old, rusty van. The windows of the van were yellowed from decades of its owner smoking packs and packs of cigs. Trash was piled up high in the back windows. The trash and the van were washed of color by years in the sun. Tre had a crack pipe in his mouth. Lit it with a lighter. His personal lighter, the one with a bent-over woman etched into its metal side. Shannon could smell that awesome, acrid smell as the crack caught and burned.

She wished that for once he'd let her hit the pipe first before having to hit his pipe. As it was, she always got the seconds directly from his mouth. She took her lips off his cock and he put his mouth close to hers, not touching her lips, of course: her lips were for his cock only. He blew the sharp-tanged smoke into her mouth as she inhaled with all her might, desperate not to let any go to waste.

"That's a good bitch," Tre said, his voice husky with the shit that now seared through him. "Good little bitch." And with that, he pushed her head back down on his cock.

———

William Lucas rolled over on his bed made of flattened cardboard boxes and a threadbare Mexican blanket he'd found folded and left on a trash can behind an apartment building over on Eddy. *Man, still fucking day out?* He'd gotten up too soon. Night was his time. Like a vampire, he had to sleep during the day and get the fuck up at night to roam the streets looking for a high. Or for food. *Whichever happened, happened.* That was his motto. Couldn't remember where he got that shit from. He'd eaten late last night, so he was good for a bit longer. Okay then: the high.

Checked his pockets. Just about ten bucks in change and ones. The locals were dead to him. Thank fuck some of the tourists that came to this town had some heart. Ten of them would maybe give him just enough of some garbage to keep him happy overnight. Maybe he would have to raid a dumpster behind some fucking eating joint for food. Or, he guessed, he could go to the church nearby and get fed. But shit, man … he hated going there. Fuck them and their God. God only shit on us now. We weren't his great experiment: we were his great bowel disorder. *Fuck God.*

He'd need to make more dough. Thought over who he could intimidate into giving him money, but he'd just about intimidated everyone he could this month, and it was a long month. Maybe he'd be able to find something to hock. Roy had that boombox he'd shown up with one day. Said he'd gotten the money from this dude in a big van, one of those motorhome things. All fitted out like a lab. Dude was even in a lab coat, like out of some science fiction movie. All he had to do, Roy told him, was let this dude in the lab coat take some blood. Weird, that. But, Roy'd been paid. And paid not too bad. Roy had told him (and where was Roy, anyway? Hadn't seen the shitbag for days) the motorhome was usually parked down in the Mission, just above sixteenth. Maybe he'd just truck down there and see.

The day was turning cold. Lucas zipped up his old cold-weather army coat and pulled up the hood of his faded, black sweatshirt. He headed over to the Mission, stuffed-to-the-seams World War II army pack over his shoulder. So he had to give some blood? So fucking what? He'd done that before.

———

The walk down to the Mission had been a fucking pain in the fucking ass. It seemed like Lucas hit every red light, forced to wait at every corner with the zombies. His thermostat seemed to be broken, and he sweated more than he could ever remember. Maybe he was getting weaker? Being on the street could do that to a guy. He'd seen it happen a thousand times. Predators end up prey at some point. No. Fuck that. Not him. What was wrong with him today, he couldn't guess. He just needed to be high. That would fix everything.

He went to the usual place. A strip of block on 20th street, near Harrison. Shitty place. Didn't even know the name. There was some faded sign on the wall outside, but it might've said The Sandbox as much as it might've said The Shitbag. Lucas knew he could find something, *something* inside here. Hoped for at least a little bud, but knew he'd settle for a painkiller he could powder and snort. Whatever.

Entered the joint, letting his eyes adjust to the smoky dimness. Looked immediately to his left and right. That's where the predators would hide, waiting to leap the moment he walked in. He had nothing to steal, except the small amount of dough in his pocket, but he also knew that would be enough. Shit, he'd been rolled once just for his hoodie and his shoes. That's just the way the world worked sometimes.

Despair was about to set in when he didn't see anyone he could score from, but then he saw Viv. She sat at the end of the bar, hands wrapped around a glass of clear liquid he figured was vodka. He'd heard that's what she was drinking now, her liver giving up the fight. Her black hair was pulled back in a raggedy ponytail. Her clothes looked like she'd been sleeping in them. Probably had been. But Lucas knew that she'd be carrying ... something. He went over to her. She barely looked his way as he stood at the stool next to her. This was the part he fucking hated the most: having to be all like a begging dog. Anger slammed him. He wanted nothing more than to clamp one of his hands over her face and with the other punch her in the throat. *Bitch.*

"Hey Viv," he said. "How's it going?"

She took a drink. Looked at him like he was the most insignificant thing on the planet. Shrugged like she couldn't be bothered. "Fine."

"Hey, was wonderin', you know? Got ten."

"You're going to break the bank, buying like that. Or maybe have the FBI down on your ass." Took another drink.

*Fuck you, cunt.* "Yeah, but I'm working on something that will net me a fucking lot more. You know I'll come right here, too."

"Uh huh."

He pulled out his dough. Put it on the bar. "What will that get me?"

Viv sighed. "Just because I like you, right? I'll give you some bud I picked up yesterday. I'll even do 1980s prices, since it came from some asshole's back yard." She reached under her dirty skirt. Pulled out a small baggy. He hoped she pulled it from something other than her hole. She tossed it on the bar. It didn't look like shake. Looked like small buds. Very small. Very wizened and dry. He scooped it up as she scooped up his money. "Goodbye," she said in a monotone.

Lucas nodded. Walked away fast, knowing that this was the most dangerous of times. Now people knew he had something. Something they wanted. Everyone seemed to want something. Especially that something that would get them the fuck out of life, any way they could.

He was heading to the door when the bartender, Crow, waved him over from behind the bar. Lucas always figured that Crow got his name because the fucker possessed black hair, black eyes, and black painted nails on his fat, sausage fucking fingers. Crow led him away to the other end of the bar, out of earshot

"Someone lookin' for you," the bartender said as he wiped down the bar.

That wasn't what he'd expected. Lucas had expected Crow to ask him for some of the weed. Carrying charges, for letting the deal go down in his joint. "Yeah? Me?"

A nod. "Some guy. Dressed in black. Mallen. Guy used to be a cop. Then was a needle freak. Then was nothing but some fucker walking around asking questions."

He thought hard. He'd never known anybody named Mallen. "You sure he was looking for me?"

Another nod.

Why would this guy be looking for him? And how would he *know* to be out looking for him? Nobody knew about him. He was a nothing. A dark hole. Man, he was more under the radar now than he was a year ago before anyone in his family even realized he was gone. What the living fuck? "You sure?" he asked again.

Crow almost threw the glass in his hand at him. "You think I don't know my shit, asshole? I just said someone was looking for you. Doing you a fucking favor. And what do you do? You question my authority." Crow then turned his back on Lucas and moved down the bar. End of session.

Lucas stood there a moment. Why would some ex-cop, ex-junkie, be looking for him? He hadn't done anything wrong. Well, not that wrong. His mind raced over all the crap he'd done in the last couple weeks. All the people he'd fucked up or stolen from. There was nothing. No one that would even have enough dough to hire a dude to look him up. Nobody even cared about him. Nobody had—

*Wait . . . .*

He remembered then that he *had* given out his name in the last couple weeks. Just once.

That fucker Hendrix. Hendrix had found some shit to pawn. Lucas and Shannon were sharing the butt end of a joint when Hendrix walked up and showed them what he'd stolen. It was some good stuff: an iPod, gold watch, and some rings. Hendrix said it would look less suspicious if Lucas and Shannon walked in carrying some of the stuff, instead of him walking in on his own with all of it. If Lucas and Shannon walked in after, or before him, with some of the pieces it would be more … quiet. *Asshole.* And that's when Lucas got it all squared away in his head.

The pawnshop fucker. That money-lending fucker. That shop was the ONLY place Lucas had given his name recently. Why had he done that? Oh yeah … he'd been desperate. Being desperate fucked with a guy's judgment. A guy would do anything when he needed to get high. That day, Lucas would've pawned his mother's asshole for something to take him away.

*Shit….*

# TWELVE

It took Mallen the remaining hours of the day before he got a tenuous lead on one of the two names Blackmore had given him. At this point, he felt a former shadow of himself. The only thing keeping him going was finding the answer to what had gone down. A Shannon Waters was known to hang her shingle out in a bar on the corner of Larkin and Turk. Nobody seemed to know where she lived, but everyone knew she had a protector. Tre. That was as much as Mallen was able to get before he ran into a wall of silence. It was one of the first times he'd had to pay for information. Didn't really mind though. Realized this was just how it was going to be for him now. Hell, maybe it was a sign that he was truly away from his old world, but not far enough that people wouldn't talk to him. Now he would just have to pay up for what he needed. What the fuck else could he do? Fold his tents and go home? Not fucking likely.

The bar was called Refuge House. Mallen laughed when he

heard the name. Seemed to be trying too hard to fit in. Wondered if it would be too neat, too carefully aged, and he wasn't disappointed when he went in. It was just like he'd suspected. Mostly hipsters, the hipsters who were slowly, inexorably moving into the hood and dragging it into gentrification, kicking and screaming. Maybe this time it would take. Probably not.

When he walked in, he almost thought he'd walked into the wrong place. *This* was gentrification? They could fuckin' have it. Pre-darkened wood paneling purposefully carved with fake graffiti that ended up looking too artful. The carved hearts with arrows through them and the fake gang symbols were too clean, too symmetrical. Even the placing of the graffiti was obviously thought out. Bullshit. What a depressing place. And Shannon Waters hung *here*? When he'd learned that she'd been seen here, he'd also heard a little about this protector of hers, Tre. About his need for the pipe. Protector? Try pimp, right? Six of one, half a dozen of another. Pimping her really wasn't a shocker, but pimping her here was. Here among the hipsters? She must be something other than what he pictured in his mind.

And she was.

Mallen spotted her after spending a handful of minutes at the bar, drinking a Well Whiskey. She sat quietly at the opposite end of the bar. Blonde, or mostly blonde. Face not totally eaten up by the pipe, but the heavy makeup she wore would cover up some of that damage. Her body though, that hadn't been eaten by the pipe, not at all. Not yet. She was attractive and healthy enough … enough to get her into the position to take someone outside, and … and then he got it. *That's* what was going on here. Tre wasn't pimping her; he was using her as a lure. He'd throw out the hook, then when Shannon found her fish, they'd leave together and Tre would come out of nowhere and slam the guy and take his wallet. Hell, Mallen figured it beat working in a fast food joint.

Well, there was only one way to play it. She was alone, a drink in front of her. Every time she took a sip, her eyes scanned the room, wanting to make eye contact. Mallen moved down the bar, catching her eye. Prayed she didn't know him. Seemed she didn't. A smile. Forced and worn. Maybe she was hoping for one of the younger, more hipster guys. Guys with more money. Guys with more faith in humanity, enough that they couldn't fathom being rolled for their phone and cash.

He smiled as he came up to her. Looked at her drink. Something red and bubbly. Smirked, "What the hell do you call that?"

"A drink. Why? They call it something else where you come from?"

"No. Well, if it's really a drink, then let me buy you another one." He motioned to the bartender. Pointed at both their drinks. The 'tender nodded and started to make them.

"Thanks," Shannon said, eyeing him for a moment. Probably wondering if he was for real, or a cop. Oh the irony of life, he thought. "What's your name?"

"Mark."

"Mark? And?"

"And Mark. Does it have to have a tail?"

She shook her head. Took a sip of the drink the bartender put down in front of her. "My name is Shannon."

"I like that. Had a sister named Shannon."

"Bet you did." She laughed then. Eyed him again, as if trying to see if her game was having the desired effect. Mallen made her think it did. He moved in a little closer.

"No, seriously," he smiled. "I had a sister named Shannon. She's in a nunnery now."

"Nunnery? What the fuck is that?"

"Well .... It's place for religious women who have given up this world for the next."

She took another drink. Seemed to be nearly drunk. "For the next? What fucking next, Mark? There's no 'next.' Only 'here.'" And that seemed to make her sad, a sad that reached through the drunk and choked her by the throat, just a little.

He didn't answer. Only took a sip of his drink. Caught her looking at him over the rim of her glass. They had a couple more drinks but he could see she nursed hers, not wanting to get too stoned. Checked her watch. "I have to go now, Mark. Sorry I can't stay longer."

He slid off the barstool. "Oh, really? I thought that we ...."

A smile. "That we what? You want something more, Mark? I can do that for you."

Mallen had to admit, that at that moment, she was indeed very sexy. She knew how to play it. "You can? Yeah?"

"Yes. I have a place just around the corner. A small flat. We can go there and have a couple more drinks. See what happens."

"And what would that cost me?" he said. "Come on, that's what this is about, right? Okay, cool. I'm okay with it. Just want to know how much."

She slid in closer. Put her hand to his hip. Trying to find the gun she thought might be there. Before he could slide away, she brushed against the Glock. Froze. He stepped closer. Grabbed her wrist and held it firm. Said quietly, "No Shannon, not a cop. Just another guy who wants to wear a gun for shits an giggles, okay? But not a cop. Now you and me are going to walk out of here all calm like. You just have to lead me out, so we can really talk."

There was a brief flex of the arm he held firmly in his right hand. "About?"

"Tommy Hendrix. You hear he's dead, yeah?"

"What's all this bullshit to you?"

"I'm trying to find who took Trina Marston's kid. Hendrix was a part of it. Let's go somewhere more quiet." He walked her out of the bar. She gave no resistance.

Out on the street, she shrugged out of his grasp, but didn't run. "I don't know this Hendrix guy," she said as she turned and started walking east down the street. Mallen knew she was leading him into the trap that Tre had set. That was fine. She knew he was armed. Hell, maybe she *wanted* him to off Tre?

"Yeah, you know him," Mallen said as he walked with her.

"Yeah? How do I know him?"

"Stop that shit. I know you know him. You know you know him. What I need are the names of the other people he hung with. Maybe somebody you'd never seen before until recently."

"And why would I tell you anyfuckingthing? So you have a gun. So fucking what. Lots of guys have guns." She quickened her pace down the street and he let her lead him. She stopped in front of a closed-up 99-cent store and turned to face him. The shadows were on his left and he turned around just in time to avoid a fist aimed for his face. Could even feel the displaced air as the fist skimmed his cheek. There was Tre. He was smaller than Mallen imagined him to be, but with a wiry build. Mallen dodged another fist and then Tre's hand went to his waistband where the butt of a pistol stuck out. Mallen rushed in, snatching the pistol butt before Tre could, yanking it out and shoving it under the man's chin. Suddenly the world had stopped. Shannon stayed still the entire time, watching, and in that moment he knew he'd been right: she wanted Tre dead.

Tre had frozen in place the split second Mallen shoved the gun under his chin. Tre's eyes went to Shannon, pleading for her to do something. Mallen risked a glance over his shoulder. She cowered there, acting scared, but he could see she was anything but. Behind those eyes was glee.

"Tre," Mallen told him quietly as he moved him back toward the shadows, the gun pushed up with all he had under the man's chin, forcing his head back, "we're going to put you to sleep for a while, okay?"

"Fuck you," Tre replied. Crazy-ass crackheads. Always copping an attitude when they went around with a gun in their waistband.

Mallen didn't have any more to waste. He took the gun and clocked Tre across the temple with it. Tre went out like a light, falling to the ground face first. There was a huge crack as the man's nose broke. Mallen rolled him over onto his side so the man wouldn't choke on his own blood. Dragged him into the even darker recesses of the abandoned store's doorway. It smelled of piss and shit and garbage. Probably on par with who Tre was. Mallen turned to Shannon. She hadn't moved an inch the entire time. Stared at him now. Scared. Like she thought she'd found a liberator, but was wondering now if she'd only found another jailor.

He went over to her, putting Tre's gun in his pocket. "So," he said quietly, "we were talking about Hendrix."

She looked at Tre. Shook her head. "He's going to wake up, and when he does he'll be angry. Angry with me for not trying to stop you."

"He'll be in no shape to hurt you. You'll have to find another answer."

"It's not that easy."

"Look, you know something, yeah? Or why all of this? Were you just hoping to get me to shoot your pimp? Leading me on? If that's it, then I'm out of here and you can nurse him until he comes around."

She chewed her lip. He could see it was for real: she wasn't just playing for time. "No, but I . . . ."

Mallen sighed. Nodded. "I get it. Hang on." He went over and delivered a kick to Tre's face that broke the man's jaw. Blood flowed and the man gurgled and tried to come around but failed. Mallen made sure that the bag of shit pimp would stay on his side, the blood running out of his mouth. Checked Tre's pockets. Found a few rocks of crack in a dirty baggie, a pipe, and about fifty in cash. He went and handed the pipe and money over to Shannon, who looked at him like he was either crazy, or her savior. Held back the crack that she'd seen him take out of Tre's pocket. "Now," he said quietly, "this fucker's going to be out of commission for some time. Way too busy on painkillers to fucking care about you. I've bought you some time. That should buy me some info."

The items disappeared into her purse. He could tell she wanted to go, find some rock, and smoke out. Like right now. He blocked her way. "I don't know what you want to know, man," she replied. "Seriously. I didn't know Tommy barely at all."

"Yeah, but you did. You probably even pawned shit together, right?"

"Who told you that? Lucas?"

He had to remember to steer clear of getting Blackmore involved. Shrugged. "That doesn't matter. What matters is that you know Hendrix." He moved a little closer. "Look, this isn't about some bullshit crack deal, or some low-bone theft. This is about a little girl. And her time might be running out. Hendrix is the only lead I have. Did you ever see him with someone outside of the norm? If you pawned crap with him, you hung with him, and if you hung with him, then you might've seen something." He looked down at the bag of crack in his hand. Then he looked at her. Didn't need to say shit. She got it.

"Okay, look..." she started, "there was something weird. One day, me and Hendrix and Luc, Lucas right? We were trying to find something to pawn to that prick Blackmore. We needed *something*, man, and Karachi wasn't around, hadn't been, and—"

That set off Mallen's memory. The note in Hendrix's car. The written name, torn in half. Too weird a coincidence. *Kara*. "Karachi?"

"Yeah. He was an alternative for us, but we didn't like going to him unless we had to." She shuddered. Said, "But I don't want to talk about him, okay?"

"Okay. So, what happened?"

Shannon continued, "Well, Hendrix usually had something.

He lived in that fucking wagon over south of Market. But it was never fucked with. Never. Everyone knew he was a snitch, but he tried to play it like he was some undercover dude. Everyone knew the truth though. Anyway, he had nothing this one day, right? Then he goes away, and me and Lucas don't see him the rest of the day. Then a couple days later we find him flush with money, and dope. I mean a LOT of dope. Wouldn't say what had happened. Wouldn't say shit about shit. He doled out a bit to us, but he was with money, man. So, me and Luc, we follow him back to his wagon. Trailing him. Lucas, he dug that shit. Like in a movie, right? Well, we get back there, and we see Hendrix about to get into his car when a big car pulls up behind his wagon. We know it's a dick wagon. We hang back. Just watch." She paused. Eyed the baggie in his hand. He knew she'd say anything now. Anything to get what she needed.

"And?" he said as he pocketed the baggie. "What happened then? Who got out of the car?"

"A cop. Dressed like a high-priced, executive type of fucker. Asian-looking. Face fur. Ponytail."

And Mallen stopped dead. His right hand started to throb, like the mem ory of the nails being pounded into it all of sudden kicked down the door and barged in. *Winstons Wong.*

"You sure," he said as he grabbed her shoulder. Squeezing it so tightly she winced and tried to get away, "you are fucking sure it was an Asian cop in a fancy suit, with a ponytail? A goatee? You fucking sure?"

"I am!" she said, tears coming into her eyes. "I think his name is Winstons something or the fuck other. Because he's always smoking."

Mallen let her go. Gave her the bag of dope. "Get out of here," he said quietly, his mind traveling back in time. To a hammer. To some nails. To a meeting under the Palace of Fine Arts dome. To what happened to Chris.

*Winstons Wong.* You fucking son of a bitch. He didn't even register Shannon running away down the street. He turned and headed back to his truck, his mind wondering what the fuck he was going to do next.

# THIRTEEN

Lucas waited across the street, in a patch of darkness made even darker by the overhang of a burned-out sign from a business that closed down over a decade ago. With his faded black clothes and backpack he was pretty much invisible. Doing a "Casper the Ghost" as his friends would have said back in the day.

Blackmore came out of his store. Locked the door behind him. Pulled the heavy security gate across the windows and bolted them shut. Snapped the heavy lock into place. Shook the gate once, the old, rusty metal sounding like off-tone cymbals. Lucas watched the man check his watch, and then move on up the street, out of the Loin. Whether that fuck lived nearby or on the other side of the moon, Lucas knew he was going to follow him.

He watched Blackmore walk to the end of the block at Golden Gate and cut over to Van Ness. Shit, Lucas thought, if the guy was going to bus it, then it would become problematic. He quickly checked his pockets. Not enough change for a bus.

Shit, didn't matter anyway: this was San Francisco. He could scoop up onto the back of the bus through the rear doors. It's done all the time.

To his luck, however, Blackmore only crossed Van Ness. No buses. Lucas smiled to himself as he traveled with a pack of herd animals. They gave him good cover, and a wide berth. No way that Blackmore would ever think he was being followed. Why should he? Lucas trailed behind Blackmore as the man walked along the street. It was a bit of a slog as he followed the man to Laguna and then left until he hit Birch Street. The street was only a block long, windows and windows of apartments staring down into the street. A quiet street to be sure. He'd have to be careful.

Lucas dumped off his backpack in the entryway of a neighboring apartment building. Pulled his ice pick. It was something he'd found in a dumpster months ago. Large size, not like what you'd see in a bar. Industrial strength, the handle wrapped in electrical tape. Helped with the grip.

Blackmore went up to the third building on the right. Lucas could see Blackmore dragging his keys from his pants pocket as he went to the door. That was when Lucas struck. He ran up, a blur of dirty wind, right at Blackmore who'd turned at the last moment, only then realizing what was going down.

Lucas shoved the point of the pick up underneath the man's solar plexus and froze it there. Blackmore became a statue, the only sound the keys dropping from his hand. He began to shake with fear.

"Pick 'em up, shithead." Lucas backed off enough to let the older man grab up his house keys. Blackmore had to try three times to pick up his keys. Held them out to Lucas, like a child that knows it's done something bad. But Lucas shook his head, saying, "After you, shitface."

"What do you want? I just run a pawnshop."

"And run your mouth. Now open it. We're going to go inside and have a chat. Then I'll bury you in some nice, quiet place. Fair trade for some talk, right?"

Blackmore didn't nod. Didn't shake his head. Only slipped the key into the lock and led Lucas into the lobby. "Look," Blackmore said at that point, "Why are you doing this? You pawn crap at my place. So what? I don't understand what it is you want?"

"It's about some fucker that's been looking for me. Knew my real name. You understand that, right? Knows my real name. And it's your fault, asshole."

"It wasn't me, I'm telling you," Blackmore said with desperation in his voice. "Why do anything to me? I didn't do anything, didn't talk to anybody."

Lucas shook his head. Grinned. "Oh yes you did. I know for a hard fact you talked to someone named Mallen, and you sent him off on the chase to find me."

"Mallen? I don't know any Mallen!"

Rain started to fall outside, the faint background noise filtering in through the glass.

"Yes you do," Lucas said as he threatened Blackmore with the pick. "Yes you do."

———

Shannon ran off into the night after dropping the bomb that Winstons Wong had been seen at Hendrix's wagon right before the man was killed. Mallen went back to the truck, jumped inside, and dialed Gwen's number. She picked up right away. "Saunders."

"It's Mallen."

"Oh, my long lost has returned to me."

He ignored the sarcasm. "I need some knowledge. Some knowledge about one of yours."

"Mine? Who?"

"Wong. Winstons Wong."

In that silent moment before she responded, he knew she had something. He knew she was debating on how much to give him, and he knew that he needed to figure her angle on this, and fast.

"What do you want to know about him for? He's got a heavy rep, I can tell you that."

"So I've heard."

"I've heard, once or maybe twice, that he knows some pretty powerful people. Moonlights for them."

"Uh huh. What else?"

"What else do you want to know?"

"Quit being so fucking cagey. You asked me in, and now you want to play coy? At this point? I don't care. I can go my own way."

"Woah, wait. Wait. What's up? We're supposed to be a team."

"Team? Right. I need info. Wong is mixed up in Hendrix's death."

A pause, then: "How sure are you?"

"Eyewitness."

"Shit … really?"

"Yup. And nope: you don't get to know who. All you need to

know is that someone has placed Wong outside of Hendrix's rolling home not long before he was found dead."

"Well…" Another pause. "What do you want to know? If it's bad, I'll have to go to Internal Affairs. You know that, right? It'll bring you into it. It'll bring you back here."

And that gave him pause. *Shit…*. And he remembered the nails. Flexed his right hand, staring at the dark scars there on the flanges between his middle, ring, and pinky. Thought of Chris. Of what they did to her. Of what Wong said to him with a smirk as he left him and Chris under the dome at the Palace of Fine Arts. "See you around," Wong had grinned. Grinned like he had all the time in the fucking world.

"Then you have to go to IA," Mallen said. "Fuck it. If this shit-sack is wrong, than he's wrong. I know IA is filled with assholes, but if Wong is in on something that involves killing civilians, fuck him. He needs to go down. That's not what being a policeman is about."

There was another silence. He waited, silently counting to ten. If he hit ten, he'd know she wouldn't be of any help anymore. But it was on nine that she said, "Wong's been linked recently to moving narcotics. Quietly, or well… it was supposed to be quiet. Word is he's getting cocky. Due to his backing. Everyone would love for him to go away, or …."

"Or what? Retire and live a happy, ex-cop life? Or … cash out completely."

"Those are your words, Mallen. Not mine."

"Yeah, they're mine. But all this doesn't explain his connection with Hendrix. I need you to access records. See if you can find some link between the two. I'll do it from the street."

"This isn't getting us any closer to finding the Marston girl."

"Hey, you said you thought Hendrix was involved, yeah? Well, now we have a connection between Hendrix and Wong. A cop. Hendrix was known to be a snitch, but then why kill him? The timing is weird, right?"

"Right," she answered.

"So I need the latest on Wong. Who he's been seen with on the street, that sort of thing."

"Okay," Gwen said. "You have anything else on the kidnapping? Any other leads?"

"Nothing right now. It all leads to Hendrix. You want your money back?"

"Well, I'd consider the package unpacked and used, sort of."

"I'll stop working with you, Gwen. But I won't lie and say I'll drop this."

"What's the deal, Mallen? I know you want to find the Marston girl, but all of sudden you're like Clint Eastwood. What gives? It's Wong, isn't it? What's up with you two?"

"Just an old joke about Jesus and three nails. But forget about that. Just get me what you can, and I'll work my angle from here. See ya," he hung up before she had any chance to say another word. Instantly dialed Oberon's number. The detective picked up immediately.

"Kane," the detective said.

"Should I be offended you haven't put me in your contact list, Obie?"

"I would have done exactly that, but then it would remind me that I know you. You have the rent for the month, by the way? My mailbox is quite lonely without your check residing inside it."

"Fuckin' ouch, Obie. Did I interrupt another date?"

"No." And Mallen couldn't help but notice the tone of regret there. Decided to leave it alone. That was a conversation for over a drink, if even then. He'd known Oberon for so long but didn't really *know* him. Figured he never would. And really, why should he expect that? Not everyone wants to be personal with every other person out there. He and Oberon had shared a lot of life and death moments. Maybe that was enough.

"Obie," Mallen said. "About Hendrix. I found something out that I know will just make your ever-loving day, man."

"About Hendrix? What is it, Mark?"

"Winstons Wong."

There was a long silence, and Mallen knew he'd hit home. "Wong? What? What did you find out? It better be good and a hundred percent steel, Mark."

"Well, he was seen outside Hendrix's wagon, not long before the guy was murdered."

Another silence. He could almost smell Oberon's mind smoking like a train's stack over this. "Mark," Oberon said quietly, "You need to be sure about the answer to my next question. Are we on the same page with that?"

"Yeah, we are."

"Who told you this? Who's the witness."

"Shannon Waters. Her and this other street dude named William Lucas hocked stolen stuff with Hendrix. Hendrix shows up a couple days later, flush with dough and junk. Won't share, so Waters and Lucas follow. She swears she saw Wong parked nearby and then get out of his car and approach Hendrix's wagon. They watched him knock on the door and the door opening.

They figured no way to get shit now, right? Everyone on the street was starting to figure that Hendrix was informing for the cops. How the fuck else could he park his car there all the time?" Mallen lit up a cigarette. Blew smoke up at the sky then said, "Wong's into it, Obie. I know it, and you know it."

"Did you tell Detective Saunders this?"

"Had to, man. Had to give her something. She didn't like it, any more than you do."

"Yes," came the reply, "but maybe for different reasons."

"What do you mean?"

"Well," Oberon said reluctantly, "it was said they dated for a while."

"Oh. Yeah?" His mind ran back over his conversation with Gwen. Her fucking Wong would've for sure made her reluctant. Or . . . .

"You told me that Gwen was driving it hard. Wanting promotion, yeah?" he said to Oberon.

"Yes. But I can't say that she'd go *this* far. She might . . . embellish a report to make herself look better, but that's about it, Mark. This? This is murder."

"I'm not saying she had anything to do with murder," Mallen replied, "I'm just saying that she might get in with some bad people who are themselves shooting upward in the department."

"But Wong is not one of those people. He's being tolerated, but that's all. Probably because he must have something on a lot of people. You know what I'm talking about, too."

"Yeah, I do." He thought hard for an angle. "So, what do I—" His call waiting signal cut in. Not a number he recognized. "Just a sec, Oberon. Be right back." He switched lines. "Hello?"

"Mallen, it's Gwen."

"Been a long time."

"We need to talk."

Every fiber of his being tightened up. "About? Like I was reminded, just recently, I'm out looking for clues on the Marston's girl's abduction. I don't know that I can come in on command."

"I need to see you, Mallen."

He figured she was about to lay on him that she'd been fucking Wong, but instead she told him, "I just heard that they found a man out at the beach. South of the park. Shot dead."

"Okay. And? What does that have to do with us?"

"He had one of Jessie Marston's toys in his coat. The … that mother of hers ID'd it."

"Where are you?"

"On my way to the scene. I'll wait off-site. You'll find me. I'll be where no one will notice, Ulloa Street."

"Okay. Be there as soon as I can. Thirty minutes, tops." He clicked back to Oberon. Filled the detective in on what had just happened.

"I don't like it, Mark," Oberon told him. "Things are beginning to be too coincidental."

"I know. Well, I'm going out to see her. Just wanted to let you know…." and here he added a smirk to his voice, "in case I don't come back."

"If you don't come back, Mark," Oberon replied, "I swear to always toast your memory."

"That's all, Obie? You'd just toast my memory?"

"Uh huh. I figure once a month is enough." And with that the detective hung up.

# FOURTEEN

MALLEN DROVE QUICKLY OVER to the scene of the shooting. Cops were everywhere. He drove around for some moments, a couple blocks out from the scene. Found Gwen's car, parked up ahead, away from the street lights. He pulled to the curb and got out. She got out, too. Walked toward him. He didn't like it that she'd hooked her jacket back behind her gun holster. Like she was expecting trouble.

"Here I am," he said with a smile. "Just like a faithful dog. Now what the fuck happened? Who's the body?"

She pulled out her notebook, and that action made Mallen's hand involuntarily move to his pocket. He thought Gwen was trying for a gun and he knew he would've done anything to keep her from getting the drop on him. He tried to unclench his shoulders and act naturally. Didn't want her to know how much he didn't trust her. And he didn't trust her at all. Not now.

"The body is of a guy named Randy Yates. They're running a

check on him now. I busted him a couple times, but that was a year or so ago."

"What'd you bust him for?"

"Narcotics." Here she stopped and smiled at him like she was pulling his favorite dinner right out of the oven. "And he's a registered sex offender."

"So? He's dead, the kid is still missing."

"Hendrix had a boner for kiddies. And so does this Yates."

Sure, he thought, it was pretty coincidental. Coincidental beyond the law of averages. *Both* guys end up dead, and *both* guys were baby lovers? It just didn't make sense though. He still would not believe it was a revenge-type thing. He knew those, what they looked like. That was usually done with a gun. And Hendrix hadn't been shot, he'd been shot up. "Where was he shot? Tell me what you have."

"He was killed just over near the great highway." Consulted her notes. "One bullet. Right in the head. Not close range, per se, but within talking distance."

"And you said that one of Jessie's toys had been found with him?"

A shake of her head. "No, it was found in his car, which was located nearby. Only a block away."

"Can you get me in to see that car?"

Hesitation then. "Why? I could be getting into a ton of shit for letting you do that."

"I need to see that guy's car, Gwen." His eyes glinted in the moonlight as he stared at her. "Look, I'll find a way on my own, if I have to. You know I will. Hoping that I don't have to."

Gwen chewed her lip for a minute. Finally nodded. "Okay,

come with me. But don't, *don't* say anything to anyone unless I give you the word. Got it?"

"Yeah, I got it."

They walked over a couple blocks to the Great Highway. Gwen turned left, heading south. The buildings on that street, open to the constant ocean air, were rusty and faded, beaten by decades of sand, fog, and drear. On his right, the black waves crashed on the sand, the sound muted in the night. The air was alive with salt. He suddenly missed his home back in Sausalito.

They came up on the car. It was surrounded by cops, lights, and more cops. Mallen's apprehension rose the closer he got. There might be cops here that knew him, way back when. But he had to see the car. He needed a line on Yates. Yeah, the cops would have gone over everything, but there was a chance. Slim, but still a chance. You can tell a lot about a man from his car. How he keeps it. Is it in good shape, even though it's a clunker? Conversely, is it an expensive ride, but not cared for? How dirty is the interior? Lots of garbage? His finding out would depend on how much the cops had already gone over it. He was hoping he'd see something the cops had overlooked. His eyes might see things the cops would miss, no matter how long their experience.

Gwen led him closer. Her partner stood near the scene, and started to come over when he saw her but she waved him off. The man almost did a double take when he recognized Mallen. Glanced at Gwen, then looked away. So, Mallen thought, she hadn't told her partner everything she was up to. He filed that little bit of information away. He just couldn't figure her angle. Maybe because Wong was involved?

At the car, she stepped aside, pointed out a couple things but it was just for show. The car had been dusted already, so that meant that probably anything of worth was gone. However, she handed him a pair of gloves, just like he was still a cop. He went to the driver's side door and opened it. Sat in the seat. The glove box was open, and empty. The sun shades had been pulled down. Empty. Yates hadn't been tall, judging by how far the seat was forward. He felt under the dash, and heard Gwen scoff. He then felt along the underside of both front seats. Looking for anything now. Anything that might also vindicate the reason for Gwen's bringing him "under the tape."

But there was nothing.

He hauled himself out. Pulled the front seat forward. It was a hatchback, so it was hard for him to get inside. He felt around first. Nothing under the carpet, and no sign of the carpet having been rigged for a stash. He checked under the backseat. Nothing. Then he ran his fingers over the inside stitching, the stitching that held the fake leather down to the backseat frame. And there it was. The stitching was gone, and the fabric was held to the underside by Velcro. He used his left hand to search around as his right gently pulled the Velcro apart. He coughed to cover the sound. The Velcro pulled apart. Only enough to allow his thumb, index, and middle finger access. He tried to keep his left hand searching as he moved around, his back to Gwen and the night covering some of his motions.

"Mallen," Gwen said urgently and quietly, "no more time, okay? We need to get you gone."

"I'm there," he replied as he pulled out, of all things, a flash drive. Palmed it as he pushed himself out of the car, standing as he dropped it into his coat pocket, the side that was away from

Gwen. He'd tell her about it, sure, but only after he'd had his time with it. The find brought him all the way back to that first night out on his own as a uniformed cop. Finding Veronica Sloan's cell phone. He'd had to examine that piece of evidence first, the call records and contacts list, before turning it over to someone else. Just like now with this flash drive. The finding of that cell phone, and the way he handled it turned out to not only define if he was going to be a good cop or not, but *how* he was going to be a cop. Well, mostly. Hadn't figured on the disgraced leaving, the years afterward wallowing in a haze of heroin. Nodded at Gwen and she quickly led him away from the scene. Once they were well away, she stopped and turned to him. "Well?"

Shook his head as he felt for his cigarettes. Found the pack and pulled one out. "Your boys did a good job."

Gwen stood there, looking at him. He knew she was trying to read him. Kept his face calm as he lit his cigarette. He shrugged. Sighed. "Sorry for all the trouble. I really thought there might be something there that your side would've overlooked."

"You have a habit of expressing yourself in terms of conflict," she replied. "Your side? Your boys? I thought we were in this together."

"So did I, Gwen."

It took a moment, but then she relaxed and he figured he'd passed some sort of test. "Okay, so that little maneuver whimpered and died," she told him. "I'll try to trace any and all of Yates's known acquaintances. I'll give you any names I can come up with, and you run 'em down."

"Yes, Ma'am," he replied. "I'll let you know if I find anything.

I still like the Hendrix/Randy's both being into kids angle. Definitely something there."

"That's why I'll keep checking. There's got to be someone else that knew both of them. That might be something."

He gripped the flash drive he'd found in his pocket. "Yeah, might be something. See ya." He turned and walked down the street.

# FIFTEEN

MALLEN WANTED THE MOST non-descript, anonymous place where he could rent some computer time, and he'd found it. The all-night copy and computer-time rental store sat out on John Daly Boulevard, only a few blocks from the ocean. For some reason, he always found a sense of safety with his back against the ocean. The store did what anyone would expect them to do: make copies, send faxes, get your computer repaired. Rent Internet time. In the back of the place were a row of computers along the wall. The screens faced into the store, probably to keep people from renting them long enough to jack off to some porn. You could rent them in thirty-minute increments, but you had to rent at least an hour to start. Cute, that. Mallen paid the dough and went to the computer that would be the hardest for anyone paying attention to see. Not like the place was full. It wasn't.

He sat down and inserted the drive into the back of the

screen. Felt a little too much like he did when he and Gato found the tapes that Teddy Mac had been carrying around with him, using them as protection for his life. At that thought, Mallen wondered how his friend was doing in Vegas as he looked for Lupe. Hoped G was all right.

The drive came up on the screen and he clicked on it. There was only one folder there. He clicked on that. Inside were other folders. Each folder had two letters for what he guessed was a name, separated by a period. D.H. F.R. C.L. He chose the first one, D.H. Inside that folder were two documents. One was called "bio" and the other was called simply "album." He couldn't click on that file right away … it was just so ominous. After a moment, he took a deep breath and then just clicked on the bio folder.

It was a biography of a child. A child named Daniel Harris.

The biography was complete. Daniel Harris was really just a toddler. Three years old. It had his complete medical background, along with the medical background of the mother. It mentioned what part of the Bay Area the child now resided in. And then, at the end, was the part that made it all fit. There was a price at the bottom of the last paragraph. Like what you'd see in any catalog.

"Jesus fucking Christ…" Mallen said under his breath. It didn't take a brainchild to know what that bio and price meant. He clicked on the "album" file. Pictures and pictures of Daniel, all taken like a candid camera had captured him. Some of them had the mother in them also. There were a couple close-ups, but the angles were off. Sometimes the lighting wasn't good. Made Mallen think of some sort of hidden camera had taken those pictures. He closed that file and backed out so he could look at the initialed files. Clicked on a few. Yup, all the same format. That was when he saw it. The initials were "J.M." He clicked on that file and it was indeed Jesse Marston. The only thing different about Jessie's bio page, and he'd seen this in a few of the others, were the letters "O.U." Looked at the photos and they were of the same sort, candid shots of Jessie watching the street as she walked, or of Jessie with Trina.

He closed that file. Closed down the flash drive and pulled it out. With the way the files were set up, the info inside them, he felt it must be some sort of black market adoption ring. That's why Jessie had been taken. To be sold. But, Jesus … to who? Where to even start looking? He had to find the person who shot Yates. And before the police got to him. Or Wong. He had a hunch that if Wong got to the shooter first, it was over. He stood up, looking at the flash drive in his hand for a moment, bouncing it up and down in the palm of his hand. Walked out of the store. Once outside he heard the roar of the ocean. The ocean was out there. Always, it was out there. Took a deep breath, bringing in the salt air. Took another deep breath, to clear his head. It would unfold in time. Things were moving along and he knew from experience you had to find that zone between letting them unfold, and forcing them to. First on the list was to go and check on Trina. Tell her he was making strides and for her not to give up hope.

———

He parked nearby in a parking garage. Walked the couple blocks to Trina's apartment. Noticed a homeless guy sleeping in the doorway of an abandoned store. Realized it was the same guy who'd been sleeping there for over four years. Four years on the street.

Got to Trina's door. Knocked. Waited. Took another knock to bring her to the door. He knew immediately that she was high. Had also been crying. "Mallen," she said as she wiped at her eyes. Tried to hide them. Tried to keep the crook of her arm out of view.

"Stop it," he said as he entered. "You think I don't recognize the signs?"

She went and sat on the couch. "I know. I had to get away, man. Just get away."

Mallen nodded. Shrugged. "My offer of helping you get clean still stands, okay? I'll take you anytime. When I find Jessie, I'll babysit her while you run the gauntlet of getting clean."

"When you find Jessie," she echoed. Shook her head. "You sound so sure," she added quietly.

"I'm making some strides, Trina. I'm onto a thread that might lead to something bigger."

She looked up at him then. "Really? Really, Mallen?"

"I think so, yeah."

"What did you find?"

"I don't want to go into it, or say too much, too soon. I just wanted you to know that I haven't been lying around, forgetting what you asked me to do. I'm on it, and I'm running the streets trying to find her. You just try to hang in there, okay? Just give me some time before you go and blast your head off your shoulders. I said I'll find her, and I'll find her."

"You can't tell me anything, Mallen? Nothing at all?" Her

eyes pleaded with him. Begged him for something she could cling to. Hell, he could understand that. A hundred percent.

"Okay, what I *can* say is that I don't think she was taken by a pedophile. It's not about that. That's what I feel, anyway." And it was true. The records he'd found on the flash drive, coupled with the photos, made him think something different. If it were pedophiles, those photos would've been of the children nude.

Trina sat there for a moment, like she didn't believe what she'd just been told. "Not a pedophile? Then why? Why would someone take my daughter if it wasn't to abuse her?"

"I'm working on the answer to that. Just give me some time."

"Okay. I will," she replied. Seemed to be getting drowsy.

# SIXTEEN

GATO GOT TO VEGAS at 3 a.m. But that didn't matter of course because it was Vegas. He'd taken the pearl white Falcon, because that car was his good luck car, and man he needed some *buena suerte.* If Lupe was here, he'd find her. He knew he would. He didn't have any connections in this town, outside of one person: *Mama Lobo.*

Everyone seemed to know Mama Lobo here in Vegas. Hell, she was known even as far away as Chicago. The stories on her would fill a book as thick as the Bible. How she came to be known as Mama Lobo alone would make any action film look like a Bugs Bunny cartoon. It was told that she came up from South America back in the fifties. Her husband was one that everybody avoided. Didn't want his evil eye on them. If he *did* put that eye at you, you were dead within twenty-four hours.

No doubt.

No way out.

Nothing left for you but a grave out in the desert somewhere. But, if he liked you? Well, he'd bury you deep enough that the animals would have to work a little harder to get to you.

Her husband had come into town, and had set out immediately to deal. Not cards, but heroin. He'd done well, too. At first. Then he'd pissed off the wrong people: the mob. Encroached a little too far. That was his death warrant. The button men had come for him. Some witnesses later testified that they'd never seen a man take so much lead and not die. The mob lost some good men that day. At least seven known high-level guys. They knew what they were going up against and still they almost lost the day.

Then they went after Mama Lobo.

She fled, so they say, as far north as she could go. Into Canada. It was eight years later that she reappeared. Began to set herself up in the same territories her husband used to own. Like she was taunting the mob to come after her. And they did. But she wasn't alone. She'd smelled out a lot of the street boys that roam the streets of Vegas, selling on their own. Very low-level stuff. Lower than low-level. She went to work and quickly converted the majority of them to her side. So as the mob came to move her out, her army of street boys moved in. They loved her. Idolized her. She was beautiful beyond beautiful. It was said she could be nurturing and deadly, all in the same breath. That day? When the mob came for her? The mob lost way more than seven button men. They lost streets. They lost respect. It was like Mama Lobo had come in on a magical carpet armed with the sword of vengeance and not only cut off their lives, but their nuts, too. After that bloodbath they left Mama Lobo alone. She'd taken her vengeance and that was enough. Now she just wanted to make a living. And she wanted to live well. So the mob let her stay. Quietly though. Acting like they didn't even know she was there.

And she'd only been twenty-four.

Now she was a venerable seventy-six and still as dangerous as she'd ever been, and as beautiful.

———

Gato pulled up to the Four Queens, not even tired. He was too wound up to be tired. He had to find *Lupe*. Fuck her street name, he thought, *Paloma*. She was *Lupe*. He silently thanked Ali again for hooking him up with her mother.

He wasted no time. Checked in to the hotel, ate some late night horror food that some people call Shit on a Shingle, grabbed up his gun, shoved it into the back waistband of his pants and went out to the streets. Mama Lobo would not be where she usually was, not this time at night. He'd have to wait about six hours. She always rose at seven. Then she would go and have breakfast at a small diner just off the north strip, then go and light a candle for her husband at the church she'd gone to ever since she'd come back. The church where legend has it they had christened Teddy Mac, Ali, and Carpy.

He didn't take the Falcon. Instead walked along the street, looking at the hookers that strolled up and down the streets. It only made him sad to think of his sister walking these same streets in the same way.

"You know Paloma?" he asked a hooker who was passing him but giving him the eye.

A shake of her pink dyed hair. "Don't know that name," she said, never breaking stride.

Gato knew it was a waste of time, but time was all he had until Mama Lobo showed up for breakfast. He'd give it another hour then go and crash for a couple hours before seeing her. There ended up being nothing. No leads, not that he really thought there were would be. Nobody was that lucky. Went and crashed, setting the alarm on his phone so he'd be up, showered, and coffee'd in time to meet Mama Lobo at her breakfast.

The few hours of sleep did him well. Woke and showered. Coffee'd, then went and got the Falcon. For this trek he would need the wheels. Drove through the early morning desert sun to the diner. It was called the Sand Dune Diner. Looked like something he would've imagined out of some 1950s movie about Vegas. This one had seen better days. Broken neon, the building worn at the edges. Yellowed stucco outsides. There were faded and yellowed signs in the windows, taped to the glass. Whatever meals they'd once advertised were now barely readable due to the extreme sun damage. They must've been from a long-ass time ago. No *pendejo* had paid a couple bucks for *dos huevos y bacon* since like 2000.

There were a few cars outside the place, and he knew by them that she was there. Lots of old, cherry low-riders, mixed with some new Jaguars and Mercedes. How she managed to keep people in line, he had no idea. Maybe he'd find out once he met here. If she was anything like her daughter, he'd understand immediately.

He entered the old diner and stood in the doorway. A chipped linoleum counter ran from the right side to the left, turning at the back wall. A row of booths stretched along that back wall. That would be the north wall and would save the diners in those booths from the hot desert sun. He spied a man moving about in the kitchen, but the place didn't smell of cooking food. He had to wonder just what was going on. Wondered if the man was another bodyguard for Mama Lobo.

There were only four other people in the place, plus that cook. Gato glanced back at all the cars. Where were the drivers?

At one of the booths sat a beautiful old woman he knew had to be Mama Lobo. The shape of her face was exactly like Ali's. She also had the air of someone who knew authority and how to deal it out. She sat there, reading a newspaper as the other two men in the booth watched him. Both men dressed like *vatos*. White t-shirts, baggy jeans, and Army-issued black boots. They sat in such a way that both the front and back doors were covered. There was another man, long and lean and dressed in a suit, tie loosened. This one sat at the counter just ahead of the booth. A gatekeeper. Gato knew that for sure because as he came closer the man slid off the stool and stood blocking his way in a move so smooth you'd think it had been performed by a snake.

"*No tiene negocio aquí, hombre.* Go."

Gato glanced at the booth where Mama Lobo sat. "I need to see Mama Lobo."

"So do a lot of people, *vato*. You go now."

"Ali gives me passage, man. Mama Lobo knows my name. *Gato*. Tell her that *Gato* is here to speak with her."

At that the old woman looked up from her paper. Looked him over. Smiled. "Let him come, Peter."

The suit stood aside and Gato moved to the booth, one of the men getting out to sit on the stool opposite the booth. He kept his eyes directly on Gato.

"Mama Lobo," Gato said with a glance at her bodyguards, "your daughter got word to you, *Si?*"

Mama Lobo gazed at him with eyes the color of opals. Her brown face was lined, deeply lined, and she wore her snow-white hair down around her shoulders. For clothes, she wore a simple dress of black cotton. Her only adornment was a thin, gold chain from which hung a slim, simple cross. But she exuded authority. Authority mixed with beauty that was a recipe for control. Gato knew immediately that he would follow her anywhere, just like he knew he'd die to protect his *madre.* "*Si,*" she replied, with a voice that was old, but had an underlying timbre, a resonance that made him sit up straighter. As if he were back in grade school. "Yes, I got her message. You are looking for your sister? *Paloma* she's called?"

He nodded. "I have to find her. Our mother is sick."

"What is wrong with her?"

Gato looked out the window. Sighed. "*Su mente se va. Está perdiendo su capacidad para cuidar de sí misma.*" Her mind is going. She's losing her ability to care for herself. "I need Lupe back. I can't take care of her. And to leave her to others? I don't like that."

Mama Lobo looked at him with deep sympathy. "I wish my boys had felt the same. You are a good son, to come so far to find your sister."

"It's my *madre*," de said. What else was there to say? It was his mother. What should he do? Not honor her wishes?

She nodded. Smiled at him again. *Man ... what a smile.* Then she sighed, her eyes going sad. "I know of a woman, a prostitute, who calls herself *La Paloma.* She arrived only a couple months ago or so. Works the Copa. Or did."

"Did?"

"I have heard that she hasn't been seen there for some days. I did some checking when my *niña* told me to look out for you, and why you were coming here."

Gato looked back out the window. The desert continued on into infinity, just like his search seemed to now. But before he was about to seriously give up hope, Mama Lobo told him, "Gato, I will send out some people to help you in your search. See if we can track down where your sister went. I'm sure she's still here, in this city."

"But if that's so," he replied, "why has no one seen her?" He then thought that maybe Lupe was still running because she didn't know that Teddy was dead and that the episode with the VCR tapes was over. Who would've been able to tell her? Yeah, that had to be it.

Mama Lobo shrugged. "She's a prostitute, Gato. They do all manner of strange things, all manner of the day. I have no idea, but I'm sure we can find out." Here she smiled that smile at him again. "If it's to help your *madre*? You can count on me and anyone who works with and for me."

With a smile, he took her hand and kissed it. Then took a napkin and put his cell number down on it. "I will keep looking," he said to her. "Thank you so much for your consideration, Mama Lobo."

For an answer, she only smiled again and looked him dead in the eye as she said, "It could be me, one day, Gato. And I can't be sure my youngest or my *niña* would be doing this, trying to find me should I disappear. *Estoy rindiendo homenaje a la gracia de Dios.*"

# SEVENTEEN

LUCAS SAT IN THE Cornerstone. Alone in the corner as he worked his way through a double Maker's Mark. First time in a long time he'd had booze this good. Man, that fucking Jew pawnbroker had been loaded. Grinned as he took a sip. Had money now for days and days. Not only for drinking and getting high, but for some new camping gear. Maybe even a bladed weapon better than the short knife he carried, had been carrying, for what seemed like forever.

He was here in this shithole bar because he found out from Blackmore that this was the only, *only* place that this Mallen cat called home when he was in the city. Seemed the piece-of-shit, ex-undercover faggot had found the Get Clean God to be one to his liking. Well, he could go fuck. Lucas had been told that all he had to do was wait and Mallen would for sure appear at some point to talk to that fat fucker behind the bar. Or maybe even Dreamo, who word on the street was starting to say had turned ear for the prick. Went to the bar and ordered another drink. The fat fuck that he'd been told was Bill brought it to him fast. At least the guy was a good bartender. He left a shit tip of two dimes, wanting to see what fat boy would do. But Bill did nothing, just left the dimes there as he went off to wipe down another part of the bar. Lucas felt insulted that his insult hadn't insulted. Went back to his corner seat and sat. Checked the new watch he'd bought with some of Blackmore's money. It could tell you the time in China if you wanted it to. Hell man, he thought, soon your watch will surf the net. Will be able to tell you about your hemorrhoids before you even have them.

Fuckin' world we live in.

Sat back against the chair. Put his hand in his pocket, his hand wrapping around the other toy he'd bought with that Jew's money: a small .22 pistol. A Sauer that its owner had never taken care of. He'd gotten it for a song, and the "for sure" it would shoot. This would teach Mallen to fuck with him.

All he had to do was wait. He knew that. But, if this waiting didn't work out, and Mallen never showed? Well, maybe he'd just have to go over the water to the other side and shoot the bastard as he opened the door to his fancy-ass houseboat everybody knew about.

———

Mallen was on his way back to his truck when his cell went off. Didn't recognize the number. "Hello?"

"Mallen?"

"Yeah. Who is this?"

"Shannon. You know?"

"I know. How'd you get this number?"

A soft laugh. He could tell she was out of doors. She was walking, and fast. "Please ... this is the Loin, right?"

"Right. And so?"

"You did something for me, so I want to do something for you. I never liked to be owing somebody something. Unless they were my dealer," she added with another soft laugh.

"I hear ya. Thanks for calling. What's up?"

"That pawnbroker dude that me and Lucas and Hendrix went to?"

"Yeah?"

"He's dead."

Mallen's hand gripped the phone tighter. "Blackmore? You sure?"

"Hey man, I just saw the cop cars. The body wagon. He's dead."

"And ... and why are you telling me this?"

He could almost see the shrug through the phone line. "You'd asked about him. About Lucas. About Hendrix. Seemed weird to me. Fucker's dead, and that's what I was calling about." A pause, then she said, softer and warmer. Truthful. "Thanks again for the chance," and with that she hung up.

He just stood there, the whirlpool of the Tenderloin swirling around him. Oblivious to him and what had just happened. Blackmore. Dead. The timing was off-the-charts coincidental, and very bad. He knew that. Blackmore's last words to him echoed in his head. *"You won't tell anyone about this, right?"*

*"Fuck no, man. We're good. Rest easy."*

He'd somehow blown it. Let Blackmore down. Let a source

down. Yeah, Blackmore had sold stolen goods, but by all accounts he wasn't a bad man. Just a man out to make a dime. How many of those were out there in the world? Ten million times a million? A lot of them were even politicians. Mallen knew he must be responsible. *Shit…*

Went and got his truck and drove over to the store. The cops were still there, but you could tell they were playing the outfield. The real game was somewhere else. Blackmore's apartment, or house. He'd never been there, but word was that Blackmore had walked to work every day for the last twenty years or more. He cruised up and down Polk. Up and down Larkin. Started doing wider and wider sweeps. Finally found the cop convention just off Laguna, on Birch. Parked as near as he could. Jogged back to the crime scene.

There were too many cops around the street entrance, and he saw nobody he recognized. Shit, this was going to be difficult. But he owed Blackmore. Owed him bad. Walking away wasn't an option. Mallen knew he had a name on the street now not necessarily associated with the word "Junkie." Maybe he could parlay that into at least getting under the tape to talk with a detective that *wasn't* Oberon.

It was only a few steps over to the nearest uniform. Not a rookie. A little weathered. The cop stood there, guarding the yellow tape with a mixture of boredom that he tried to hide so he could look important.

"Not a nice night, yeah?" he said to the cop.

"Nope," came the reply.

"Which detective caught it?"

Now the uniform looked at him. Studied him. "I'm not sure. Your name, sir?"

"Mallen. Mark Mallen. And I need to talk to whatever homicide detective is in the lead on this. Just need to talk to him for a few, okay?"

The uniform nodded. Only briefly, like he didn't want anyone to know. "I know the name."

"Can I get upstairs?"

There was a pause, then, "You really think you have something? Something that would help?"

"Yeah, I do. Fuck yeah I do."

The uniform stood there, undecided. Mallen added, "Look, I know that if you know my name then you know what I was. On the force, and off. I'm just trying to help solve a homicide here. I need to know what went on upstairs. I think I can help, okay?"

After a moment, the uniform cop nodded. Held up the tape. "Inspector Scheider is in charge. Good luck."

Mallen passed under the yellow tape. Scheider was a name he didn't know. He wondered as he went up the stairs how he would handle this. How much resistance he'd run into.

And there was the entrance to Blackmore's apartment. Lots of cops stood in the hallway outside. He acted like he belonged there as he made his way into the apartment.

It was a bloodbath. There were signs of destruction everywhere. Broken furniture, smashed glass. Blood spilled all over the carpet. There were explosive patterns of blood here and there on a nearby wall. Like a basketball had been dipped in red paint and bounced against it. Mallen knew what had happened.

A detective came up to him. Young. Freshly shaved. Immaculately dressed. Said, "What the hell are you doing here, Mallen?"

Mallen didn't recognize him. "Do I know you?"

The detective smiled. "A lot of guys have heard of you. How you got back your life after losing it. How you took down some big guys before you lost that life." Held out his hand. "David Armstrong."

Mallen took the offered hand. "I had no idea that I was anything but a dark memory."

"Well, learn to live with the change, I guess." Armstrong indicated the next room. Smile disappeared. "Scheider's in there. I guess it's him you came to see, right?"

Mallen glanced that way. Caught a glimpse of the far bedroom wall. A lot of blood there. "Yeah," he replied. Added as he went to the doorway, "Hope to see you around, Armstrong."

Stopped as he got to the room. His mind did a flip. Inside were two bodies. One was Blackmore. The other could only be his wife. Nothing left of either of them but bloody husks. Someone had beaten the fuck out of them. Probably shot them both as an afterthought. Blackmore looked like he got it in the neck. His wife looked like she got it in the face. If he hadn't seen things like this most of his adult life as a cop, Mallen knew he would've puked his guts out at the sheer brutality of it. A brutality of pure, dark violence. If Lucas was really responsible for this, and Shannon's call to him made that pretty clear that it could be, then Lucas needed to be brought in. And right then Mallen didn't care if it was in cuffs, or on the slab. He'd somehow let Blackmore down. He knew it. Somehow, Lucas had tripped to him, and had done this.

He'd have to make that right. Any way he could.

That was when he caught one of the detectives looking at him. The detective stood with two other cops. As soon as the detective saw Mallen, he came over. First thing Mallen noticed was the man's nose. It'd been broken, and more than once. Lots of weathered lines on the face. He was taller than Mallen by a good five inches, built like a defensive end. And he didn't look like a friendly, given the expression on his face as he came over.

"Mallen," he said. The word was a simple one. The tone carried way more. "What are you doing here?"

Mallen put on a smile, trying to play it light. Didn't want to come out swinging, knowing that he had no fucking right to be there. "You're Inspector Scheider?"

"Yeah. And you didn't answer my question. Why the fuck are you here?"

Mallen glanced over at the bodies. "I'm here because I might be able to help out a bit, you know?"

"Really? And why to God's holy asshole would you know shit about this?"

"Because I'd talked with Blackmore earlier today."

"What did you talk about?"

He didn't want to give it all away so fast. Countered. "What did you and your guys pick up? Anything?"

"Hey," Scheider replied, "who the fuck are you? What we did or didn't pick up is none of your business." The detective took another step closer, said quietly, "I know all about you and your dope years, okay? Horton told me all about you. So have other guys on the force. You can go fuck, okay?"

Horton. Man, that brought back memories. All bad. Horton

going at it with Oberon at the scene of Dockery's shooting. When he'd just been trying to find Eric's killer. Horton seemed like the sort of asshole to hold a grudge and go to bat if it meant fucking him up.

"Inspector Scheider," Mallen told him, "Okay. I hear you. But when I tell what I know to other cops, *they* will listen. And then they'll be just a step or two, or three, ahead of you, yeah? And you'll look like a dickhead for not listening to me now. You don't have to fucking like me, okay? I don't think I like you. But that doesn't mean we can't try to grab the bucket of shit who murdered these two civilians."

Scheider stood there a moment. Considered. Then he looked at Mallen and smiled, spoke over his shoulder to a couple of uniforms. "Get this fucker out of here. Toss him back to the gutter. He's lost his fuckin' way."

Mallen had no time to react as he was grabbed and pushed out of the room, then down the hall. They even took the time to push him along the stairs and shove him out through the lobby and onto the street. He almost fell onto the sidewalk but caught himself. Stood straight. Looked back up at the apartment building. So, he thought, that's how it was going to be played. Okay, he'd play it as it was.

It wasn't like he had no idea who the murderer was. He had a VERY good idea. A good, steel jacketed idea. Pulled out his phone, swearing he'd never forget Scheider's name. Dialed Shannon's number. She could tell him of some places she'd seen Lucas. But there was no answer. "Shit," he said. The thought of Blackmore and his wife being killed because he'd fucked up tore at him. He needed to do something. *Something*. But what? Maybe

Dreamo would know Lucas? It was a long shot, because Dreamo didn't deal to, and with, people that he felt were dangerous or looked like they'd be a problem. But he had to try. Had to look under every stone for Lucas.

He needed to find Lucas. Oh yeah he did.

———

The Cornerstone was hopping and that made Mallen happy. Anything that made Bill's life easier. He went to the stick and Bill somehow, between making all the other drinks, got him a double scotch, neat ....

———

Lucas watched a tall guy wearing a dark coat walk in and go to the bar. That fat fuck of a 'tender sure knew him. Put a drink out for him before the guy had even had time to settle. The tall guy had an air about him. One different from anyone else in the place. It was a war-weary vibe. There was something in the way the guy stood at the bar. Occasionally glanced at the back hallway. The hallway that led to the bathroom where Dreamo dealt his junk out of.

Lucas knew straight away the tall man in the dark clothes was Mallen, the guy who'd been looking for him. The description that the sack of shit Blackmore had mumbled out right before he'd died was to the letter.

———

Mallen had only enough time to smile at Bill and finish his drink. He had to talk to Dreamo. He put the glass back on the bar and headed for the back hallway....

————

Lucas watched Mallen go. Put his hand in his jacket pocket. Around the butt of the gun, his finger resting lightly on the trigger. *Fuck you, Mr. Shit Detective Wannabe....*

————

Mallen walked down the graffiti-littered hallway and pushed on the men's room door. There was some short guy at the urinal. Mallen went to wash his hands to buy time before the guy left. But the guy didn't leave. The guy then went into the stall where Dreamo presided. Mallen had never seen anyone else buy from Dreamo. Ever. Always felt as if Dreamo could make some sort of ethereal appointment book take shape and make sure no buyer ever met another. Mallen moved to the urinal and pretended to take a piss....

————

Lucas finished his drink. Got to his feet. Walked across the bar, hand in pocket, eyes intent on the hallway. He'd show that fucker to leave him the fuck alone....

————

The short dude finally left. Fast and smooth. Just like a junkie who had the proverbial bag of golden dust. Got to go. Go now.

Got to shoot. As soon as fucking possible. It was hard to believe, no … it was only now *starting* to be hard to believe, that he was ever that way. That thought made him feel good. As soon as the door shut, he crossed the floor, his boots crunching on the broken glass. "Dream," he said as he put his hand on the stall door, "it's Mallen, man."

"Ah," came the thready reply he knew so well. Would always know. "Come ahead, favorite ex-customer of mine."

Mallen pushed on the door and there was Dreamo. The Mohawk was now a vivid white. Whiter than white. Dreamo seemed even thinner than the last time Mallen had seen him.

"Shit, Dream," Mallen said as he pulled out his cigarettes, "can I get you some food? Maybe some soup, at least?"

For a reply, Dreamo smiled as he brought his gaze up to Mallen's. There was actual warmth there. "Thank you, ex-customer. That would be cool. That Thai diner has Tom Yum that I really dig. I would appreciate that. I can't leave the office right now, dig?"

Mallen took a drag off his cig. "Yeah," he replied, "I dig."

———

Lucas put his hand on the men's room door. His hand was shaking. Why? Because this fucker Mallen was so well known? Well fuck. Now *he'd* be well known. As the guy that shot that fuck. Yeah … now *he'd* be some tough shit.

He pushed on the door. Entered the room. Walls were covered with years of graffiti. Sink permanently stained. One urinal, one stall. It at first looked like no one there. Then he saw the feet of two people in the stall. One had to be Mallen, the other Dreamo.

He pulled the gun from his pocket....

---

The bathroom door squeaked. Mallen heard it. Looked at Dreamo, who shook his head and put out a hand for Mallen's cigarette. Wanted a drag. Mallen had no idea that Dreamo smoked anything but H through a needle. He heard the glass crunch as someone came toward the stall. Could be some newbie, needing to take a dump....

"Dream," Mallen said quietly, "You know of a guy—" And the stall door opened and Dreamo was suddenly up on his feet, pushing Mallen to the side and then there was the blast of a gun going off, shattering the rest of the world, and Mallen was falling to the floor as he heard running feet and felt Dreamo fall into him, a heavy weight, and then he was grabbing at Dreamo as he heard screams and yells outside and he heard Bill yelling something like "get that fuck!" and then the door slammed open and Bill was there. Mallen held Dreamo in his arms, trying to keep him from hitting the floor, a sack of cement in a cold and dark world. The bullet had entered his upper chest. Blood still pumped, but it was fading already as the heart wound down. As he died, Dreamo grabbed Mallen's coat, stared at him a moment, and said, the faintest of whispers, "Mal... you care...."

Mallen laid Dreamo on the floor. The dirty floor that the guy had spent hours above dealing out dope. Dream had taken the bullet meant for him, and now there were two people that had been dealt death because of him.

Bill leaned against the wall behind Mallen. The large man took a heavy breath that sounded more like a deep hiss. "He's ... ?" Bill said, unable to go further.

Mallen only nodded. He was numb. Yeah, this guy was a dealer. Dealt H. But he'd also possessed some strange code of honor. Never dealt to kids. Never dealt to the violent. Just stayed here in his little world and quietly dealt and shot dope. Mallen couldn't count how many times the guy had helped him out since he'd gotten clean. Only helping him once would've been enough.

"Call the cops, Bill," Mallen said as he looked down at Dreamo's dead form. At the blood there. "I'll find the guy who shot him, Bill. I swear I will."

Bill nodded. "Then get the fuck out of here, Mal. I'll deal with this. You go and find the prick who did this. I'll deal with Justin." The bartender then shoved by him into the stall and grabbed open the secret stash place in the wall that Dreamo had used for his "vault." Threw all the heroin into the toilet and hit the lever. "Get the fuck out," Bill repeated.

"I'll leave by the back."

"Then fucking go, all right?" Bill replied as he shoved Mallen out of the stall. Mallen looked again at Dreamo's corpse. He wanted to fix that image in his mind. This was a guy he'd traded quotes with as he'd bought dope from him. It was crazy, yeah ... but Dreamo had been someone he could trust during a period of his life when he could trust no one.

# EIGHTEEN

As he walked away from the Cornerstone, the sun heading low in the western sky, Mallen's mind could not wrap itself around the fact that Dreamo was dead. That his ex-dealer had taken a bullet for him. Dreamo was now the second man that had died because of him. In his mind, he wrote Dreamo's name under Blackmore's.

*Lucas…*

He needed to stop that man. That man was dead as soon as he met him.

Made it back to his truck. Got inside and started up the engine. Couldn't put it into drive though. He didn't know his next destination. What was the best next step? He was up against it, and knew it. And in those situations, there was really only one person he could rely on to help, to at least be a sounding board. He pulled out his phone and dialed Oberon.

"Mallen," came the familiar detective's voice. "What's happened now?"

He smiled at that. "At least you put me into your contacts list."

"Only a matter of form, trust me." Then he heard Oberon put his hand over the phone. Said something to someone. Then after a pause, said something again. "Now," Oberon said when he got back on the line, "what's going on?"

"Sorry for bothering you, Obie, but it's like this . . . ." He outlined everything that had just happened. About Blackmore. About Shannon and Lucas. About the files he'd found on Randy's flash drive, and under what conditions he'd found them.

Oberon swore under his breath. "Mark, goddamn it, you're withholding evidence you illegally obtained."

"I know, man," he replied quickly, "but I have the feeling something is going on with Gwen, too. I had to take the chance."

"I want to see those files, Mark. And right now."

He felt for the flash drive. Clutched it firmly. "Okay. I'll be wherever you need me to be, and fast-like."

_____

And Mallen was. Fifteen minutes of pressing every traffic law on the books, and Mallen arrived outside of Oberon's house, not far from Sutro Tower. He'd been there only one time before, during a case that had worn everyone down. He and Oberon were up all night and into the dawn, talking it over, looking for angles, figuring how the case had fallen out, and then figuring on how to get the evidence. The all-nighter had worked. The guilty were found and sent to jail.

Just like how it was supposed to work.

He parked nearby and leapt out of the truck. Walked quickly up the street to Oberon's house. Just in time to see the door to the house open and Oberon step out, along with another man. This man was Oberon's age, dressed more like someone at an office would dress on "Casual Friday." Both men seemed surprised to see him there as he walked up the steps to the door. The man glanced at Oberon, then over at Mallen. Oberon only shrugged. Leaned in and kissed the man on the cheek, squeezing his shoulder.

"I'll call, okay?"

"Okay." The man walked down the stairs and as he passed, said with a slight smile, "Hi, Mallen."

After a moment, Oberon said, "Let me see those files." Mallen nodded and went up and into Oberon's house. Handed the flash drive over to Oberon, who glanced at him for a moment, then went to his computer and attached the drive. "Any ideas yet?" the detective asked.

"It involves Hendrix. And I think Wong, too, like I said. Also that guy Yates that was found shot out at the ocean. There was evidence that he'd been there to meet someone. He had this drive in his car."

"And Saunders?"

"She got me access to the scene, but she's also slept with Wong and how far back that little fuckfest goes I have no goddamn idea. Those two sharing the same bed bothers me all to fuck and back." Paused for a moment, then continued, "To her credit, though, she got me access."

"Yes, to her credit." Oberon went through the files, sighing many times. He seemed to get it straight away. Then, quietly, he said, "His name is Dylan."

It took Mallen a moment to understand. Shrugged. "Legendary musician. Legendary poet. Good name."

Oberon nodded. Looked again at the computer screen. "You were right. It's a baby- or child-selling ring of some sort. And not babies from China or Africa. Babies right here. White. Black. Hispanic." His eyes scanned the screen as fast as he could change the page. "It seems that it is indeed low-income, poverty-types they're targeting."

"Right," Mallen replied. "People who might not call the police. Maybe they'd feel no one would help them. Or they didn't want to draw attention to their lives."

"Yes, that would seem a possibility. I'm sure you're correct, though. What else do you have on this?"

"Hendrix. Wong was seen at Hendrix's car, right before he may have been killed. I'm sure Yate's knew Hendrix, and I *think* they both knew some guy named Karachi."

"Karachi?" Oberon mused. "That's a man who I would very much like to see inside a box."

"Really? What do you have on him?"

"Not much," the detective mused, "but enough to know he's the type that would do anything for a good dollar. Not some low-level street five-dollar thing, but up in the hundreds. Bad guy. Deals sometimes, too. If he has to. Been in and out of jail. Been connected to a few molestation cases, but they never took, no matter how much we wanted them to."

"Why's that?"

"No one would testify."

And that also seemed to dovetail nicely to the direction this case was moving. A bunch of street guys, herders, really...looking for lambs to turn over to the adoptive parents. That didn't make sense though. You don't hire molesters to bring you a child all clean and healthy. Somewhere, somebody had got it all wrong. *Wrong*... Then Dreamo came to mind. "You hear about Dreamo?"

"No. Why?"

"He took a bullet tonight. A bullet meant for me."

Oberon blinked. "I did not hear what you just told me, am I correct? Dreamo, dead?"

Mallen nodded. Said, "You know a guy who goes by the last name of Lucas?"

A moment, then, "No."

"How about the pawnbroker over on Polk, Blackmore."

"Sure. Sells stolen goods. Clean other than that. We were thinking of developing him into an ear for us. Why?"

"He's dead. In a very bad way." Mallen then told Oberon about his dealings with Blackmore, and his run in with Scheider.

At the end, Oberon just shook his head. He flashed a brief smile. "You're in it again, aren't you? I know the feeling by now. You're into something deep. How does Saunders fit into this?"

Mallen shrugged, "I don't know. I still don't know why she wants my help. That bullshit about needing an ear on the street is that: bullshit. I'm sure of it. I can't figure her angle. Not yet. But I will. What makes me nervous about her is her involvement with Wong."

Oberon couldn't help himself. He glanced at Mallen's hand. "They *were* pretty hot and heavy, if for a short time."

"Honestly, Obie … I'm not sure what to do. I just wanted to help find a kidnapped little girl. It's gotten way big, way fast."

The detective leaned back in his seat. Stared at the folders on the screen. A lot of folders, and each one representing a child. "Reminds me of where we've just come from, Mark."

"I know, man. I know. People are just a commodity for so many rich bastards. These kids? People wait years to adopt a child from out of the country for fuck's sake. Adopt one from inside here, in America? It's a nightmare. Everyone knows it. Sure there are the happy endings, but those are for the few. Then some wealthy fucker comes along and just buys his way to the front of the line? Or even sets up a network to help *other* wealthy pricks get what they want without waiting? And we're talking children, Obie. Little children." He glanced at the computer screen. "I've got to stop them."

# NINETEEN

Lucas stood in a dark alley, his backpack on, bedroll under his arm. He swore quietly as he shoved the gun deeper into the bedroll. He'd have to sell it. Couldn't believe he missed that fucker Mallen and hit Dreamo. There'll be a lot of people pissed at him for that. Lots of junkies just lost a good dealer. Yeah, they won't come after him themselves, but they'd not bat an eyelash at sicking someone who *was* capable of fucking up his shit if they could get a little something out of it. *Shit shit shit shit!* Maybe now was the time to leave this town. His shoulders sagged. He didn't want to leave. This was a good town for street living. It was easy to get around, and if you kept your head down, you were pretty much invisible. Goddamn it! How the fuck did he miss Mallen? The gun sight must be fucked. It wasn't me shaking, he thought, I was just too strung out. Should've waited until that prick came out. Shoulda followed him down the street and then put a cap in the back of the fucker's head. How would he get a second chance now?

Then it came to him. He knew how to get his second chance. The fucker would eventually show up *there.* Had to. Everyone goes home at some time.

———

Gato got the text on his phone at 11:43 p.m. It was from one of Mama Lobo's crew. Said, "Behind Treasure Island."

Vague, but good enough. He left the hotel. Walked to the garage to where the Falcon was parked. No *valet* bullshit. Nobody drove this baby, nobody but its daddy. He hopped inside and roared down Ogden and made the turn onto the strip. Yeah, it was a crazy town, and he could see the attraction, but it just wasn't for him. He'd take his city anytime. He did wonder what New York would be like. Maybe he'd see it one day, once he'd found Lupe.

He made Treasure Island and drove around to the back service area. The place was huge. Behind the building was an army of dumpsters. Jesus, he thought, how much garbage did a place like this make? Over at the edge of the lot, he spied an old Chevy Impala parked in the shadows. That had to be the guy.

The Falcon pulled up next to the Impala, driver's window to driver's window. Gato's right hand was wrapped around his Sig 239. He'd taken to keeping it near at hand, no matter where he went. The guy in the car was bald, head completely tatted with biblical quotes in a bold, Gothic font.

"Gato, right?" the man said.

Gato nodded.

The man indicated himself. "Hector."

"Okay. Why the text?"

"Found your sister, man."

And here was that moment that he'd hoped for, for so damn long. But was it for real? "How you know it's my sister, man?"

"She answered to Paloma."

"Answered? That's passed tense, *vato.*"

"She ain't Poloma anymore, man."

Gato's first thought that he was about to be shown her grave. And if that were the case, he wouldn't stop until the *pendejos* who did it were hanging from burning trees. His hand tightened on the handle of Sig. "What do you mean?"

Hector grinned there in the darkness. He had a gold tooth, inscribed with a fancy "H." It caught some of the overhead light from a security lamp. Glowed and shined. "She not on the street anymore, by all accounts, man."

"You hear why?"

He was met by a shrug. "Heard a lot of stories, man. Been out workin' and listenin'. Some of the stories say she got taken in by a pimp named Metal Mike. Some say she left the streets on her own. Livin' in a room outside Old Vegas."

"Where is that place?"

"On North Twentieth. Some place that should be condemned. An apartment building that still looks like a hotel for people who can't do better. Second floor, rear. Number six. Heard she barely goes out."

"Barely goes out? What's the reason?"

"Dunno. I was only told to give you leads. And there you are. Two of 'em. Follow 'em down, kitty cat."

And Gato knew then and there he didn't like Hector. "Thanks." He rolled away quickly, wanting to get away from the man and follow up on the lead. She was close. Gato was beginning to feel it.

He put the car in gear and checked the GPS on his phone. It wasn't far to north Twentieth. He went fast. It was late enough that maybe he'd even catch her there. Mama Lobo wouldn't steer him wrong. He was sure of that. Those eyes weren't the eyes of someone who would hurt him.

———

It took longer than he would've liked, but Vegas really never slept, so there was traffic all the time. Only when he got away from the strip did the traffic thin out. As he drove, Gato wondered what he'd really say. When he first started tracking Lupe down, he thought he would let into her the minute they came face-to-face. Yell at her about how could she leave their *madre* like she did. But now? Now he just wanted to put his arms around her, tell her about their *madre*. About how much they needed her help.

He turned the corner onto Twentieth and pulled to the curb, cutting the engine. Looked up and down the street. Considered the information Hector'd given him. There was no way his sister would live *here*. Maybe Hector was setting him up for an *emboscada*?

The place put the worst halfway houses he'd ever seen to shame. Pulled his gun from under the seat. Sighed. Ran his fingers through his dark and stringy hair. Time for another shave job. He had to believe that Mama Lobo was playin' it clean. That she wouldn't send him to his death. She was Ali's *madre*. He got out and walked to the lobby door. Hector had told him the second floor. It was suddenly feeling too easy. Maybe his time with Mallen had made him more paranoid than in the old days? Was she really here? He turned the knob on the lobby door. It opened. He would've felt better if it'd been locked. Wouldn't have made it seem like such a trap. The other side of him told him that in a neighborhood like this, a locked lobby door would've been asking a lot, so don't worry.

As soon as he was inside, instinct took over and he pulled the gun. Walked quietly up the stairs, gun held low and a bit behind him should he run into a civilian. But there was nobody. The place was as silent as an empty closet at midnight. He moved to the second floor and down the hall at "double stealth." He found number six at the end of the hall on the left. His high tops made no noise at all on the thin, threadbare hall carpet. Got to the door. Stood off to the side. Tapped lightly with the barrel of his gun.

Heard movement inside the room. He tapped again. "*Lupe, hermano pequeño de Eddie.* That was the name they'd used on him when he was a kid. Always "Eddie." Had always pissed him off. If he'd been able to choose, then Eduardo was the lesser of two evils. She would know it was him. No one else knew how much he hated the name Eddie.

Movement inside the room. Then nothing. Even ambient noise from outside had ceased to exist, it seemed so totally quiet. "Lupe?" he asked again, almost a whisper.

Then there was a voice from the other side of the door. Soft. Feminine. Young. "Eduardo?"

It was her. Her. It was. "Lupe!" he said urgently. "Let me in. I've come for you. I gotta take you home."

Another pause. There was the rake of the safety chain. The release of the locks. The door opened ....

Her eyes were dark, but with the faintest mix of hazel. Skin the color of brandy. A face that, like her mother's, was a face that artists would've used in their paintings of The Virgin, but with Lupe it would also include a touch of Mary Magdalene. Taller than Gato by just an inch, but that inch meant a lot to the both of them.

Her stomach was swollen. A large round globe. She carried her baby low.

Gato took one look at her, then at her stomach, and then threw his arms around her. "Oh Lupe! Lupe! I found you!"

She started to cry. He could feel her warm tears on his neck. All she said was, "*Hermanito.*"

He hugged her tightly. As tight as he could with the fact that she was indeed very pregnant.

"What are you doing here?" she asked. "Why are you here? You shouldn't have come."

"It's mama. She needs your help, Lupe. She's not—" There were footsteps in the hall outside. He felt Lupe tense as she whispered, "Miguel."

"Metal Mike?" was all he had time for as Metal Mike came round the hall corner and down toward them.

The man wasn't large. Only a couple inches taller than Gato. Wasn't more muscular, either. It was the eyes that set off warning signs in Gato, as if he needed more. They were pale blue, almost white. Gave the man an air of one who is beyond caring about the pain he inflicts. He dressed in a grey suit, tie a few shades darker than the suit. Gato could see the bulge of a gun under the jacket, under the left arm. He'd expected, with a street name like Metal Mike, for the man to dress like a street dude. The fact he was dressed the way he was put Gato even more on his guard. Mike wasn't putting you on: he had money.

Mike looked from Lupe to Gato. "Paloma? Who is this?"

"I mentioned him to you once, awhile ago. This is my brother."

A smile then. "Eduardo?" Came forward, putting out a hand. "What a surprise."

Gato hesitated, but then took the hand. The man did not have a firm grip. That also set him on his guard even more. Like he was being set up to feel superior right before the takedown. "I would've called," Gato said with a slight smile, "but I had no idea where *mi hermana* was."

Mike smiled back. Put his hands into his pants pockets. "Well, she's right here. Where she belongs, right Paloma?"

At that, Lupe didn't answer. Instead she said to Gato. "You said something about our mother?"

"Yeah," Gato said as he turned to face her. "She needs you, Lupe. Her mind … it's not good. Leaving her with strangers only makes her feel worse." Looked over at Mike for a moment, then said to her, "You have to come home."

"Your *madre* is very sick … Eduardo, was it?" Mike said.

"Yes, very." His gun was still at his side. Mike had noticed it and done nothing. Gato's mind screamed at him that this was going to go south. Way south. Instead Mike only nodded.

"Well, then, Paloma," he said to Lupe, sincere warmth in his voice. "You have to go."

She stared at him for a second. Put a hand to her stomach. "Yes, Mike?"

"Yes, you can go." He stepped aside to let them past. Gato put his hand on Lupe's shoulder and guided her forward. That was when Mike reached out, his fingers just touching her shoulder.

"But the baby stays, Paloma. My son stays."

"What the fuck, man?" Gato said and then three men entered the hall from the apartment opposite Lupe's. They were all armed, all ready to throw down. Gato wanted to shoot it out but couldn't, not with his sister so close. Motherfuckers had him stone cold.

Mike held out his hand to Gato. "The gun? Or guns?" Gato was forced to give up his Sauer to Mike. He said nothing about the small Ruger LCP he kept in his boot since he'd left San Francisco. If they missed it, that was their fucking fault, the *pendejos.*

Mike looked at the gun for a moment, then at Gato. Spoke over his shoulder to his men, "Take him outside." Two of the men bull rushed him, taking him off his feet and slamming him into the wall. Mike went to Lupe, saying, "It's my boy, Paloma. Once you've given birth you can go home, or go to hell. I don't give a shit." And here he pointed Gato's gun at her face. "But you are NOT going to take my boy from me and go merrily on your way. No. Not going to happen, my Paloma." Turned to Gato. "It's only a month or so you'll be out of commission, *vato.* You'll have to stay here, too. I know my Paloma and if she knew you were out there, she wouldn't stop to get a message to you, or bring you back into all this. Count yourself lucky." He pocketed Gato's gun.

135

"This will be almost like a holiday for you." He glanced at the men holding Gato and indicated the stairs with a nod of his head.

Gato was dragged kicking and fighting down the stairs. The two men were good. Held him tight.

"How we going to keep him cool for a long while, man?" one of the men said as they dragged Gato through the lobby. "Look at this little shit. He's got a lot of fight in him."

The other man looked at Gato for a moment, then spoke to his friend. "We'll just dope him up to keep him quiet. No fuckin' biggie."

# TWENTY

MALLEN KNEW HE'D HAVE to stay away from the Cornerstone, at least for now. That fact killed him. He wanted Bill to know he was there for him. But if he showed up too soon that would only invite eyes. Mostly SFPD eyes. He had a history with Dreamo. A lot of people knew that. He'd have to play it cool, no matter how he felt. Bill would understand. Or so Mallen hoped.

*Karachi.* After he'd split from Oberon's, he'd driven right back to the Loin to try and find a line on Karachi. There was something going on with that name. He could feel it. After a very short time, he found one of the rarest of rare things in San Francisco at night: a parking space east of Van Ness. It was late now, the moon up, but he needed information. Dialed Gwen's number. Got voicemail and hung up. Dialed again and this time she picked up. She'd been sleeping. "Detective Saunders."

"Informant Mallen," he replied, adding, "Karachi. Need a line on that name. Fast like."

"And who the fuck is whose informant?"

"You want the child found, right?"

"Of course."

"Then I have some information, and I need to run it down. I need info on Karachi in order to do that. He might be a missing piece." When she didn't answer he said, "Sorry I woke you by the way."

There was a soft laughter. "Fuck you, Mallen. I'll see what I can get, in the morning, okay?"

"Thanks. I'm getting close, Gwen. I know I am." Hung up, knowing that he was basically lying to her. He wasn't getting close to finding Jessie, but he *was* getting close to finding the people that had taken her and probably handed her off to somebody who wanted a kid, like a quarterback hands off to the running back. Gwen would check in the morning. But there was something tugging at him. Something that told him he couldn't wait around for Gwen to get back to him.

He would need someone to do some work for *him*. Smiled at that as he stood there on the dark, Tenderloin street. Been a long-ass time since *he* needed a snitch. Some ears on the street that weren't Dreamo's.

Shannon Waters.

Would she do it for him? Fuck … why should she? And if she did, what would it fucking cost him? This would've been a perfect time for Gato. Wondered how his friend was making out, out there in the desert. Dialed his friend's number. Got voicemail. Shit, was everyone letting every call go to fucking voicemail? "Hey, G," he said, "call me, man. Need to hear what's up, yeah?"

Now it was about finding Shannon Water's address. It didn't take too long, as everyone that crawled around on the streets at night seemed to know her. He'd been told, time and time again as he searched for her address, that she would do anything for a fix. Anything. Especially if she'd really split from Tre. Mallen just nodded when he'd been told that last bit of information. He knew that Tre wasn't splitting anything right now, with anybody. And wouldn't be for some weeks. He had to admit: he loved it when predator became prey. It took about three quarters of an hour to find Shannon Water's address. Checked the time on his phone. Well, fuck it, right? He had to take the shot. As The Great Gretzky had said, "You miss a hundred percent of the shots you don't take." Dialed her number.

She answered. "Yeah?" Her voice seemed strained. But not the strained that came with dope. No, it was the other kind of strained, the one that came with no dope.

"It's Mallen," he replied. Cautiously added, "Didn't think you'd be awake."

"Well I am." Left it out there like a dare.

"The shit that Tre had no good, yeah?"

"Fuck you. Can't someone try to put shit behind them sometimes?"

"Yeah. Of course they can."

There was a very long pause. Mallen looked at his screen on his phone to make sure the call was still connected. It was. "I used to be a ballerina," she said, and he had to strain to hear it.

"Okay. I was sorta hoping my daughter would take that up, but she's more suited to being a wide receiver than a prima."

"Why'd you call me, Mallen?"

It took him a moment to work up to it. "I'm working on this missing kid thing, right? For a friend. Her kid was taken. The

139

first card on the table was Hendrix, but now it's getting … bigger than that. There's this other name that surfaced again. That name you mentioned. This guy named Karachi. And—"

"And you need something, right? Like me, helping you out?"

"Well, I'd ask a friend but he's out of town."

"Karachi," Shannon intoned. "But why the fuck should I help, or care, about you or anything you're dealing with? I'm trying something and I need to stay as far away from you, Tre, and the streets, as possible."

"I hear ya. How long has it been?"

After a moment, she said, "Only a day."

"Hey, it's not 'only a day.' Never is it 'only a day,' right? A day without is a day won."

"You want me to go and set off balloons now?"

"No," he replied, "I'm just saying that I know what it means to do a day without. What it means to do a fuckin' *hour* without. Even ten fucking minutes without, yeah? You're being strong, and that's good."

There was a silence. Then she answered with, "I guess it's not as bad as getting off cigarettes. Hear that's worse."

"Personally? I think it's hard to quit *any* habit."

"Yeah, suppose so."

"You need anything?" he said. "I can bring you in some food or whatever if you don't want to go out. Seriously. I'll do that."

"Really? You'd do that? Really?"

"Yeah, I will."

"And you don't want anything in return, right?" Distrust. Hell, he figured, how many times has this woman been used?

"Shannon," he said, "not anything like what you might be

thinking. Just a line on Karachi. Where I can find him. I need to talk to him. Bad."

He could hear her breathing. Could almost hear the struggle inside her. Then she said, "I'm only doing this because I hate that fucker, alright?"

"Alright."

"Then bring me some groceries and we'll call it square after I tell you what I know. I'm at 872 Ellis. Apartment D." The line went dead.

Mallen shoved the phone in his pocket as he went searching for a store that would be open.

———

The building was an SRO, a single-room occupancy. Turned out to be one he'd been in a long time ago. Not for drugs, though. Actually as a cop, back when he'd just started undercover. He was sent here to put fear into the heart of some guy who'd thought he could buck the establishment. He was told to break limbs if necessary. Happily, that hadn't been needed. He'd broken a couple items of furniture, pushed the barrel of his gun into the guy's left nostril. That'd been enough to make the guy submissively urinate, and that was that.

The elevator wasn't working so he had to hoof it up the four flights. The smell of not only cooking food but also of cooking crack assaulted his nostrils. Must be driving Shannon crazy. Didn't even have to knock on her door. She opened it immediately as he approached. Must've been camped out waiting for him. He offered up the bag of groceries and she took them immediately over to a broken-down, fake wood table in the corner of the room near the bachelor kitchen. The studio was bare of pretty much everything except the bare essentials. Gave off the feeling of being just a way-station for her. A mattress on the floor. A beat-to-shit dresser. An unframed mirror on the top of that, leaning against the wall. The kitchenette looked like it had only recently been scrubbed, judging by the bottle of 409 and can of Ajax on the counter, along with a few wet and soggy rags.

She caught him looking at the cleaning supplies. "It kept me busy for a couple hours. Took my attention away." Ended it with a shrug. She then went through the bag, pulling out each item and putting it almost reverently on the table. "Man, you spent a ton of dough on all this stuff. Thank you, Mallen."

"Couldn't go out? Or didn't have the money?"

After a moment. "Both. I would've done anything for a hit once I was out. But I was starving. Of course there was no food here. I . . . ." After a moment she continued, "When you called, it was like the universe aligning for me. A delivery man." A smile. Shy.

Mallen smiled back. Bowed. "I'll do what I can for you, Shannon. As long as you're serious and not trying to burn me."

"I'm not. I swear, I'm not."

He studied her for a moment. The look in her eyes told him she was either an awesome fucking actress, or was really trying to turn it all around.

"You know," she said as she went over to a kitchenette drawer and pulled out a knife, "I really have to move." Went back to the table and started to slice off some of the Swiss cheese he'd brought her.

A memory tugged at him. Yeah . . . he'd said the same thing,

142

right before he'd gone to the drunk tank to clean up, back when he was trying to find Eric Russ's killer. He thought then that moving would change everything. Of course at the time, while still hooked to the end of a needle, it was just jack-off bullshit. The things that junkies tell themselves when the guilt of their wasted lives and opportunities press down on them too much. They pretend to hope that tomorrow *will* be the day they stop, that they can move away from their old life, to a new life where nobody knows them ... maybe even move away from the needle. He looked around the room again, and wished he could do more for her. For anyone who seriously wanted to tie up their addictions and throw them off the pier.

She made herself a sandwich of the cheese, bread, mayo, and a little of the ham. She obviously wanted it all to last as long as possible. Grabbed one of the bottles of water he'd picked up last minute, realizing that water from the tap was too depressing a thought. She went and sat on the mattress. Sighed with contentment as she dug in. "So," she said after a moment, "Karachi."

"Yeah," he said as he pulled out the rickety wooden chair near the table and sat. It was the only chair in the place. He wondered if it would last through their conversation. "What do you know about him? Can you give me a lead on where I can find him?"

"Why are you looking for him?"

He shook his head. "You don't want to know. Trust me on that one, yeah? Let's just say that once I find him, he'll be out of play. Once he's told me what I need to know from him."

Shannon took another bite from the sandwich. "What are you, Mallen?" she said. "Some kind of private eye dude? I don't get what makes you do these things. You got Tre away from me. Then you gave me his dope. I've heard other things, too. Like you're some kind of avenger dude. I mean ... you bring me food when somebody else who wanted me to talk would've brought a knife or the back of their hand. I don't get it. Why do you do this? Why are you involved at all?"

Mallen shrugged. "Some people went to bat for me. I just want to do the same for other people."

A smile. "That simple?"

"That simple."

"I think I like that," she replied. Took another bite, then said, "Karachi is someone who hires himself out for whatever bullshit you need. He'll break legs. Deal your dope for you, if you can trust him. Run stolen goods to the nearest pawnshop. Take 'em even as far as the East Bay. For a price of course. He's almost like a business. The farther away he has to travel, the more it'll cost you. He'll even guard your girls so you don't have to," she added bitterly.

"He have that arrangement with Tre?"

"No, Tre never had enough money for that. But he did give Karachi some rock once. Tre had to go to jail for a few days, and he wanted someone to keep tabs on me."

"And Karachi did that? Kept tabs on you?"

A nod. "And ... other things. He's a fucking dog. A fucking animal."

"Would he ever do things like hook people up with things they wanted? Like if someone wanted a woman, or even a gun, would Karachi get that person together with the woman or the guy who could get the gun? Would he even go out and get the gun and exchange it for the money?"

She thought a moment. Nodded. "If the person who gave over the money trusted him enough, yeah. And yeah … Karachi would be Mr. Go Between any chance he got. Anything that would get him a cut of something."

"Okay. Where can I find this shitball? Do you have any ideas on that?"

"Mallen, I heard about Blackmore. You're not going to do me that way, are you?"

It stung, that statement. Made his blood boil. He had to find Lucas, too. The list of people he had to find was growing, not getting smaller. "No fucking way would I do you like that, Shannon. No way. As far as I'm concerned, once I walk out that door we don't know each other." And here he gave a faint smile, "Unless you need help staying on this side of the addiction fence, you know?"

"Deal." She took another bite of the sandwich. Chewed for a while before saying, "I know that Karachi lives in Bayview. At least that's where the fucker has his coffin stashed."

"Coffin?"

"He usually only comes out at night. Unless he needs to score."

"Okay. Any ideas at all where in Bayview? Even a street would help."

"I could get in a lot of shit if this gets out, Mallen. I could get dead."

"I know. It won't happen, trust me. You have my cell number.

You call it if you even suspect someone's tripped to what you're telling me. Trust me, Shannon. Okay?"

Another bite of the sandwich as she looked pensive and conflicted. Finally, she said, "On La Salle. There are these blue and grey apartments there. Bars on the lower windows. That's where he took me. Once."

"He took you there?"

"When Tre paid him to keep tabs on me. He took me there and locked me in the bedroom for three days. He'd only let me out to go to the bathroom or when he … .." She got up and busied herself with searching through the grocery bag again. Came out with a box of donuts. Held it up to him like a toast. "Well, I'll be fat, but at least I'll be clean."

"La Salle," Mallen said to himself. Not far from the bay. "And you think he'd be there more likely in the day?"

"Yeah. Most likely, anyway."

"And what does this piece of shit look like?"

"I think he's part Indian. Like from India, not American Indian. Your height. The times I've seen him, he was wearing a black leather trench coat. Wild hair, parts dreading. Deep scar running down the side of his neck. Dark eyes. Angry eyes. Always angry." She ended with a shudder, remembering something horrible.

"Thank you, Shannon," he said as he got to his feet. "I'll come back with more food tomorrow or the next day."

But she shook her head. "No. I'll have to go out eventually. You got shit happening. Can't be looking after me like I'm a sick little doggie or something."

Mallen considered this. It was true, but she ran the risk of falling back. It'd only been a day. But she did have a point. What if he couldn't make it back in a couple days? He pulled out his wallet and laid three twenties down on the table. Shannon's eyes went big as she saw the dough. "I figure you still have the money I gave you from Tre," he said. "I'm giving this to you because I'm trusting that you will use it for food. I don't want you to have to do anything you don't want to for money, got it? If I can't be here for the next few days, than at least I know you'll have money for food and you won't have to hook for it, or whatever."

She got up from the mattress. Came over and looked down at the money, then up at him. Threw her arms around him. Held him tight. "Thank you, Mallen. You give me a little hope that not all the guys in this world are assholes looking only to hurt and abuse us women. Thank you."

# TWENTY-ONE

GATO WOKE UP SLOWLY. Painfully. Waking was ugly. Took a moment to remember where he was and how he'd landed here in the shit. The room was the size of a meat locker. Almost as cold. His right eye was swollen. Jaw ached. Head pounded. He felt around the back of his head. Dried blood there. Probably when it hit the floor. That was all he could remember. Oh wait. He remembered something else: he'd broken that one motherfucker's jaw. That was a nice kick ... a nice kick? It was then he realized he had no shoes. The gun was gone. So was his shirt.

Looked around his cell. Nothing. No toilet, no nothing. That was when he spied a small hole in the corner. Just about the width of a pipe. Went over to it. Yeah, there had been a sink here at one time. Realized then he had to piss. Stood over the hole and aimed as best he could for it. It worked for a moment, but then backed up. *Motherfuckers ... I will kill you all and leave your homes a burning mess for this ....*

Seemed the hole *did* drain, but slowly. Hoped he didn't have to crap for a while. Maybe they'd let him out. As his mind began to clear he wondered what Lupe had gotten herself into. And pregnant! And his *madre* back at home, needing them both. He had to get the hell outta here. Who the fuck was this Mike guy, anyway? Drugs? Girls? Was he a pimp like that fucker Teddy Mac, but on a higher level? Had the look of a drug bastard. And man ... Mallen didn't even know where he was. Paced back and forth ... back and forth, wondering how to handle this. Prowled the cell. They'd come for him. Of course they would. He had to be awake when they did. He'd fight his way through this. Oh yes he would.

There was the sound of heavy steps approaching the door. Two people. Heard the jangle of keys and a lock being opened on the other side of the heavy wooden door. He went and pressed his back to the wall, right behind the door. Right hand balled in a fist. If he had to die, he was going to die fighting. The door opened wide, but outward. There was a moment of quiet, then laughter.

"Come on, fuckhole," said one of the voices from before. One of Mike's guys. "Like you're going to catch us unawares? You better get used to the fact that you'll be our little doggie until that cunt hooker sister of yours squirts out that brat Mike is so up in arms about. Come on, man ... don't be a pussy about this. Take your medicine like a man, not like some little bitch."

Gato didn't move. *Medicine? Madre de dios! No!*

The two men rushed into the room fanning left and right. Gato leapt at the one with the broken jaw. Grabbed the jaw and twisted it, bones crunching. The man screamed and Gato leapt over him, bolting out the door and down the hall. Didn't know which way was out. The walls were concrete. Got the impression he was underground. The thud of boots behind him. He kept taking lefts and then rights. Where the fuck was this place? Then there was a gunshot and his right leg shot out from under him. A ton of bricks fell on him and everything went black.

It was only dreams then. Faint images and stabbing pain as he watched from outside looking in. His jaw was broken, or so he thought. Was that drool, or blood? Tried to move. Everything was so heavy. His body, the air, even the pain was a ton of lead. A pinprick, and then the pain receded .... Was that someone talking? Something about a junk car ... junk .... *no?*

———

Another period of blackness ended as he opened his eyes. Still couldn't move. Barely registered that he was tied to a cot. A cot? Tied? Why was that? His jaw ached and he could barely see through his swollen eyes. His pants were wet, and smelled of shit and piss. Or was that shit, piss, and dried blood? What was this place?

"He's waking up," said someone somewhere.

A face loomed over his. Weird how the wires around the face shined like hot lead. Pain shot through his head and every fiber of him when he was slapped. It had all happened so fast. Waking was bad. Just like it had used to be. And how long ago was that since waking had been so bad. Who cared?

"Shoot him again," said wire face. That brought him back a little to the surface. Horse. Needles. His sister. His *madre* ... Something clamped down on his right wrist. He gazed over at his arm, and through the haze of his puffed-up eyes and drugs he watched a needle go into an arm. There was a sting, and then he realized the arm was his.

"*Punta Madres.* Go fuck yo … ur … selves …" and then he floated above it all and went away to some corner of the darkness where there were no corners and he had to search for one and then he remembered being in jail and helping this one white dude out named Mallen and how it had been cool to be this guy's friend but did he have any friends now … and … and ….

———

Gato knew he was going to die. Knew it. But every time he'd get right to the cusp where death … where dying … meant seeing God, the messengers would come in and put the chains back on his being. At one point, he finally saw his *padre.* After all these long years. Then he saw the Lord. Saw Jesus. Tried to cross himself but the straps, the bloodied straps, wouldn't let him. Every time he tried to breathe, the smell of shit and piss made him vomit, but it was a dry vomit now as he no longer had a concept of water, or what it tasted like. It could've been a day … or a lot of days. Had no idea. All he knew was the pinprick, and how sad it made him feel. His mind traveled back in time, retreating from the present … a present that held nothing now but pain and agony. He'd been a kid at the time, maybe eight or nine. He'd tried to grow a plant for his *madre.* Worked and worked on it to make it grow big and strong. The leaves were large and a shiny, dark green. Then one day he'd come out to water it and the plant had been knocked over and stamped on. Some kids he knew from the next block had done it. Had laughed at him as he stood there, almost crying but trying to be strong. His *padre* would want him to be strong. What he'd done, if he could remember right, was to go out to meet those *putas* with a broom handle. They'd laughed at him ... until Gato swung the broom handle against this one kid's head who was in his gym class. Broke the kid's nose and they all went running away.

Man, had his *padre* beaten the crap out of him!

But now, *padre* was dead and he was sad. It was then that he realized someone stood over him. At first Gato didn't know the man, but eventually the man came into focus and it was then that he recognized Metal Mike.

Mike stood there looking down at him, his sleeve over his nose. "Can't you at least change this fucker's pants, you assholes?"

"We thought it more fun for him to wallow in his own shit and piss."

"I don't want him to die, yet. Not until after Lupe gives me my son. If she knows her brother is dead, she'll go ape shit. She's Catholic, but not above killing her child to stick a needle in my eye."

"Hey, Mike ... this guy broke Jessie's jaw. Twice. He gets what he gets. And what he gets is to shit and piss on himself."

Gato felt his right arm grabbed. Like in a dream. Pressure around his elbow. "Jesus, you guys don't even know how to shoot up some motherfucker with dope. Clean him the fuck up. Lupe wants to see him."

"Clean him up? Jesus, Mike ... look at the spick. He looks and smells like a Port-a-John."

"I told you two assholes to keep him locked up and quiet.

You decided to treat him like a third-world political prisoner. This is *your* handy work so clean it the fuck up."

Gato tried to open his eyes at the loud voices. Metal Mike was still there, looming over him like the devil looming over a broken soul. Maybe Mike had some dope? He needed some more, the need growing faster and faster. Needed more so he could go away to where the pain wasn't. To where there was nothing. He vaguely felt a silence, then Mike said, "Clean him the fuck up, or I'll find someone who will, and then you'll find yourself where this piece of shit-out Chorizo is now. Are we clear on this?"

"Yeah," came the response. Flat and dead.

"Then get the fuck to it."

———

There was water. Hot. Scalding. They beat him like an animal between blasts of the water. Laughed at him as he crawled around the tiled floor in a vain attempt to get away from the water. His junk-encrusted mind no longer thought of right or wrong, or of Lupe. Or his mother. Those were thoughts for some other Eduardo. Being beaten, then being cleaned up. Words of apology for the beating while being beaten. There was one moment where he begged like a little boy for some junk to make the dark and jagged pain go away, but none came until the moment where he cried like a little *coño* for some. Then he was tossed to the ground, his left arm held rigid and he didn't fight anymore ... only waited for the release from all the agony.

Then it went dark again.

He was getting very used to that darkness.

# TWENTY-TWO

LA SALLE STREET WAS quiet. Not even a car sound, or the sound of people. A bit fucking unnerving. Seemed at first glance like any other quiet residential neighborhood you'd find in the Bay Area. But the security bars on all the first floor windows of every building told him how it really was. If what Shannon had said was true, then judging by the sun he had a couple hours before Karachi emerged from his coffin. Laughed at that thought. *Jesus… dude. Get a grip.*

Drove to the end of the block and did a U-turn. Parked. From where he was, he could see the building Shannon described. Reached under the seat and pulled out his gun. Didn't need to check the clip like in the movies. He was on top of his shit enough to know that clip was fresh, clean, and full. There was only one building it could be. Except… problem was it was two stories. Top, or bottom? Top would be safer, so he decided to look upstairs first.

Walked down the street, not trying to be under the radar or

anything. In this hood? Trying to be furtive or quiet would draw more attention. Just keep walking boldly. Like you have the right, or have a mission.

Got to the concrete stairs that led to the upper apartments. He just padded up them quietly, not needing to keep to the sides of the risers. Made virtually no sound, and he realized then that he was just about back to a hundred percent. He'd been the "go-to" guy when back in uniform to stalk upstairs in the dark or along some quiet corridor. Always had that ability to move quietly. Had lost it when he'd been tied to The Need, but now he was back to where he was, plus some years. *Not bad for a quickly becoming old man*, he thought as he moved up step-by-step, gun held low by his left side. Made it to the top and was confronted by a peeling, wood door. A door behind a rusty, metal security screen.

*Fuck…*

Now would be the time for a silencer. He hadn't done a hot entry in years and years. And if he was wrong? And this wasn't Karachi's apartment? His mind raced over the possible outcomes. Well, in this hood it would be long-ass minutes before the police arrived. The other side of the coin could be he'd stumble in on some sort of drug dealer mess, get into a firefight, and die. Or, the place might contain some of God's honest citizens and then he'd beg off quickly and get the fuck out of Dodge. But he just couldn't believe that Shannon would've steered him wrong. Not the sound of her voice as she spoke. He was sure of that.

*Fuck it…*

He shot the knob on the screen door and it flew into bits, the door coming loose. He ripped it open and slammed the thin wood door with his shoulder. It shivered and splintered as it blasted inward. It was all flashes after that: a living room with only a couch and TV. A man there, leaping up. Gun already aiming at him.

Mallen fired on instinct. There was a gun pointed at him and he didn't give a fuck at all if it was Karachi behind the trigger or Keanu Reeves. The first bullet chewed through Karachi's wrist, and the gun dropped to the dark brown wall-to-wall carpet. The second bullet caught Karachi in the chest. As the man dropped to his knees, he reached with his other hand for the gun that had fallen to the floor. Like he wanted to take his adversary with him. Mallen charged forward and shoved his knee nice and clean into the man's face. Mallen grabbed Karachi's gun off the floor, then went and closed the door as the man writhed and bled on the floor, blood flowing from his wrist, chest, nose, and mouth. Mallen rolled him over onto his back. Based on the description, this was indeed Karachi, and thank fuck for that. Put the gun in the man's eye.

"Karachi," Mallen said. Not a question. A fact.

The man moaned. Mallen thought about what this fucker had done to Shannon. What his part in this whole goddamned thing probably was. Couldn't help it: he swung the gun across the man's already broken nose. Not that hard, but Karachi howled. Mallen put the barrel back in the man's eye. Knew he had very little time. Either the police would get here, or this piece of shit would shuffle off to Hell.

"Karachi," Mallen repeated, "you're going to listen to questions and you give me answers. Real answers. And if I don't believe that you're giving real answers? Well, I don't give a rat fuck and I'll pull this trigger. But only after I shoot you in both hands, then your elbow, then your shoulders. You read me on this?"

There was a faint nod.

"Good. Now, about the Marston girl. Jessie. You took her."

A shake of the head.

"You fucker, you know you did."

Another shake of the head. "Killed the … guy … who … "

… *did*. "Why? Where is Jessie Marston? Where?"

"Her … buyer. Buy … er … " Karachi put his head back. Mallen banged it on the carpet a couple times to bring the man around.

"Who?" he hissed at Karachi, "Who the fuck is the buyer?"

Karachi was losing the time battle with the loss of blood. Looked up at Mallen. Then he grinned a toothy, bloody grin that would haunt Mallen the rest of his life.

And then he died.

Mallen looked around the room. No, he thought, there must be, *must* be a clue here.

Karachi's place was a ratty two-bedroom. The kitchen was piled high with rotting pizza that had died in the boxes they were carried over in. He checked the cabinets, the fridge, and the oven. Nothing, not even drugs. Went to the bedrooms. The smaller one made him want to retch. It was obviously the one where Karachi had kept Shannon and what looked to be many other women over the years. Evidence of different-sized women's clothing, of bloodstains all over the sheets and floor. Rotted and molding Chinese take-out boxes. McDonald's wrappers. The pail in the corner stunk from where he stood in the doorway and it was all the way across the room. Now he was *very* glad he'd killed Karachi , even if the sick piece of shit had taken a clue along with him. Mallen would deal with it.

Checked the other bedroom. Obviously this was where Karachi spent his money. Man cave. Huge big-screen TV, complete with every game console and tons of games. Bed covered with satin sheets. Black. He checked the entire room for some hidden alcove, but found nothing. Moved to the closet. Karachi also had a thing for black leather coats and black army fatigues. A street warrior he probably thought himself.

It was in the closet that he found Karachi's arsenal. At least six Glocks. A mini Uzi, with extra clips. A shotgun, sawed off. Tons of shells. A goddamn .44 magnum. All the serial numbers were filed off. He took the Uzi and clips. With the shit he'd seen since he'd gotten clean, he had the feeling it was better to be safe than sorry.

As he was closing the closet his eye caught something behind all the coats. Looked like just a crack in the plaster. He knelt down, and quickly pulled at that area of the wall. And goddamn if it didn't come away to reveal a goddamn wall safe. Not a combo, not that high-end. Needed a key. Mallen bolted back to Karachi's corpse. Found his keys. Ran back to the safe door. It was the fifth key he tried. The thick metal door opened. Inside were bundled dollars. Looked like twenties and fifties. But he didn't pay that any mind. It was the book. A little black book. Underneath that was a flash drive very much like the one he'd found in Yates's car out at the ocean. The man who'd been shot by Karachi. Now it was time to go. Decided to park the Uzi in his coat pocket, the clips in the other. Slipped his own Glock in his waistband and beat it out of there. Checked the outside first. It was as quiet as if nothing had gone down. Who the hell would want to get involved with a shooting? Not here, that's for sure.

Walked calmly back to his truck and hopped in. Stashed the Uzi under the backseat. His own gun went under the front. The flash drive and black book went into the glove box. The truck engine kicked over and he was down the block before anyone would've even been able to get his license plate.

# TWENTY-THREE

Mallen headed across the Golden Gate, heading for some-where he could upload and look at the files on that flash drive. God but did he need to get his own computer. Didn't want to do this in the city. He began to feel that he needed to make his trips into the city as few as possible, and as short as possible, if at all possible. His phone rang and he checked the number. *Shit.* Gwen. The timing was too good to be just a coincidence. "Hey," he said, trying to sound upbeat. "What's up, Gwen?"

The moment she answered him, he knew she was pissed. Very. "Where are you?"

"Crossing the bridge on my way back to the Batcave."

"Ha ha ha fucking funny. We need to talk."

"Not much to talk about. I haven't done that much, yet."

"You keep telling me that. It's starting to piss me off."

"Only starting?" he said with a smile. "Look, I think I'm opening it all up, slowly though. Like a rusty old can."

"You're shit at metaphors, Mallen."

"I'm a recovering junkie on a case, not a fuckin' writer. What do you want from me, yeah?" After a moment, he added, "What's this all about, anyway? You sound harried. More so than usual."

"I'm heading to Bayview."

"Yeah? Why there?"

"Because a call came in about twenty minutes ago that a neighbor heard gunfire, then nothing. Then not long after that, she saw someone walking down the street to a truck."

"And? She get a good look at him? This guy?"

"Not so good, no."

"Why are you on it, anyway? You the only homicide detective in the city?"

"I'm on it because when the uniform got there, he found Jimmy Karachi shot to shit. The uniform knew that I was looking for anyone who was a known acquaintance with Yates."

"And he's dead?"

"Dead as disco. Oh, and his place had been gone over. They'd even dug through the wall safe."

*Fuck…* He'd forgotten to close the door and return the keys to Karachi's corpse. "Any idea what went down?"

She spoke quietly then, "I lied when I said there was no description of the person walking up the street. Tall. Dressed in black. Dark hair. Went to some sort of truck and took off."

He remained silent until she spoke again. Mallen knew better than to say anything at this point. Let her open up on her own. Show her hand first. "I know it was you, Mallen. We need to talk. And I mean right now. What did you get from Karachi's place?"

"I'll be home soon," he replied. "Come there and we'll talk. I'm not doing this over the phone."

"So you did find something?"

"See you when you get here." Cut off the call. His mind raced as to what the fuck to do with all this. He needed time to look through the book and the flash drive. How to keep them both out of Gwen's hands? If he had to, he could give over the flash drive. Pulled out the book as he drove. Glanced at it, other hand on the wheel. There was some sort of code there. Each page had the same design. A large, capitalized first line, coded, then a paragraph or two more of the same code, regularly written.

He wondered about the writings. If it was the creation of Karachi, then it was fucking unlikely that it could ever be broken. Man, if there was ever a time he wished he was Sherlock Holmes, it was now. Ol' Sherlock could break it, just like he figured out that dancing man code bullshit in *The Dancing Men* story.

The moon was still high when Mallen pulled Mr. Gregor's Land Cruiser into the lot. Killed the engine and got out, leaving his newly acquired arsenal stashed under the backseat. He'd come for it when it was dark.

The salt smell was a welcome thing. It immediately relaxed him and he just wanted to get inside his floating hovel. Remembered he had to write that rent check. While he was still alive. As he went down the dock he tried to figure out what to do with Gwen when she showed up.

He glanced at Gregor's home as he walked past. There were already lights on, glimmering dimly through the crazy patchwork windows on the upper story. Every time he looked at that floating home, he was still amazed that the man had built that fucking thing on his own. Crazy.

If Mallen had been paying attention, rather than reflecting on floating homes, codebooks, and undercover cops who were acting not like cops, he would've felt someone come up behind him. As it was, one moment he was walking then the next he felt the barrel of a gun shoved into his back, just below the right ribs.

"Don't you fucking make a move, asshole," said the voice. Mallen knew immediately it must be Lucas. The voice had that weathered, used-up quality to it that long-time abuser gets. Mallen had to admit as he was walked forward to the door of his home that he wasn't so much impressed with Lucas as he was pissed at himself for acting like a rookie.

"Open your fucking door, shitbag," Lucas hissed at him. The gun was right there, pushed hard into him. "Slowly."

Mallen pulled out his keys and opened the door. He was even more impressed when Lucas didn't shove him through the door. In fact he walked Mallen forward into the main room. "Take off your jacket," he was ordered. Nice, the guy wasn't even going to take the chance of checking the pockets. Where the fuck had Lucas learned this crap? TV? Mallen's blood boiled as he slowly took his coat off, letting it fall to the ground, the gun making a dull thud. He would have to try something, and soon. No fucking way was he going to let Lucas leave with that flash drive and codebook.

No fucking way.

"Turn around," Lucas told him. "I want you to see it coming."

Mallen did as he was told. "You sound like something out of a Bogart film. You killed Dreamo, fuckhead."

"Yeah, and? Guy would never deal to me."

"Guy had standards."

Lucas's eyes turned to slits and the gun lashed out too fast for Mallen to duck or fall back. The barrel caught him across the cheek. He could feel the blood starting to flow. But if Lucas thought it would have some sort of effect on Mallen, he was very, very wrong. With what he'd been through the last couple months, a gun barrel across the cheek was a lover's caress. Mallen barely blinked. Only slowly raised his hand to check how badly he was bleeding. Not so bad.

"Ouch," Mallen said. Oh yeah, he wanted to kill this fucker. Kill him bad. And he would, if he got the chance. The killing of Dreamo and Blackmore was enough, but who knew what other shit this predator had done? Guys like this just don't wake up one day like this. No, it takes time. Time and practice.

"Blackmore gave you my name," Lucas said in a flat tone. "I got him. And now I'm going to get you."

"So fucking what if Blackmore gave me your name? I'm a nobody, man. I just needed some answers about Hendrix's death. I found him in his wagon a couple days ago. You gotta know he's dead, right?"

"I'd heard."

"He was into something. Something out of the ordinary, and—"

"Dam fucking right he was," Lucas replied. "Asshole disappears, then comes the fuck back totally flush with bills and smack. But would he share? No. And after all the times me and that cunt Shannon stood for him at Blackmore's, pawning crap with him

164

to get some dough so we could get high, man. That wasn't cool. Fuck Hendrix."

"Yeah, fuck him. But I'm just trying to find a friend's missing girl is all, so I needed to track down all leads. It wasn't personal. I just wanted to talk."

"Talk? Well, you can talk to God now," Lucas said with a smile. Like he was pleased with having replied in that way, with those words.

"You really need to work on your thug banter, man," Mallen replied. Regretted it as Lucas stepped closer. He could even see the proverbial finger tightening on the trigger. "So Hendrix wouldn't share with you, yeah?" He just needed some more time to figure out how to take Lucas down. Just a few seconds more ....

"Fuck talking man. Now you die. Can't have people asking after me, or people giving out info on me. No can do. That one time, the last time I saw that fuck Hendrix, he was running his mouth about all sorts of shit."

"Yeah? Running his mouth?"

"It was early morning. I'd run into him going back to that bullshit wagon that the cops wouldn't touch. I wish I had those kinds of connections. The fuckhole. He was all proud of his dough and dope. He practically made me beg for some dope. Told me to come back later. Then he took off, just like that. Ran off. Lying sack of shit. I told Shannon later I knew he'd been lying."

"Well, I'd heard Hendrix was a liar," Mallen answered. Figured it would keep Lucas going and that was a good thing: keep him talking, not shooting.

"Damn fucking right he was a liar," came the reply. "Always

saying he 'knew the folks downtown.' Always said it, just like that. Would sometimes brag about it. Well, everyone on the street had figured that one out. I mean .... The wagon, right? I'd only ever seen cops around there once or twice."

Mallen looked around the room then. "Hey, you give a dying man one last cigarette? Like they used to do in the movies?"

When Lucas seemed not to like that suggestion, Mallen continued quickly, "Look, I'm a recovering junkie, right? We smoke all the fucking time, yeah? I just... just wanna smoke man. I'll smoke fast, I swear."

Lucas spied a pack on the nearby table. Never took his eyes off Mallen as he scooped them up and tossed them at him. Mallen again was impressed with how cautious Lucas was. This guy had been something else before he'd become a street viper. As Mallen pulled a cig from the pack, reaching for a nearby pack of matches, he said casually, "You move like you were Army. Army?"

"Fuck you," came the reply.

"Ah. Marine." Mallen lit the cigarette and blew out the match, tossing it into the ashtray. Get them used to the small movements, he'd always been told. The small movements, then hit them with the big one. He took a deep drag of the cigarette.

"Put your hands back up," Lucas told him as he moved in. Mallen tensed, but he'd taken the cigarette out of his mouth just before Lucas has given him the order.

"I'd heard there was some Asian cop that would come around Hendrix's wagon. Had some goatee. Is that the guy that gave Hendrix his parking pass?" Mallen said.

"How the fuck should I know? Enough talk. On your knees,

back to me. I'm going to put this cap right in the back of your head."

"Oh, I thought you wanted me to see it coming. My bad," Mallen replied, every muscle fiber tightening. He saw Anna's face then. Right there in his mind's eye. "You should at least let me see it coming, man. Even Bogie would've done that."

"Okay," and before Lucas could pull the trigger, Mallen flicked the cigarette right at the man's face. It didn't hit but it made him flinch and then Mallen was on him and both men tumbled to the ground, the gun between them. A blast slit the air as the gun went off. Both men pushed the other away, like they didn't want to know each other anymore now that the door to death had been passed through. Lucas checked himself for a wound. Smiled when he saw blood seeping from Mallen's side. But the gun was right by Mallen's hand, and he'd scooped it up before the knowledge of being shot even registered. Then the pain started and he glanced down. The bullet hole was close to the outside near and just above the hip. Not much more than a deep graze. God did indeed look out for lost children and recovering junkies.

"Okay," Mallen hissed, "Now we're going to play a *different* game."

"What . . . what game, man?" Lucas asked in a worried whisper.

Mallen pulled himself over to the couch. The gun never wavered from Lucas's face. He wondered how long until Gwen showed up, or maybe some uniforms. "This game is called "You Tell Me What the Fuck Ever I Want to Know.' If you play well, you get to live with both nuts in your sack, both legs intact." Took a deep breath. "You ever play that before?"

When he got no response from Lucas, he continued. "It's played this way: if you fucking don't answer the way I think you should, you lose something. Or, well … I kill you outright. The world won't mind one less Lucas, right?"

Again, Lucas just stared at him. Sometimes at the gun. There were no sirens. Mallen grabbed up the sweat socks that he'd stuffed into his running shoes only a few days ago. Pressed them to his side. He needed to get the book away somewhere, but he also now needed for Gwen, or any friendly, to show up. It wasn't a bad wound, but it was enough that he was beginning to feel light-headed from all the adrenaline that had earlier pumped into his system and was now quickly leaving.

"So let's get started," he said to Lucas. "First question. You saw the Asian cop, yeah?"

Lucas nodded his head. "Saw him once. Knocked on the back door of the wagon."

"Spend much time talking? He hand anything off to Hendrix?"

"No. Nothing. They only spoke for a few minutes." Lucas shifted a little. "It was the other detective that Hendrix spoke more to. The woman."

And the world just blasted some cold air down the back of his neck. Hell, there were more than a few women detectives on the force. He knew that. "Yeah? What did she look like?"

"I only saw her once," Lucas replied quickly. Like he was happy he was getting through to Mallen. Like he thought Mallen would soften with the more information he got. "Red headed. Nice suit. Fine bitch."

"How long did they talk?"

"Oh man, it was like fifteen minutes. She stood outside, acted like she was writing a ticket, but it was fucking stupid. Only made it more obvious. To me, anyway."

"Then what happened?" He was losing his grip on consciousness. He'd either phase out for a very important couple seconds, or be completely out soon, and this sack of shit would take the gun and shoot him.

"Well…" Lucas replied slowly, like he could read Mallen's mind. "I don't… don't remember. Give me a moment." And then he leapt at Mallen, one hand going for the bullet wound, the other for the gun. Mallen's insides exploded at Lucas's fist slammed him in the hip. He was able to keep the gun away from the man, but then they were struggling on the ground, locked together, and this time Mallen knew he would never live through a second round. The world outside of his head was silent. There was only the sound of his breathing. Everything was happening like it was all going down underwater. Both men had their hands on the gun as they rolled back and forth on the floor, knocking over the coffee table, pushing away the couch and chair. Mallen knew there was only one chance left. He released his left hand suddenly and smashed down on Lucas's nose. Lucas flinched from the hit and Mallen knew he had him. Lucas's grip relaxed for just a second, and also just a fraction of pressure. Mallen got a better hold of the weapon and brought it smashing down but Lucas grabbed for it and it went off again and this time it was Mallen who looked at Lucas and it was Lucas who looked at a bullet hole in his body. High, and in the left shoulder, centered toward his heart.

"You…" Lucas said as he lost consciousness.

Mallen lay back, the world fading. Desperately grabbed at some deep breaths. Closed and opened his eyes. There was a frantic knock on his door. It was faint, but he could still tell it was important. Mallen thought it was Gwen, but then he heard Mr. Gregor's hurried voice, "Mallen! Mallen! You alive? Answer me or I'm storming in, son!"

"I'm here," Mallen replied. "Come ahead, sir."

The door banged opened and Mr. Gregor stood there. Scanned the room then walked in, closing the door behind him. Came over to Mallen, who only then put the gun on the coffee table and lay back. He felt weak, and cold. Mr. Gregor said to him, "Son, you live one fuck of a life."

A faint smile. "And ain't that a stone cold fact, sir."

"What do you want me to do?"

"Check him. Is he alive?"

Gregor knelt down. Checked for a pulse. Nodded. "Barely, son."

"Call an ambulance, but first take this." Mallen handed Mr. Gregor the codebook and flash drive he got at Karachi's. "You don't have this and never did," he said.

"Got it," the old man said as he shoved both into his back pocket. "We got to get you to hospital, too, Mallen."

All Mallen could do was nod. Gregor went to the phone and was about to dial when Gwen appeared in the doorway. She took one look at the scene and ripped out her phone, saying, "Anyone call an ambulance?"

"Just about to," Gregor replied.

Gwen nodded. Called it in. Shook her head at Mallen, "You're such trouble."

Mallen looked at her for a moment. At her red hair. She *was* very good-looking.

Gwen saw the gun on the table. Looked from Mallen to Lucas. "What the fuck happened?" It was then that she looked over at Mr. Gregor. "Who are you?"

"He looks after the dock. Name is Gregor." Mallen said, "He pretty much saved my life by knocking when he did." He then indicated Lucas, "*That* is the guy who killed Blackmore, the pawnbroker, and probably was into some other shit that's gone down recently."

Gwen raised an eyebrow as she came over and helped him over onto the couch, "What kind of shit, Mallen?"

Mallen tried to shrug. "Just check. I'm sure something will come up with that gun."

Gwen was about to say something when the sound of sirens rent the air. Mr. Gregor moved to the door. "I'll let them know all the action is in here," he said as he left. Mallen had a feeling the man would disappear for a moment to stash the book and flash drive, then come back. Gwen watched Mr. Gregor go, her gaze lingering there for a moment before she turned back to Mallen saying, "You have some good friends."

He tried to smile. Almost made it. "The best."

# TWENTY-FOUR

GATO WOKE TO THE sound of automatic gunfire. Automatic gunfire. Sounded pretty. Like a rap song he wished he knew. Screams. A noise of... something... outside the door to his room. A fight? More gunfire. Then the door burst open and a man fell into the room, in slowmo, his head a mess of bone, flesh, and hair. Gato had to admit, the sparkle of the blood as it splashed to the floor was as beautiful as he'd always imagined Jesus' blood to be as it fell after the soldier pierced his chest with the spear.

A man ran into the room then. Young and strong guy, like how he'd been young and strong once. Dressed in black. So dramatic. "*Vamos, gato. ¡Ven conmigo!*"

All Gato could do in response was laugh. Man, it was so fucking *dramatica*. The man came and grabbed him up. Dragged him to his feet. It hurt but not in the good way the needle had hurt. He tried to struggle out of it. "Hey *vato!* I'm good, man ... keep cool!"

"*¡Silencio!*" the man said. Pulled Gato to the door like pulling a five-year-old. Pulled him into the hall. There was a lot of noise out here, and it hurt Gato's head. Lots of gunfire. He thought it was important, but the only thing that was starting to feel important was the needle and The Need. Gato was pushed and yanked down the hall and it was only then that he realized the man held an Uzi. Nice rig, that. They went down a hall, stepping over some bodies that certainly looked dead. He'd looked at dead fucker's before, right? He was sure he had.

Then they met up with two other men, both dressed in black. That was when the bullets started to fly again. Came from the doorway on their left. Chopped up the walls, some hitting the man that pulled Gato along as they fell back, away from the fire. The man toppled to the ground, dead. There was a part of Gato's mind that begged him to pick up the gun and start surviving but the rest of him just stood there, staring at the Uzi, unsure what to do. One of the other men then grabbed him and pushed him down the hall, yelling out, "*¡Hijo de puta! ¡Vete al infierno!*" And he did. But it was such a long hallway. Finally they were at a door and he was shoved aside and there was a huge explosion as the door was blasted apart, wood shards cutting his face. The night air felt great and he realized then that he hadn't felt the night air for what felt like a really long time. A glance over his shoulder showed him some sort of abandoned warehouse but other than that it was all desert dark. Why leave that place though? The happy drug was in there! He made a move back to the building but was smacked in the face by one of the men dressed in black. There was the screech of tires and a van came into view.

"Hurry!" one of the men with him yelled out and the van skidded to a stop, the side door sliding open. Before Gato could say anything, he was tossed inside like a bag of recycling and then it was about men yelling, more gunfire, the door slamming shut, the crunch of tires skidding over dirt and then it was a roller-coaster of speed and tossing about and then he had to puke, and did, all over himself and everything.

"Fuck me," he heard someone in the dark say, "and we let Marcos die for this piece of shit? Fuck."

And then Gato passed out.

———

The first thing Gato noticed when he came out of the darkness was that he again found himself in the back of some vehicle. This time it was an SUV. His mind was fucked up and foggy. Couldn't tell who was driving. The sun outside the windows hurt his eyes when he tried to find out. The figure in the passenger side turned to look at him. Took him a moment to realize who it was and what name belonged to her.

*Mama Lobo*...

"Mama..." he said. Couldn't say the rest he was so weak.

"Quiet, *gatito*," she replied. "You've had a bad time, right? You have to leave now. Don't return. Ever."

It was coming back to him. But as that happened so did the hurting. He needed something to make it okay. Then it hit him hard. He needed the smack. He'd been given smack. *Oh... no... no... no...*

"When you didn't show again," Mama Lobo told him, "I started sending out feelers. Trying to find you. But that Mike ... " Shook her head. Her eyes turned hard. "That Mike."

"But ... I can't go," he said through teeth that had begun chattering. "Lupe."

"You forget about your sister, *gatito*. She's not going anywhere for about another two months. Maybe two and a half."

Gato curled up on the backseat. Only then noticing a man next to him. The man put a bag over Gato's mouth just in time. Heard the man curse, then the window going down. The smell left slowly and the window stayed down.

"I can't leave her," Gato muttered, his remaining strength leaving faster than the losing team's fans.

"I'm sorry, Eduardo. There's nothing else I can do for you, except get you out of town. You're sick. Dehydrated. You need food and rest and ... " She looked out the car window. "Now you go home."

"I ... can't. Oh, Lupe," he muttered. Tried to keep his eyes open but it was growing impossible. The agony was tearing his bones to shreds. His skin was on fire, the leather of the seats like a burning whip. The sun scalded his eyes.

"Where am I going" he managed to ask. What about Lupe? Even through the pain, he realized he'd failed. His sister. His mother. Himself. He'd failed. Couldn't help hit: tears rolled down his cheeks, and even those scalded him.

As he began to fade into darkness, a darkness that felt like diving into hot tar but was still welcome as it offered oblivion, he heard Mama Lobo say, "You're going to the only place I know to send you where you'll be safe."

———

Gato could never remember just how he survived the trip, survived what he'd been put through. All the way west he shook and vomited into a bag that would get thrown out the window once it was used. The van would frequently stop for the expulsion of other body liquids and solids, sometimes just in time to make sure Gato could get out. He had no embarrassment left. Would just shit right there, not caring if the entire world saw him there, crouching with his filthy pants down. The only thing that kept him going was his thirst, his driving thirst for revenge on Mike and all his crew. He knew he'd go back again. Knew he'd rescue his sister and her child. He knew he would. If he had to walk all the way back to Vegas, he'd have his vengeance. Every time he thought about what had happened to him, he thought about his cell. About how they'd kept him like a dog in a kennel. Then he'd think about Mike.

About the dope.

About the pain.

Oh yeah ... *habría jodido tener su venganza.* Yes, he'd have his revenge.

# TWENTY-FIVE

As he lay in the back of the ambulance, Mallen thought of the laundry list of things that had happened, and the things that had to be done. First on that list was to call Chris as soon as possible and let her know what happened. A hold over from the old days. Their agreement had been that if he got seriously injured, she needed to know, as immediately as possible.

He also needed to get in touch with Mr. Gregor. Man, he was wracking up red points again. And where the fuck was Gato in all this? He'd lost track of the days. Usually he wouldn't have worried about his friend. If anyone could take care of himself, it was Gato. But this time something deep inside told him to be concerned.

He looked down at the bandage on his left side, just below the rib cage. Again he thought about how lucky he'd been since getting clean. Yeah, it may not look like it, or feel like it, but he'd been very, very lucky. Something out there in the universe wanted him to survive, but it also wanted to keep reminding him just how precious his new life was. But fuck, what the hell more could he do? He'd been shot. Was on the ropes, and beat to shit.

And, as always, the answer came back in its quiet and steady voice: *whatever you can do.*

———

The paramedic truck pulled up to the emergency room doors. He was taken in on a stretcher. Not his choice. He would've preferred to walk in. He could've made it. As he entered, he caught sight of Gwen's car pulling up to the nearby red curb. Was she keeping tabs on him? Was he being crazy, believing Lucas? That Gwen knew Hendrix a lot more than she had let on. His head swam at everything that was going down, going down way too fast. Maybe he should just lay back and enjoy the chance to stand down. Even if it meant being sewn up.

They wheeled him into the emergency room and right over to a curtained bay. A doctor and team were already there, ready to go. One of the nurses came up to him with a pair of scissors in her hand, ready to cut his pants off him. He pushed them away.

"No." They all stopped and looked at him; skin chalk white, shirt dripping blood. "You know how much these cost?" he continued, working through the pain so he could get his pants open. One of the nurses helped him get them all the way off. Same with the coat. The shirt could be replaced.

Then the work began. An intern came over to him, clipboard in hand. Asked him a bunch of questions he answered as best he could. Had no insurance. Gave his address. Name. Then the question came: "Have you ever used a needle to shoot drugs?"

"Yes," he replied, eyes steady, "But that's in the past now."

A nod in response. The rest of the interview was done quickly, but he was barely there for it. Maybe he'd passed out; he couldn't remember anything when he woke up in recovery, Gwen standing there watching him.

"Well, hello," she said with a smile, "how's my snitch?"

"How do you think?"

She gave him the once over. "Pretty shitty, I'm sure."

"Right."

Pulled out her notebook. "I took over the shooting. Lucas is still in a coma."

"There is a god."

Glanced at her notes. "Gregor backs up what the evidence shows. That Lucas came after you with a gun. You struggled. Lucas got the worst of it. We're checking the gun, like you said to." Took a moment before continuing, "But what none of this shit says too clearly is why he was there in the first place."

"I think he had me mistaken for someone who was after him."

"Mallen," she said, looking him dead in the eyes, "why was he there? What's the real story?"

"Like I said earlier, Gwen, I don't know why he was there. Seemed out of his head, you know? Going on about how I was trying to frame him for some murder or some such shit." Shifted in the bed, to get more comfortable, "Like I said to you back at my place, I would see about that gun. I'd also maybe check forensics, see if you can place Lucas in connection with that pawnbroker's murder. What was his name? Blackmore? And wasn't there some dealer shot recently? With maybe the same gun?"

"Justin Jones," she told him. "Dreamo. Yes, I heard about that." Gwen wrote down some notes. "Thank you for all this. I'm sure the SFPD will be most beholden."

"Well, one can hope, yeah?"

———

Gwen wanted to stay around, but Mallen acted like he needed sleep and rest. It was lucky the nurse came in at that point, too, and reinforced the idea that the patient needed rest. Gwen gave him a look that let him know she didn't buy his dodge, but would let it go, for now. "See you soon, Mallen," she said as she put her notebook back in her pocket and walked away. The nurse soon followed, after checking to make sure his vitals were good.

His coat had been tossed over the visitor's chair. There was a plastic bag nearby, the one that contained all his clothes, bloody shirt included. The chair seemed a long world away.

*Fucking hell…*

He had to call Chris. Managed to sit up, but it was like the phone was in the next time zone. Took a deep breath. He'd had his hand hammered to a card table and lived to tell about it. Leapt into the freezing bay to escape death. He could do this. Put his feet on the floor. The world twisted. He breathed heavily and steady until the twist unclenched. Pushed himself upright. Took two steps and leaned over for his coat. Began to fall forward. Used his right hand to snag the coat and the left to rebound off the chair, pushing himself in a backward motion that sent him returning onto the bed. A demented gymnast move, but it worked. Checked the I.V. tubes. All good. Dialed Chris's number.

It wasn't Chris who answered though. And it wasn't Anna. It was Daniel. "Hello?" Daniel said, "Mallen residence."

*How cute...* "Uh... hi Daniel. This is Mark. Chris around? I need to talk to her."

A pause, a hand over the mouthpiece. Jesus fuck... the guy was actually asking if she wanted to talk to him. If he hadn't been laid up, he would've gone right over and punched Daniel in the face. After a moment, Chris got on the phone. "Hi Mark," she said, and he knew that something was up. Could hear it in the voice he knew as well as his own. "How is it going?" she said.

"I just wanted to let you know that I'm in the hospital. Like I would've done, back in the old days."

"The hospital? What happened? Not...?"

"No. Something a lot easier to deal with. I'm working on something. Trying to find a woman's kidnapped child. It's sorta gotten bigger than I'd first imagined it would be."

And she gave him a soft laugh. "When did it NOT get bigger than first imagined?"

"Right," he said back with the same amount of laughter.

"So what happened? Do Daniel and I need to come down there? How bad is it?"

*Do Daniel and I need to come down...* And that said everything he needed to know. She would've put off Daniel and come down by herself if she wasn't serious about him. Doing this was her way of introducing the man into her world. A world in which he'd now been regulated to the sidelines. He knew Chris would always let him see Anna, as long as he stayed clean, but she herself was now in another place. With another man. So much for Daniel sleeping on the couch.

"No, you don't need to come down," he said, trying to hold his voice steady. "I just wanted you to know. I'll be fine. It wasn't serious. I coulda sewn it up myself except for the circumstances."

A soft laugh, "Sounds like the old Mallen I married."

"Well, old is new again," he replied hating his response immediately. Too desperate.

Silence. Then after a moment, she spoke quietly. Like she didn't want Daniel to here. "I need someone... clean, Mark. A world that's clean; one not involved with dealers, bullets, and dead women. You can see that, right? After what's happened?"

He swallowed hard. "Yeah, I can see that. Of course I can."

"And don't you stop coming around," she said, "or start blowing off your visitation days, okay? If you have issues with coming here, I'll bring her to you. She loves you. Idolizes you. You have to see her."

"No 'have' about it. Of course I'll be there for her. And I'll still be there for you, too, Chris. No matter what, okay? You hear me on this? I will always be there for you. Even if you got married again, I'd be there."

"Married?" she replied. "We're not there yet. Not by far. But I appreciate your words, Mark. Thank you." There was a pause, then, "Are you sure you don't need us to come over? Which hospital are you in? What the hell happened?"

"Long story. I'm in Marin. Not fatal. Hurts like hell, but I'll make it. I'm leaving now. You stay home. I'll call in a couple days." He was fading, both emotionally and physically. Needed to be home. "Tell Anna I love her and we're flying a kite very soon."

She was saying "okay" when he'd hung up. Most of his energy was spent. He lay back and rested for a moment. He had to get home. Get to Mr. Gregor. Dressed as best he could in his blood-encrusted clothes. Managed to get his shoes on without passing out as he bent over his feet. Then the nurse came into his bay. Had forms in her hand, clamped neatly to a brown, fake wood clipboard.

"Mr. Mallen," she said and then noticed he was about to take out the IV. She came over and removed it the way it was supposed to be removed. "You're certainly impatient," she told him.

"You can't stop me from leaving, right?"

"No. You have to go?"

"Yes. It's very important that I get back on the road."

She looked him over. "That better be an easy road, Mr. Mallen."

"Unfortunately, it rarely ever is." Added with a soft smile. "I can get a cab outside?"

"Sure." But as he started to move away, she stopped him. She glanced once at the nurse's desk just up and over one bay. She then went quickly and grabbed a bunch of bandages and cleaning swabs, along with other things he recognized for changing bandages. She put it all in the bag they'd put his clothes in. Pushed it at him as she said, "Use it. Clean the wound every day for five days. The bullet missed anything necessary, but it took a little bit of flesh. Keep it dry and keep it clean as long as you can, alright?" she looked at him like she really cared. She almost seemed familiar, but he couldn't place the face. "You don't recognize me, do you?" she said off his look.

"I'm afraid I don't. Sorry."

She shrugged. "You helped me once, back when you were still in uniform. A very long time ago. I'm glad to pay it back."

He nodded. She walked with him forward down the ward, her carrying her clipboard, it all looking very official and okay. She stopped at the sliding glass exit doors. Pretended to writing something down, then simply turned and walked away.

Mallen left as quickly as he could. The night air was cold and crisp. The stars shone brightly between rolls of dark gray clouds. He had only his phone, a few dollars, and the bandages he'd been given.

Hell, he reasoned as he walked to the nearest taxi stand, lots of people have a lot less.

# TWENTY-SIX

GATO'S EYES OPENED AND it took a moment for him to realize where he was. In a warehouse, the ceiling three tall stories above. He was on a bed, the area cordoned off by wheeled bookcases and curtains batik'd in all sorts of crazy patterns. The bed he lay on was low but more comfortable than any bed he could remember from the recent past. Had the vague memory of knowing this bed. He tried to move but he was sore from head to foot. Insides felt like they'd been cramped up for days. His entire face was numb, and the parts that weren't numb were in intense pain. His jaw could barely move. There was a pitcher of water and a glass on the dark wood table next to the bed. He sat up, slowly, trying to be careful. Even that nearly sent him back into oblivion. He had to sit and stare at the water for a moment, almost wishing it would just rise up and come to him, but of course it wouldn't. In the end he didn't do anything but lie back on the bed. That burned him. Burned him deep.

Nothing had ever kept him so weak, so completely thrashed out. Nothing but back when . . . .

. . . . then it all came flooding back. Lupe. Her baby. Mike. The junk. Being beaten like a dog. His blood boiled. How the fuck could that have happened? How could he be taken so easily?

It was all he could do to not let the hot tears that boiled in his soul roll down his cheeks.

At that moment, Ali pushed aside the curtain and walked into what he now remembered was her bedroom. He'd only been here once. Only once. Back when both her brothers had been in trouble. He'd come to warn her. She'd asked him to stay. And he'd stayed. Ever since then he'd wanted to be here, back where he'd first met her. She was going to be his wife, he thought at the time. But now? Now that thought felt like a teenager's stupid wet dream. That dream had been shoved in his face like shoving a dog's nose in its own shit. That dream was now shelved. The world he was now walking in wasn't meant for kid's dreams. This world was too real, too dark.

Too mean.

"So," she said as she gave him the once over, "my little cat seems to be awake."

"*Yo creo que sí.*"

She came and sat on the edge of the bed. Studied him carefully. Like she really cared if he were okay or not. "My mother took a long chance bringing you here. You must've struck a chord in her."

He tried to sit up and finally did, putting his back against the wood of the bed frame. There was a faint memory. "She did tell me she wished she'd had more sons like me than the ones she'd had."

Ali smiled, but there was a lot of sadness there. "That sounds like her, alright." She checked the bandage that he only now realized he carried wound tight around his midsection. Broken rib. Or Ribs. This was definitely part of the discomfort he'd felt since he woke up. Touched the area gently, probing, but Ali pushed his hand away. "They broke the two lower on the left. Cracked a floating rib. Painful, but you'll live."

There was a feeling there inside him then. A desire that made his chest tight and his ribs hurt. It was the desire to shoot. To shoot Mike and all his gang. "How long was I out?" he asked quickly.

"A long time. Long enough, if that's what you're asking. I'm surprised you have any liquid in you at all." She reached over and handed him a quart bottle of water. "Drink it," she said as she got up. "I'll see if I can find you something you can hold on your stomach. From what mama told me, you haven't eaten in some days, *vato*."

He opened the water bottle. Drank and drank and drank. Didn't realize how dehydrated he was until he drank. After a moment he stopped. Put the top back on the bottle. Told Ali quietly, unable to look at her, "I owe you and Mama Lobo my life."

Ali smiled then, "You know it, Gato. Don't you know it?"

Then he thought of his friend. Of Mallen. His brother always seemed to find trouble. *O problema encontrado.* He had to call Mallen. "You have a phone I could use until I get my own?"

"No," Ali replied, "but I have a phone you can use to make a call, or calls, while you're here. I'm not some cheap-ass liquor store, *gatito*."

"Hell no, you're not," he said. She went to a drawer. Pulled out a phone and tossed it to him. Just some random smartphone. He booted it up and wasn't surprised to see it was completely anonymous. As anonymous as any phone could be these days. Registered to a fake person, and only seemed to be flying on local wifi networks. An extra battery was taped to the back, for emergencies. The phone was a *fantasma*. Somebody might be able to pick it up, but they would have a fuck-all load of shit trying to track it.

He dialed Mallen's number, the number he now knew so well.

But a voice answered he didn't know, and the anxiety of that worked to bring him around some more. Helped to make him more present.

"Yeah?" said the gruff, gravelly voice.

"This phone belongs to my *hombre*. Why isn't he answering?"

"And who are you?"

"You first, fucker. I need to know where Mallen is."

Silence, then after a moment, "I run the dock where he lives. He's at the hospital getting stitched up."

Gato's hand tightened on the phone. "What happened? Tell me."

A gravely laugh. "Hey man, not until you tell me who the fuck you are."

"My name is Gato. Mallen would vouch for me, if he could, *hombre*."

"Gato," the man intoned, "Yeah, he mentioned you. This is Gregor."

"The guy with the truck?"

"Yeah, that guy."

"Man, what the fuck has happened to him?" Gregor gave him a rundown of the scene at Mallen's place. Gato's answer was a string of Spanish swearing. Took him a minute to calm down enough to ask, "Where was he taken? Do you know?"

"Marin General. That woman cop he knows, the redhead, wanted to take him to the city, but he wanted to stay north of the bridge."

Gato figured it out. There was something unsafe for the moment about San Francisco hospitals. "Look," he said, "I'm laid up, but I will be out there, *will* be out there as fast as I can. How long do you think he'll be in the hospital?"

"Well," Mr. Gregor said slowly, "if it were anyone else? I'd say a couple days. Mallen? Based on what I've seen? Be home before the sun rises."

Gato nodded. Yes, that sounded right. "Okay. *Gracias. Gracias, señor Gregor.*"

———

It had taken Mallen longer to get home than he'd figured. Finding a cab in the city in the early morning hours was nothing, but finding one in the early morning north of the Golden Gate? That was something else entirely. The cab drove off but he stood still, watching the vehicle disappear into the darkness, tail lights a red haze. Didn't move until he'd looked up and down the parking lot. There didn't seem to be any cars he didn't recognize. Sighed a bit in relief, and only then did he stalk down the dock toward his home. Once inside he immediately went into the bathroom and set about checking his bandage. Still good. Made it upstairs to his office. To the file cabinet. Pulled the spare handgun out of the top drawer. The Uzi was still in the truck as was the other handgun he took from Karachi's place. At least he had something on him now. Made his way downstairs, intent on eating something before figuring out his next move.

Then he heard it. A noise coming from just outside, out on the deck. Shit, he was so beat up and tired how the fuck was he going be able to do anything? Couldn't even hunker down behind anything, his body hurt so much. He knew if he hunkered down, he'd never be able to get up. The gun was still in his hand. Aimed for the door, pulling back the hammer. Seemed as loud as hammering down a railroad tie. All he could do was shuffle to the corner of the kitchen, gun trained on the front door. He heard someone come forward from the deck and check the front door knob. Certainly wasn't making any effort to be quiet.

Then a voice spoke from the other side of the door. "Mallen. *Soy yo, el hombre,* Gato."

And Mallen could never remember being so relieved. "Ah, shit, G!" he called out as he went toward the front door, "Get the fuck in here my brother."

Gato entered the room. *Jesus fucking Christ,* Mallen thought as he looked at his friend, at the man who'd saved his life more than once. He'd never seen Gato so beat to shit, both on the inside and out. Mallen noticed, too, that there was some difference around the man's eyes, and it was more than just the fading bruises. No, he could tell right away that something heavy, bad, and dark, had gone down. As if to verify Mallen's feelings, Gato wore black pants and shirt, the shirt's sleeves rolled up just to the forearm. Not the usual white wife beater. It seemed insane, but if he didn't know better, Mallen would say his friend was recovering from a bout with the needle. But no, man.... that was insanity. Not Gato. Not G.

The two men continued to look at each other for a moment, then Gato smiled faintly. "Looks like we both were taken to Hell and back, *vato.*"

"And then some," he said as he moved to the couch and let himself down onto it. Never felt so good to sit. "Where you been?"

But Gato only shook his head as he stood there. "Not anywhere that was good."

"You didn't find Lupe?"

"Oh yeah, man. I found her." He gave Mallen a brief rundown on everything. Lupe's being pregnant. Mike. Being held prisoner. Then he walked over to Mallen. Looked ashamed he raised the sleeve of his right arm. The dark pinprick scabs showed clear, even in the low light from the table lamp across the room.

Gato looked away as he put his sleeve down. "They got me, *vato.* I have to fuck their shit *up*, man. Somehow, some way... I have to make them pay for it all."

"Where was Lupe when you last saw her?"

"With that Mike cat. I think she's safe as long as she's pregnant."

Mallen considered this. "So how much time do you think you have, G?"

"Hell, man, what do I look like? A midwife? I have no goddamn idea when she'll *dar a luz*." He took a deep breath then. Relaxed. "I think a few months."

"And you're sure he's going to kill her once the baby is born?"

A nod. Mallen had never seen his friend look so sad. "Mama Lobo told me to stay out of Vegas. No matter what. She's going to take a rash of shit for helping me, but she was willing to do that."

"Why?" Mallen'd heard stories about Mamma Lobo, but nothing that would lead him to believe she would've done what she did. He couldn't understand why she'd put herself out like this.

"Well," Gato replied, "it was more for Ali, bro. Not for me. For her."

"Ah. Well, thank God for crushing out on the right people, yeah?"

Now there was a faint smile there. Then his friend turned all business. "*Primero lo primero, vato.* I called your phone and got your truck-man. What the fuck is going on, Mallen?"

Then it was Mallen's turn to give Gato a quick recap. As he told his friend about what he was into, he'd kept talking as he moved to his bedroom and switched clothes. Came out into the living room, dressed in a dark car coat, sweater, and black jeans. Carried some bandages with him that he shoved into the pocket of his coat. Put the gun in the other pocket. "We need to go see Gregor, fast-like. He helped me out and I don't want to put him in danger. He's been a huge savior, a couple times over now."

"Then let's do it, man," came the simple reply.

They left Mallen's home and went quickly down the dock. "You have some metal on you, yeah?" Mallen asked.

"Fuck yeah I do," came the response. "And spare grain for her, too."

"Good." Mallen didn't worry about waking Gregor. From what he'd seen, the man was probably up wondering what had happened since the hospital.

As he walked up the dock with Gato in tow, he kept his head on a swivel. Until he could figure out about Gwen, he was over putting his trust in people. Especially those with badges. The only cop he could ever trust a hundred percent had always been Oberon.

There were lights on in Gregor's place, the upstairs lit up like a church on Sunday. Mallen knocked at the door. Waited. After a moment it opened and there was Gregor, Steelers cap on his head, old Hawaiian shirt on, along with the usual khaki army shorts. Smiled when he saw Mallen. Glanced at Gato. "I told your friend there you'd be home by morning."

"Can't keep a good recovering junkie down, or so it would seem, sir."

Gregor stepped back to let them in. Mallen had never been inside the place, and he was struck immediately by how it reminded him of Quint's house in *Jaws*, minus all the shark skeletons. "You two don't look like you could make it upstairs, but you'll have to," Gregor told them.

Mallen and Gato followed the grizzled old vet. Upstairs was nothing but one, long open area. Like a half-finished attic. No two windows were alike. Mallen could swear the mosaic glass windows that served as skylights were taken from an actual church. Gregor led them over to a huge worktable, covered in papers. There were maps there, of the bay currents. Also larger maps showing every walking and riding trail from the Golden Gate all the way up to Mendocino. Many of them had a penciled set of numbers at the point where the path started.

Mallen pointed to one set of numbers. "How long it took you to walk that trail?"

Gregor shook his head. "How long it took me to walk it with a full kit on my back. Keeps me in shape."

Gato shook his head. Looked at Mr. Gregor. "You're someone I could learn from, sir." Mallen had never heard his friend sound so reverential.

But the old man only shrugged. "You already know what you need to know. It's just how you go about putting it into play." Gregor then led them to his desk, an old architect's table. On the surface was the codebook that Mallen had given him, along with the flash drive. The flash drive hadn't been touched, but the codebook sat in a wash of notes and scribbled paper.

"Nobody saw you give this to me," Gregor told them, "but I could swear that red-headed cop gave the eye of suspicion as I vacated. I don't know how long I can keep this safe, if I'm right."

"I can take it with me when I leave," Mallen said.

"Well, after what I tell ya," Gregor responded with a grin, "you might not want to take it away from me."

"What do you mean?" Mallen looked over all the notes. "You mean you cracked the fucking code? Already?"

"What one man can create, another bastard can figure out," Gregor smiled with a grim smile. "Whoever did this had a military background. If I didn't know better I'd say he served in Vietnam like me. Or, he'd at least read about the codes we used back then. It's damn close to what we used back in '68."

"You can place it that far back, sir?" Gato asked. Again, Mallen was surprised about how reverential his friend was being.

"Sure. Code is a part of war, just like forgiving is a part of marriage. All our communications were picked up all the time by the other side. We needed a way to get messages to each other. A lot of us didn't have radios. The radio guys were usually getting blown to fuck, the radios along with them. So.... the grunts began to develop a coded system that only them and their captains would know. It grew, became more... refined for lack of a better fucking word. Spread, until most of us were using it." Nodded at the codebook in front of him. "Whoever wrote that code somehow, somehow, knew about that code we developed. Maybe they were there, or their father was. But it was one, or the other."

"Some guy could've stumbled upon a book in an old store somewhere," Mallen said, thinking of Blackmore and Lucas. "A pawnshop or something, yeah?"

"Well, sure. But the fucker who found that book would need the key, or have a code-breaking background. If it's NOT the real thing, it's based off the real thing."

Mallen glanced over the notes and scribbles again. "What have you gotten from it?"

Gregor sighed. Shook his head. "It's not pretty." Spread out the papers in front of him, covered over and over with code variations and possible solutions, most everything scratched out. However, there was one page that Gregor showed them. "Consider this fucker the Rosetta stone. Everything started to fall together after I nailed *this* baby."

Mallen and Gato stared at the page, totally lost. Every letter seemed to have a random letter underneath it but underneath *that* was a word. Same for the digits. There were digits underneath the original digits. Those seemed to make anything from dates to weights to lengths. Light weights. Short lengths.

"It's a catalog of sorts," Gregor said quietly. "You know what of, don't you, Mallen?"

Mallen could only nod. "Yeah, I do."

"How … what about the code?" Gato said quietly. "How'd you break it, sir?"

Gregor shrugged. "I used to know shit like this. Once I got a handle on it, it came to me. Every letter on the page is actually five letters back. Unless it's a vowel, then it's five letters forward, unless it's at the beginning of a word, or at the end, and then … " He caught himself. Smiled. "Hell, who gives a fuck, right? We broke it and that's all that matters. I just do what those above my pay grade tell me to do."

"I'm *so* not above your pay grade," Mallen said.

"You think I'd let just any old numb nuts drive off in my truck? You got another thing comin'."

Mallen smiled at that. Winced with the pain of doing so. Gregor looked at both of them. "The other side better look a fuckin' lot worse. If not, it's time they did."

"*Palabras más verdaderas nunca fueron habladas,*" Gato responded.

"Got that right," Gregor said as he sat down on an old stool and proceeded to go over the book with them. "It's a catalog of children."

"Children porn?" Gato spat out. "*Madre de Dios.*"

"No, not that, G," Mallen said to him, a hand on his friend's shoulder. "Right, Mr. Gregor?"

"Right, Captain," Gregor responded. "It's a catalog of children, but I'm almost positive not for porn. For sale. The words that are used. It's like buying a car."

"That jibes with everything I know about this so far," Mallen replied.

Gato just shook his head. "*Vato*, can't you ever stumble upon a group of illegal bunnies, or some such shit. Jesus."

Gregor laughed, then pointed to one page in particular. "This is the page for the last few 'transactions.' Was put at the back of the book. There was a secondary layer to the code here. Not that hard to figure out once I'd cracked the main code. The enemy really underestimated who they might come up against. Or, well, maybe they just got fucking lazy."

"Did you find anything about the transactions?" Mallen said. "The exchange of money for a kid?"

"What do you think they pay with? Jellybeans? Now see? This one?" He pointed to the second to last entry on a page. "This one shows height and weight and sex of the ... package, as they use the word. There's a code here I can't make out. 'O.U.F.M.' Don't know what the fuck that means, but I been trying to figure it out."

Mallen remembered another code he couldn't figure out. That code had two of those letters in it, and was also something to do with Jessie. His gut told him that it was very important to figure that one out. Very important. "No idea where the package was taken?"

Here Gregor smiled. "There IS a sort of location. There were initials, buried under some half-ass attempt to bury the original code under a newer one. And a bad newer one at that. Seems like the guy who received the original code tried to be slick. Was a dick, not slick." He glanced down at the page again. Checked it against some notes he'd made. "This is a Marin address. Up in the hills by Mount Tam. No name, just an address. It's the only address that's mentioned after the stats on a child. You gotta wonder if the boy who owned this was going to try some blackmail on the back side."

"Yeah ... ," Mallen said. "You gotta wonder."

"We need to go right out there, man," Gato said. "Before any more children are taken or hurt, man."

"I know. I hear ya." Mallen said. "Mr. Gregor. You pretty sure about that Marin address?"

A nod. Studied the book a bit longer. Smiled as he wrote down another address, saying, "This one seems to be on ... well, the other side of the ledger. Can't understand it all." Showed it to Mallen. This one was below Market Street. From the high to the low, Mallen thought. Wrote them both down, then turned to Gato. "You up for a drive?"

Gato smiled faintly. "I left the Falcon in Vegas, but I brought another baby. We're good."

"Then we're good," Mallen replied then turned to Gregor. "I can't thank you enough for all this. I'm going to owe you a long time."

"Forget that. Just buy the damn truck already. I could use the money."

# TWENTY-SEVEN

"Is he able to talk?" Wong asked the nurse. "We have some questions for him."

"Talk?" she replied. "No, I'm afraid not, officer. The doctor feels, however, that he'll be able to speak with the police soon, but not yet."

Wong went to light a cigarette. Realized where he was. Put the pack back in his pocket. Smiled at the nurse. "Thank you. I have him being in room 304. That right?"

"Room 306," she replied, then went off to do what could be one of another thousand tasks. Wong watched her go for a moment. It really paid being a cop. You could say anything and no one questioned it. There was no one around, so he lit up a cig, fast and smooth. Took a bunch of quick drags and dumped the burning stick in a nearby water glass someone had left by the drinking fountain. Made his way down to Lucas's room.

Why did everything have to be like this? Seemed that no

matter how much you sewed, some stuffing always snuck out between the stitches and had to either be crammed back in and sewn down, or just cut off. And he'd wanted to stay home today. Well, overtime, man. That was something at least. Maybe jack-off there in room 306 would never wake up, and everyone could go back to their homes happy and safe.

*Hafuckingha. Bullshit, and you know it ....*

Yeah, how many times had someone actually woken up and done the smart thing? Maybe Mallen had. He took Detente. That was smart. But man ... he'd wanted to fuck Mallen's shit up more than just hammering his hand to a table. He'd wanted to tell him that he'd raped his wife. Cum all over her while she wept. *That's* what he'd wanted to tell Mallen, but he'd been told not to. No, actually he'd been *ordered* not to say anything. They knew the wife wouldn't say anything. She'd been told she'd have to watch her daughter die if it ever got out. Man, he'd taken a lot of heat for screwing her, but man ... it'd been fun. Hell ... hadn't all that bullshit been about bitches, blood, and fun? He shrugged as he arrived at Lucas's door. Maybe it was good all of those guys belonging to that organization had gone back underground. He didn't need more than one superior officer at a time.

Entered into room 306. There was Lucas, hooked up to a lot of tubes and machines. The room was filled with the steady, pulsing beep of the heart monitor. Just like in the movies, Wong thought as he went over to the bed. Looked down at the idiot who tried to move up the food chain without any real knowledge or skillset for that type of thing.

What a stupid asshole. *Well, this is the price you pay for thinking above your station ....*

Wong glanced one time over his shoulder at the door, then grabbed one of the pillows under Lucas's head and forced it down over the man's face. Sweat broke out on Wong's forehead as he pressed and pressed. He just wanted the dumb sonofabitch to fucking die already. Shooting him with a silencer would've been easier but he didn't own a fucking silencer. The heart monitor beeping took off like some dance song, and Wong knew he now had only seconds.

Finally Lucas's body muscles quit working, realizing they were on the wrong end of a losing battle. The heart monitor went solid tone and the room filled with the stench of urine, shit, and cum. Lucas was dead. Wong left quickly.

He was at the elevator a couple doors away when the nurse came rushing down the hall to Lucas's room.

———

Mallen and Gato drove across the Golden Gate, in a cherry 1968 Olds Cutlass S 350, painted a dark green color that Mallen had no idea existed. "Another one from your garage, G?" he said with a smile.

Gato nodded. "The last one, too. I have to make them last." After a moment, he said, "I need to go back to Vegas and get a couple things, *vato.*"

"I know."

"I would go now, right? But man... somebody's kidnapping kids? Those guys? The ones doing it? Man...." Shook his head. Considered a moment, then added, "You know, man? We've seen some dark things since the drunk tank. Some crazy-ass dark shit."

201

The sky outside the car was black. It was late. No stars. Only clouds. Mallen could feel it was going to rain, and very soon. "Yeah," he finally replied, "it's a dark world, and that's a fact. I feel though that if I never did another thing in my life after we've found Trina's daughter, I would feel it was a life well-lived. I may have made some *major* fucking mistakes, but I've always tried to play on the side of the angels. What more can we do in this life, right?"

Gato remained silent for a long time, then said, "I can't think of a thing, Mallen. Sounds good to me, bro."

They made the rest of the trip to below Market Street in silence. Gato couldn't find parking so parked in a parking garage a few blocks away from the address that Gregor had given them. Mallen checked the piece of paper. The last name was all they had. Reading was the name. They walked down the street, through the late-night crowd of people who had no home, and the people who would sell their home for some drugs. People huddled together in doorways. People walked up to each other to shake hands then parted ways quickly. Drug deals. Some people, dark husks, sat on the street or on building stoops. Nowhere to go, nowhere to be.

They found the address and Mallen went and looked at the registry. No "Reading" there. But there was a "Redding." He smiled at that; Gregor was a little rusty at code breaking. Had to be the same person. He pushed the buzzer. No answer. Not at first. Then a woman's voice was heard.

"Hello?"

"This Ms. Redding?" he said, using his best cop voice.

"Yes. Who is this?"

"My name is Mallen. Mark Mallen. I just want to talk to you about your daughter."

Silence. Then, "My daughter was taken. They never found her." That was followed by a click. She'd hung up.

"Well," Gato said, "we got the right place, man. You want in?"

He looked at Gato. "We need to talk to her."

His friend nodded. Went to the front door. Mallen couldn't see what he did, but the door was open in record time and Gato stood aside to let him in. Mallen went into the building lobby. Not badly kept up. Someone even made an attempt at sprucing up the joint: over on a small side table by the elevator someone had put a vase with flowers. On the walls were prints of van Gogh and Picasso paintings in frames that looked like they'd been found on the street. Overall, it worked to fight off the desperation and fatigue that existed right outside the lobby door.

From the numbers on the directory, Mallen figured the place to be on the second floor. They opted for the stairs instead of the elevator. He had no idea which apartment it would be. Didn't want to knock on each door.

They got to the second floor and he slowed down, Gato instantly doing the same. No two cops could've been more in tune. They walked past each door quietly and slowly. Every fiber of Mallen's being was tuned to any noise coming from behind a door.

It was the second door on the right that he heard it: the faint noise of a woman crying. Had to be. He'd called, dredged up the hard memories. Had to be the place.

Used his soft knock. Spoke quietly, but enough that she'd hear. "Ms. Redding? This Mark Mallen. I just need to speak with you. There are other children going missing. I believe you can help me track down the people responsible for that."

It took a moment, but then she answered the door. She was older than he'd thought she'd be. But there was the same air about her that Trina had. Desperate. Infinitely lost and sad. Tired, deep blue eyes. "What do you want?" she said.

"I wanted to talk to you about your daughter's disappearance."

She regarded them both. "Why the hell do you want to talk about Lucy's going missing? The cops never found anything. Then they just went away." A shrug. "Moving on to the next crime, I guess."

"There was another child taken. Maybe a lot of other children taken. Can we come in? Please?"

She studied Mallen's face. Nodded and stood back from the door. The two men entered. It was a homey place. The people who lived here were poor but hadn't given up. Not in the least.

"I heard about you," she said as she went and stood by the dining room table. It was worn, but obviously cared for.

"Me?" Mallen said.

She nodded. "Yes. Out there," she said. She could've been talking about "out there in the jungle."

Gato kept back by the door. "*Eres famoso, hombre*," he said with a faint smile.

"Not likely," Mallen replied over his shoulder. "What's your first name, Mrs. Redding?"

A scoff. "Ms. And it's Jenny."

"I'm Mark. This is my friend, Gato. What have you heard about me?"

Jenny studied him for a moment. "Heard you liked to help people. Didn't take any shit. And if you did, you'd come back and make the other guy eat even more shit."

He heard Gato chuckle behind him, then say, "Well, that does seem pretty accurate, *vato*."

"Yeah, I guess so," he replied softly. Asked Jenny, "Your daughter. How long ago was she taken?"

She sat down at the table. Looked at the peeling edges of the fake wood on the table's top. Eyes tuned now to a station back in her past. "Three weeks ago."

"What happened?"

She took a deep breath. "Happened at night. While I was asleep on the couch. Never heard a thing. I've been so tired lately. Working shifts at both jobs, back to back. I was whacked-out tired."

"Somebody broke in through the bedroom window?"

With a nod, she got up and led them into the bedroom. The marks were still there on the sill. The lock was one of those cheap brass pieces that turn into a flange on the lower window. Not like the window in Trina's apartment. This window had been forced. Still traces of fingerprint dust there from the police. "Doesn't seem right at all," he told her. "You bust your ass providing for your kid, and you end up being too exhausted to hear something like this happening? I'd be feeling shitty about it all, just like you probably do."

A grateful smile there. She'd obviously been blaming herself, just like he thought. "That's just about what the detective said."

"Well," he replied with a smile, "that guy's opinion pretty much makes it unanimous, right?"

"A woman."

"Oh, yeah?" On a hunch, he said, "Redhead, right? Nice suit?"

"Yes. I have her card around here. Told me to call her if I remembered anything." Jenny left and came back a moment later with a business card. Gwen's business card.

Mallen handed it back to her. "She help you out? Has she called you back with anything? Anything at all?"

Jenny looked down at the card. Bitterness crawling into her voice. "No. Nothing. I even called a couple times and left a message."

He nodded. "Well, sometimes the cops don't move as fast we'd like."

"You always seemed to move fast, from the stories I've heard."

"Stories get blown out of proportion. I'm just another guy."

She smiled at that. Like she'd caught him in a lie.

"What had you been doing in the days leading up to what happened?" he said, wanting to change the subject away from him.

That was met with a shrug. "Just the same stuff. Going to the store. Taking Lucy to the park. Taking her to a nursery school day-care sort of thing."

Just normal life, he thought. "Nothing out of the ordinary, yeah?"

She thought for a moment. "Well, this guy took our photo when we were walking down the street. Just down on the corner."

"Oh, yeah? Did you mention that to the police?"

"Didn't think to, actually. Just some guy taking photos of people. He was taking shots of lots of people. We just happened to be there."

Gato came forward. "What did this guy look like?"

She looked at both of them. "Why? Do you think it has something to do with her disappearance?"

Mallen put a hand on her shoulder. "I don't know. We're just trying to get to the bottom of it all. Find the people doing the taking."

Tears started then. She tried to hold them back. "What is this world? That people abuse children?" She broke down, went and sat down on the couch. Wept. Mallen went over to her. Sat down next to her. Put his hand over hers.

"No, it wasn't for that. We have no reason to think or believe that."

She looked at him then. Eyes desperate for some answers. "Then why?"

He took a deep breath. "I'm just not sure, but it wasn't about that."

"And you know that for a fact?"

"All I know is that I need to find these people before they take any more children. I really believe, with every fiber of my soul, that Lucy is still out there. And I'll find her. I will."

Jenny wiped at her eyes. Worked at a smile. "It's just like I'd heard. You never give up."

He shrugged as he got to his feet. "What's the point of giving up? We have to keep fighting for the answers and the truth, or we're nothing."

# TWENTY-EIGHT

MALLEN COULDN'T LEAVE THE city without stopping in to see how Bill was doing, and how it'd gone down after Dreamo… Justin… had been killed. Even though Dreamo was gone, Gato still seemed to not want to be there. Mallen understood. What happened to his friend in Vegas had left its mark. Brought him closer to a world he'd struggled to get away from. And maybe now the question that everybody in recovery asks themself was again in the forefront of Gato's mind, after a very long hiatus: will I make it another day without using?

Bill was there, as usual, but he also seemed a changed man. Had aged some years. He'd tried hard to keep his nephew from hurting himself, but it was still his family that had died back there, on the floor of a dirty bathroom.

When Bill saw Mallen, he automatically went and grabbed up a glass. Filled it with scotch. Put it in front of Mallen. Looked over at Gato.

"Beer," Gato replied. Bill pulled the beer and set it down on the bar.

"How're you holding up?" Mallen asked. "What happened after I left?"

Bill went and poured himself some whiskey. Shrugged. "What you'd imagine when a known drug dealer is shot. 'It's a drug thing.'"

"I got the guy who killed him, Bill. Sent him to the hospital. Didn't kill him, but he won't be walking anytime soon. Or maybe even a year from now."

The bartender's mouth curled into a small smile. Held up his glass in a toast. Took a sip. "Why was he after you?"

"I'm not really sure. I think it originally had something to do with me looking for him. I think he saw something he shouldn't have seen, regarding Jessie's disappearance."

Bill looked down at the drink in front of him. "I can't believe, that after all this time, Justin got killed over something he *didn't* do. Crazy."

"I'm sorry, B. I never meant for this to happen."

"I know, Mallen. Can I ask you a favor, though?"

"Name it."

"Will you come to his funeral? It's tomorrow morning. Down in Colma."

"For sure."

———

Heavy clouds hung low over the cemetery that next morning, making the sky feel close and suffocating. Mallen felt that this was appropriate, given the occasion. He stood there, looking into the gray sky, he realized it suddenly felt like all time stopped. That's the way it should be when someone died, he thought: the entire world should just fucking stop. Maybe, he figured, that was one of the major problems with man and his society: the world *didn't* stop when someone died.

Dreamo's coffin was of dark, lacquered wood. No ornament. Mallen wondered at Dreamo's being buried in a place like this. He'd felt that ashes thrown out to sea, or a nameless grave in a pine box was how it would've ended for Dream. To his surprise, this seemed to the "family plot." Lots of the same last names. Bill stood by the graveside next to a couple of older women and a younger man who could've passed for Dreamo's brother. He was thin, dressed in a loose-fitting black suit. Unshaven. Mallen looked around at the cemetery to avoid staring at the coffin. Gato, who had insisted on coming with him, stood at his side and crossed himself from time to time, saying a prayer under his breath.

Then Mallen saw the woman. She stood off by herself, underneath a nearby Cyprus tree. Had a white rose in her hand, and was dressed in dark clothes. Hair a dyed red, with black roots. Mallen could tell by her jerky movements and agitation that she was strung out. She gazed sadly at the coffin. Looked like she wanted to come over, and made a move to do so, but in the end instead placed the rose against the tree trunk. Then she turned and walked quickly away. As he watched her go, Mallen knew it was just one more mystery to add to Dreamo's life.

His thoughts went back to Monster Mallen. His father. It sure seemed to be the ending of this phase of his life, if life really ran in phases. Chris, moving on with Daniel. His father dying. Now

Dreamo. Even Gato seemed to have moved on into another phase of his life. Mallen wondered if it was just possible that he was entering the last phase of *his* life. He was about the right age for a guy to think he'd lived two thirds of his life. Was he okay with that? Yeah, he had to admit that he was. Had to also admit that he was lucky to have gotten this far, having thrown himself against the wall as much as he had.

Mallen had never believed in an afterlife. Had never given thought to one. However, as he stood there near Dreamo's coffin, he hoped that whatever did come after, if something did, had room for people with decent hearts, no matter if they weren't very good at being human.

There was no priest or minister or whatever to say anything resonating about Dreamo. There was only the sound of the ocean, and the wind. After a moment longer, the two women and the man walked silently away. Bill came over to Mallen and shook his hand, his eyes moist. He then, to Mallen's surprise, gave him a quick hug.

"Thank you, Mal," Bill said quietly, then turned away and walked to catch up with the women and the man. Mallen watched them go, a small group of people who had cared for a person who had once lived and then died. Mallen felt then that Dreamo had been one of the lucky ones: there were people to stand over his grave and be sad at his passing.

Gato crossed himself one more time, then said, "Come on, Mallen. It's time to leave the dead to themselves."

———

As Mallen and Gato left the cemetery in Gato's car, Mallen's cell rang almost on cue. Checked the number. Oberon.

"Obie," Mallen said, "what's up? Rare that you call me."

"It would seem my luck ran out," came the reply. "I heard about an incident that happened out at your home."

"Yeah, something weird with some guy named Lucas who thought I was chasing after him. Turns out he had something to do with Dreamo's getting killed, and the pawnbroker Black-more's death, too."

"Busy man, this Lucas was."

"Was?" Now Oberon had all his attention. "Was?"

"Yes, was. I'm at the hospital now. He's dead. And it wasn't complications from his many injuries."

"I have an alibi, if that was going to be your next question."

"No, it wasn't. Not the next one."

"What is the next one?"

"What are you working on? Or more specifically, what have you found yourself in?"

"You know. The same thing we discussed before."

There was a silence there. "Then we need to discuss this more. In person."

"What's up?"

"Better we talk face to face, Mark."

"Okay. Where?"

"Park at the lot over Sutro Baths. I'll be there as soon as I can." And he hung up.

Mallen looked at his phone for a moment. Then over at Gato. "How much time do you have?"

A shrug in response. "That girl I got to look over my *madre* is doing a pretty good job, no matter what *madre* throws at her."

"I think Oberon has something important. Wants to meet out above Sutro Baths."

Gato nodded. "Then we go, *vato.*"

————

The eternal wind blew in the from the west, sending dancing sand over the parking lot as Gato's car pulled in and up to a parking slot facing out to the water. Oberon was already there and turned at the sound of their car. Mallen noted that his friend must be cold, as he was wearing the rare wool overcoat. Looked very noir.

Mallen got out of the car, telling Gato just to hang back. As Mallen approached Oberon the detective told him, "Let's talk as we walk." Oberon then headed to the trail that led down to the shells of what the baths used to be. Mallen began to feel more and more worried. This was all very out of character for his friend. He'd known Oberon since his first night out on his own in a black and white, and the man had never acted like this. So wound up and unwilling to be overheard. This had to be bad. Very bad.

Once they'd started on the gravel path, Mallen reflected he liked it better when the place was just dirt and unkempt. Now it was an official "attraction." After a moment as they walked, he asked, "What's going on, Obie? Why the top secret shit?"

But Oberon wouldn't answer until they were well down the hill and approaching some of the old stone buildings that looked like the remnants of a war zone, not the remnants of an earlier time when people had things like indoor pools and spas for the public.

Once they were out of earshot of any of the tourists or anyone else, Oberon turned and said, "It's about Lucas's death."

"What? What about it?"

"Let me ask you this: how did you trip to him?"

Mallen put his hands in his coat pockets to keep them warm. Maybe it was the coldness of his soul when he spoke about people he felt he'd let down that made him do that. "Blackmore," he said. "Blackmore told me about Lucas and this woman named Shannon Waters. They would come in with Hendrix to pawn stuff. Lucas intimated, when we last spoke, that Hendrix showed up flush one day. That he saw a woman cop outside of Hendrix's car, talking to him through the window. He described Gwen, man. Down to a 'T.'" Mallen brought out a cigarette and lit it. "Also said he saw another cop hanging around Hendrix's car. More than once. Described a detective that sounds a fuckin' lot like Wong." He held up his right hand, the nail holes healed but still very visible. "Yeah, Wong."

This all seemed to be exactly what Oberon did not want to hear. Reached for Mallen's cigarette but stopped himself. "Obie, what is it?" Mallen said.

Oberon took a moment to work up to it. "Lucas was found dead in his hospital room last night. Preliminary cause of death is suffocation. A man that could match Wong's description was seen leaving the room only a minute or so before Lucas's body was discovered by a nurse. She missed him but the first cop on the scene interviewed an intern who remembered this one man getting into the elevator. Very calm. Very collected. The man stood out to this intern because the intern said the man smelled of cigarettes."

As Mallen's mind raced over all that Oberon had just told him, a large part of him was actually happy. He was glad that Wong was involved. That gave him all the reasons in this fucking world to break that man's face, and career. Mallen took in the scenery. Shrugged. "So why the secret-style meet, Obie? You could've told me this over a drink at any bar of your choice."

"I've been down to records. I was curious. Wanted to look at Gwen's record and at Wong's. Their arrest records. And I found out two interesting things. One is that since the time Gwen made detective about two years ago, there have been only a handful of cases where Wong was not also involved. Same for Wong's cases; Gwen was always there."

"So? Some cops work better together than others."

"They *weren't* working together. Weren't partners. But each one always ended up being the cop that gave the other the *one clue* that led to the solving of whatever case was on the table."

After a moment, Mallen said, "I'm not scanning this, Obie. What do you mean?"

"I think they've been fixing cases. Creating scenarios where both could benefit from the solving of a case, *after* they've rigged it to be successful."

"That's crazy, Obie! Not possible."

Oberon glanced at Mallen's right hand. "Really? Like it's not possible that a detective could be involved with a huge conspiracy involving snuff films and a huge underground organization involving kidnapping and murder? Really?"

"Okay ... okay, point taken." Mallen looked over at the ocean.

Why was it the world had to be so dark? So fucking dark? If not for his family, he thought it might just one day get the better of him. It was one of those moments where a little bit of him wished he'd stayed in the Tenderloin high on smack. It probably would've killed him one day, but at least he wouldn't know the kind of darkness he'd seen ever since he'd gotten clean. And once again that answering little voice inside him told him that if the world was a dark place, then he better get to fuckin' drowning it in light. Any way he can. Every chance he had.

"They have to be stopped," he said quietly as he took a drag off his cigarette. "I'm sure that both of them are involved somehow with these children being snatched. I know it, man."

"How do you think?"

"I don't know, yet. Look, both of them were seen with Hendrix. Hendrix knew Karachi. Both are dead, and we've found some facts about this group that's snatching children." And this is where he dropped the bomb. He knew he'd have to tell Oberon at some point about the codebook. "And I found a codebook at Karachi's, Obie. Gregor has mostly broken the code, too. That's how I found one of the other mothers whose kid has been taken. Jenny Redding. I have the address of another place. Maybe the family where another kid was taken. I think it's got to be that. This address is the only one that ISN'T in the Tenderloin, but over in Marin." Took another drag off his cigarette.

Oberon just stared at him for a moment. Shook his head. "Mark," he said, "I know you've done some completely insane things in the past, but all this really hits the wall. Why can't you just stay home and heal from your gunshot wound like anyone else would be doing? Why, oh why, do you have to fuck with my life like you do? As I've had to say to you oh so many times before: you realize how many laws you've broken, don't you?" After a moment, he continued, "And just how did you know that Karachi was dead? That has not been made public yet. No names mentioned. How do you know?"

"A little bird told me."

Oberon turned away and walked over to the wall of one of the buildings. Turned and put his back to it. Looked up at the sky for a moment and Mallen wondered if he'd finally pushed his friend too far. When he came back, he knew the answer to that question.

"I don't know you anymore, Mark. I've looked the other way, many times. Many times. We've seen a lot together and I've tried to help you every chance I could, but I cannot look the other way when it comes to shooting and killing another man, no matter what type of criminal he was." Held out his hand. "Give me your firearm."

"Come on, Obie. You know that I've always made good on my cases. I can bring in the bad guys on this one. We can do this, man. Just listen to me, okay?"

The detective stared at Mallen for a moment. Shook his head.

"Obie," Mallen said as Oberon approached, "I can fix this. Make it work. You have to trust me, man. You don't understand. Who knows what's happening to those children! I'm on the trail! I—"

"No, Mark, *you* don't understand. I'm sure it was involuntary manslaughter. That's how I'll paint it, and I'm sure the evidence can back that up. But what were you doing at Karachi's, instead of reporting what you'd found out to me or anyone else on the force? That's obstruction, Mark."

"Look, just listen to me for a second. Please, Obie... just listen. I know how we can do this."

———

Gato sat behind the wheel of his car and watched the exchange down below between the two men. He could see that his brother was not being heard. That older cat, Oberon, kept shaking his head. Paced back and forth. Then Mallen grabbed the man's shoulder. Spoke urgently to him. Oberon paused. Glanced up toward the car, but Mallen tugged on him again and the two men paced back and forth together. *Vato* really seemed to be pleading his case. Then Mallen turned suddenly and clocked Oberon a good one across the jaw. Gato sat there, unbelieving. No way he'd just seen Mallen hit his cop friend and knock him on his ass. No way. But no matter how much he stared, there was the limp body of Oberon, propped up against a broken concrete wall, head down on his chest.

Gato watched as his friend left quickly, walking like a man on a long march back up the trail. Got to the car and leapt in. Gato stared at him. "Mallen... what are you doing, bro?"

"We'll need another car."

"*Vato*..."

"My friend," Mallen said, "you tell me to get out and walk, I'll do it. I don't want to get you more involved. As it stands, no one can prove anything on you because you haven't done anything. I don't want to take you down with me if that's how all this turns out. I'll follow whatever you do, but you have to do it like now."

He looked back at the building, at the figure down there, propped up against the wall. Already a couple of tourist types were standing near Oberon. Probably trying to decide whether to get involved or not. "Like now," Mallen repeated.

Gato started up the Olds and put it in reverse. "I'm running out of cars, Mallen," was all he said as he backed out of the parking spot.

# TWENTY-NINE

GRIFFIN STARED OUT THE window as he sipped from his beer. Below him was Eddy Street. He could see Ben and Tony down there, sharing a crack pipe. Up near the corner was Old Man Papa, passed out in the gutter. Nothing new there. Regretted his taking the kid at the beach. He shoulda just left her. But he'd wanted the dough, not realizing in the heat of the moment that there was no way to contact the buyer. He'd read the article on SF Gate about Yates. About the bullets. No mention of the kid at least. This was supposed to have been a ... what do they call it? Yeah, a "windfall." It sure the fuck hadn't happened that way.

The kid started up crying again. *Fuck...* Got up, went into the room to see what Lazy Suzy was doing.

He walked into the small room to find Suzy trying to tie the kid's hands behind her back. He came over and swatted Suzy on the ear. Pushed her away. "What the fuck do you think you're fucking doing?" he asked. "This kid has to arrive safe and sound, all of this a bad dream that will take years and years of therapy to get over. Leave her alone, you hear me?" He turned and looked down at the crying child. His eardrums seemed to break as he picked her up and carried her out to the living room. Put her down on the couch. Petted her head, "There, there ya go … big ugly woman won't hurt you again. I swear."

He grabbed up the stuffed animal the kid seemed to want around. A stuffed aardvark. Pushed it at her, then tried to pet her head as best he could. Tried to do it like he was petting a puppy. *Same thing, right?* Whatever he was doing, it seemed to work well enough. The waterworks stopped, as did that fucking screaming. He couldn't help but think though: the poor kid; looked wiped out by it all. Griffin went to the freezer and brought back some vanilla ice cream. Gave her the spoon and let her dig into it for a bit. Smiled as she seemed to forget everything in the world except the spoon and the contents in the spoon. He had to laugh: she lapped it up just like a junkie. After awhile he took the spoon away from her. Put her down more comfortable on the couch. He woulda been a good father, he thought, if given half a chance. Drew the blinds. Took a deep breath, and brought his head back into the "here an' now." He knew he needed to unload this kid, and like right the fuck away. What the hell was he gonna do?

"I wanna see momma," she whimpered.

He turned to face her. Looked down at her. Hell, he would've been a fucking better father than his old man had been, the abusing cocksucker. Suzy came into the room, eyes glazed, fixed on the kid. Hands worked spasmodically, like someone possessed. He smelled the meth on her. Fucking bitch. Never trust an addict. Dried up old cunt.

"You'll see your momma, trust me," he said softly to the little girl, "Your momma will be very happy to see you."

"And until then, you sit the fuck there," Suzy slurred as she came forward. Griffin stopped her. Dragged her back toward the bedroom door. "No," he said quietly so only she could hear, "she will be comfortable as possible. Kept happy, as fucking possible. The people on the other side won't want some more than necessary freaked-out kid, you got me?"

"She's a pain in the rear," Suzy said, her eyes red, face pale. Must've smoked a full bowl while in the other room. Wondered where she got it. That fucker Hendrix, probably. Before he croaked.

He grabbed her arm tighter. Spoke more quietly, just above a whisper. "So? We're gonna take care of her, because there's money on the other end of the ride."

Suzy began to say something, but he jammed his hand up under her jaw to keep it shut. She was scared now. He'd shown her enough times what he could do, and the dumb bitch still stepped out of line from time to time. But, this time, she dociled the fuck out quickly. Went limp. Gave in, gave up. "Like I said," he continued as he released her, "we are going to take care of her. And if you make me have to choose between the two of you?" He looked once over back at the girl. She was watching this exchange, a worried expression on her little face. She'd start crying again if it went on much longer. Griffin leaned in, close to Suzy's ear, making it look like he was nuzzling it. Whispered to Suzy, "If you make me choose, I will, repeat, *will* choose her. I don't need some old, bashed-out useless cum bag. What I DO need is some money, and that kid is money. So shut the fuck up and treat her nice, or I'll treat you dead. Got it?"

What he got in response was a quickly nodded "yes" from Suzy.

And if in an answer from God, his phone rang. Pulled it from his pocket and checked the number. Didn't know it. "Hello?"

The answering voice sounded nervous. "Is this... is this the partner to... Karachi?"

"Who the fuck is this?"

"The... the... the one this was all for."

Griffin laughed. "Yeah, fuckin' right. You just got my number from Karachi after he told you to call? Yeah, right."

A pause. "Karachi is dead."

Griffin's hand tightened a bit more on the phone. "No way. Not him."

"He was found in his apartment, shot."

It was too much to deal with. He needed something to calm him down so he could think. "I don't know why you're calling me. You have the wrong number." And he hung up. What the fuck was going on? Karachi was dead? What the fuck? Yates. Hendrix. Now he was thinking he should just put the kid on the street and be done with it. But what if the little kid *could* give the police enough to go on? What then? Looked over at the couch. At the kid. No, he couldn't do it. Even if it meant his life, he couldn't do *that*.

Suzy asked quietly, "So... this means trouble?"

"Shut the fuck up and let me deal with my thoughts, okay?" His cell rang again. Again. Just like God putting his finger on

Griffin's shoulder. *Maybe it's time for you to take the lead in things, friend Griff?* It was the same number as before. Answered the call.

"Please, okay?" the voice said. "We just want what we paid the first installment for. Is that so hard to understand?"

*First installment?* Griffin thought fast. Shit, this was sounding like there was going to be much dough in this. Much. "I really don't know what you're talking about, you know? You're going to have to be very fucking clear here. What did you pay for?"

"You know." It was definitive. "What you have in your possession. What we want." A sigh. "It's got indoor plumbing. About three feet tall. You need more? Or would you rather me send you a fax?"

"No, no … I get it. Okay. We're good. Yeah … I got what you want. You paid the first installment. Karachi's dead. Now that second installment comes to me, so we can close the books on this bullshit."

"I know how much I was supposed to pay him. I'll know if you try to make me pay more." Man, did this dick brain sound like a fish out of water. Was trying so fucking hard to sound "street."

"And I'll know if you try to fuck me on the price," said Griffin. "Karachi told me how much. Look, let's just get this the fuck over. She wants a home, and I want money. This should be fucking easy, right?"

"Yes. Easy." A pause. "So … where and when?"

Shit, this guy was lost. Griffin's mind raced over the possibilities. Where was the best place to meet? Not in the city. Someplace alone. Where no one would be, late at night. Where?

Where O fucking where? Then it came to him. Yeah, it would be quiet there. Easy to deal with things if it all went bad. "You know Battery Spencer? Just across the Golden Gate?"

"Yes." He could almost hear the fuckhead gulping on the other end. He was beginning to enjoy this. Fuck this lame-ass faggot.

"Meet me there in one hour."

"Okay. I'll be there. Come alone, though. I'll bring the money."

"Be there, on time, or I'll package this up and dump it in the drink." And he hung up. Suzy came out of the bedroom. He hadn't realized she'd gone back in. Eyes redder than before. She glanced at the kid. Hands worked spasmodically. The hair on the back of his head stood on end, actually fucking stood on end when he looked at how Suzy was staring at the little girl. *What the fuck was wrong with this bitch?*

"You make the deal for it?" Suzy said. Never took her eyes off of the little girl.

"Yeah, we meet in an hour. Across the bridge at Battery Spencer."

A nod was all he got as she cast one more glance at the little girl who lay curled up on the couch, thumb firmly in mouth, arm firmly holding the stuffed aardvark.

Hell, Griffin thought as he went and retrieved his battered .22, there were worse ways to earn a living. Not that he could think of them at the moment.

———

After Mallen's encounter with Oberon, Gato had driven them right over to the garage around the corner from where Gato shared a flat with his mother. Told Mallen to wait while he went and checked on her. Mallen looked around at the tricked-out classic muscle cars. Whoever Gato's father had been, he still owed that man a thousand thanks. How many times had Gato's ability to grab them some new wheels saved them? More than he could count.

Gato came through the side door of the garage. He'd seemed grim since he'd returned from Vegas, but now he seemed like a barely controlled fire. "How's your *madre*?" he asked his friend.

"Okay," came the flat answer. Went over to the 1967 Mercury Cougar. Black as black. Hitched up rear-end. Centerlines.

Mallen thought the car seemed to perfectly match his friend's mood as he went to the garage door and pulled on the chain that rolled it up with a clang of corrugated metal. Gato started up the engine and the car growled out onto the street. It may be stealth black, but the double headers made it anything but. Mallen lurched under the door as it slammed back down. He then locked the gate and jumped into the car.

"Is that woman you have looking after your mother still working out?"

"Pretty much," came the flat reply. "Where to, man?"

"My place. I have to get the book and some shit so I can camp out for a while until this is all over. Don't know what Oberon's done since he's woken up."

Gato's only response was a quick nod.

They drove the rest of the way in silence. A couple times on the way over he caught Gato mumbling something under his breath. Fingers would tap relentlessly on the steering wheel. Mallen again wondered just what the fuck was up with his friend. He could tell that whatever went down in Vegas, it must've been heavy. Very heavy. He owed Gato. He knew that, and embraced it: He'd lay his life down for his friend, as his friend had done for him many, many times.

As they crossed the bridge, Mallen used that moment, as had become his habit, to think about what to do next. The cops were not an option for now. He couldn't stay at his house. After he got the codebook and flash drive from Mr. Gregor, then what? Gato seemed to be reaching crisis point with all this, and he couldn't push the man any further. Maybe Chris? Pulled out his phone.

And after the third ring, a man answered. He recognized it. Daniel. "Hello?" the man said.

"Hi Daniel. It's Mallen."

A pause. "Hi Mark. You want to speak with Chris?" Guy couldn't wait to get off the phone with him. Mallen checked his watch. Late. Late and the guy was still there. At least he didn't sound like he'd been sleeping.

"Yeah, please."

There was a silent moment. Then there was the hand over the speaker followed by the muffled sounds of people talking. Again. That made him very mad. Again. Jealous mad. But he took a deep breath, reminding himself that he no longer had any claim on the world that was at the other end of this phone. Chris came on the line. "Mark? Is everything okay?"

"Yeah, it is. Sorry for calling so late, I…" Tried to think up something, but there was nothing. "I just wanted to know that Anna was okay. That's all."

"She's fine," Chris answered. "Got another 'A' on an art project she did. You'd be proud."

"I don't know any other way to be when it comes to her. You've done a great job, Chris."

"No, I mean you'd be out of the ordinary proud of this. She made her first kite, Mark. Received an "A" on it."

And like any good parent, he choked up. His girl? Got an "A" on a kite she'd made herself? Oh, Jesus fucking Christ... "Seriously?" he replied. "I'm... I, well, I don't know what to say, except 'Hell yeah!'" Cringed at that. Almost like they were suddenly playing roles.

"Mark?" she said to him then, "I was going to tell you the next time you came to get Anna, but... well, now I feel I should just tell you."

His hand tightened on the phone. Here it was. Here it came. "Yeah?" he asked. It really felt like one of those times where God just seemed to want to shovel his shit right down your mouth for an entire fucking day, just for the hell of it. "What's up?"

Another silence. Man... fuck those goddamn silences, he thought. Just spit out his sentence and he'll take it like a man. "Chris, what is it? Does it concern Daniel?"

"Yes. Yes it does," she replied. "Remember what I told you a couple days ago? About the use of the couch?"

Even with all that had gone in his life, fuck yeah he still remembered. Her question also told him the answer. "Not any longer, right?" he said. "That what you want to tell me?"

"Yes."

"Thank you for telling me. I really, really appreciate you playing it this way, Chris. Seriously." He added, trying to put as much a smile into it as he could, "I still get to see Anna just like before, right?"

"Of course you do, Mark. You're her father, idiot." But there was humor in the way she said it.

He looked out the window. Gato took the exit into Sausalito. He could tell that his friend had figured out a bit of what happened, just by listening with half an ear. "Anyway, you kiss her for me, and I'll call in the next couple days to set up some time with her, okay?"

"Okay. Take care."

And he ended the call. Seemed like it was the time for endings of a sort. This was one thing that sure couldn't be fixed with a gun or some plan of action. This was beyond his reach now. All he could do is just go with it, as best he could.

# THIRTY

GATO PARKED THE COUGAR in a far, dark corner of the lot near the dock that led to Mallen's home. They got out and moved quietly over the gravel.

As they approached Gregor's place, Mallen saw that the lights were off. *Shit…* Didn't want to wake the man. Mallen had hoped Gregor would still be up, poring over the codebook or his Marin walk trails. Maybe even watching a taped Steelers game. He needed that book out of Gregor's hands. It was time to keep people *out* of it, not in it. He'd been an idiot, gotten lazy. Lost his edge. And now innocent people had paid. Nobody else was going to pay for his mistakes.

Knocked on the scarred old door. Suddenly felt he was being watched. Glanced at the windows. Thought he caught the movement of a curtain on the second story. After a moment, the front door opened and there was Gregor, dressed as always: Steelers t-shirt, khaki shorts, and no shoes. The man didn't give any indication at all that Mallen had woken him up, if indeed that's what Mallen had done. The alert gaze in the man's eyes made Mallen think that's exactly what he *hadn't* done.

"Sleep lightly, yeah?" he said to Gregor.

"Never sleep on a mission, son. That'll get you killed," Gregor answered with a slight smile. "Don't stand in doorways longer than you have to," he added. A teacher, giving a lesson.

Mallen and Gato went right in. Gregor turned on a lamp, and Mallen saw there was a gun in Gregor's hand. The older man had him dead to rights, but only smiled and laughed softly. "No, son. Not for you."

"Who then?"

For an answer, Gregor went to one of the front windows, but only after shutting off the light. Carefully pulled back the curtain, but only a little. The hairs on the back of Mallen's neck stood up. He'd known Gregor long enough to think he knew what this answer would be, too.

"You've had visitors," he said, voice flat.

"Yeah? How many? When?"

Gregor moved to the stairs. Motioned for Mallen and Gato to follow. They went up to the loft area. Only then did Gregor turn on a light. A cone light that shone on the tabletop. There were mounds of papers there. All pencil scribbles and diagrams and letters. Gregor had been busy. He dug through a nearby pile of papers. Came out with the codebook. Handed it over, saying, "Mallen? You better burn that fucker."

"Burn it?" That was crazy. "Why the hell would I do that? All the answers are here."

A laugh. An old, crusty laugh. Gregor dug under the pile of

papers again. Came out with a pack of cigarettes. Lit one up and tossed the pack on the table. Blew out some smoke, then smiled. Dug under the papers once more and this time came out with a thick sheaf of paper binder-clipped together. "You want to do that because I copied the whole fucking thing for you. Something you should've done immediately, youngin'."

"*Capitan*," Gato said with reverence, "that's amazing."

Mallen's mind was numb at the work the old man had accomplished, and in so little time. "Look, I can't let you get into this anymore, Mr. Gregor. Hell, I still want to buy your truck."

The old man laughed at that. Nodded. "I appreciate a soldier who can crack wise in the face of trouble. Good to know that about you, Mallen."

"Who was here?" Mallen said.

"Only an hour ago, a man came down the dock. Went up to your door. Knocked. Looked back at the dock gate. I was watching the whole thing. You know, after awhile you recognize the step of someone, right? Well, I know how the locals sound as they walk past my place. I can tell when it's someone who doesn't come around often, or someone who's never been here before. I saw him look back at the land. There was a couple of men standing there in the shadows. Sentinel-like. You didn't answer your door, so after about minute or so, they left."

"You get a look at any of them?"

"It was dark, and I don't have as good vision as I once did. Plus I was looking from a concealed vantage. The guy that knocked at your door was thin. Wore a suit. Chinese, or Japanese. Can't be fuckin' sure."

Wong. Who the fuck else? Mallen glanced at Gato, who only

nodded in response, then pulled out his automatic and checked the clip. That was definitely Gato's vote. Mallen looked down at the book in his hand. "I can't ... can't involve you any deeper, sir." The "sir" was pretty much automatic at this stage. If Gregor wasn't still on duty in the service, he still exuded that aura. "This runs deep into some really bad places."

Another old, throaty laugh. "Well, it's you, right? Where else would it be running?"

Mallen chuckled at that. "I'll burn this straight away. Did you make anything else from all the writing?"

Gregor scanned over the papers on his desk. "Partial. It's definitely a ledger of sorts. If I'm right, there's a lot of money changing hands."

Mallen's phone ringing almost made him jump. Checked the number. Gwen. He paused before answering it. What way to go? His gut said to take the call, so he did, stepping away from the other two men. "Hey, what's the latest?"

A soft, mocking laughter was his answer. Knew immediately she was not happy. "Heard something through the vine. About Oberon."

"Really? What about him?"

"Look, where are you?"

"Look, what's up? Why call now? I just don't have anything to report."

"Bullshit you don't. Where are you?"

"So you can tell your blue brotherhood? Why would I tell you where I am?" Fuck it, he thought, I'm burning up the world, might as well do it right. Like Ol' Monster Mallen had always said: Play it to the limit.

"I won't tell my 'brotherhood,' you asshole," she said. "I still need your help and we haven't exactly been playing open hands, right?"

"Got that right. I know about you and Wong."

Silence. "Look, we have to do this face to face. Where are you?"

Thought for a moment. "I'm still in the city. In the Loin. At St. Luke's. They let homeless sleep there. I figure I'm about homeless, about fuckin' now."

"Okay. Let's meet in the morning. I'll buy you breakfast. At Han's. They're not far from your ... motel."

It was only a handful of blocks away from St. Luke's. On Leavenworth and Sutter. He could be there in the morning. "Okay. Nine?"

"Okay." Then the call went dead. As he put the phone in his pocket, he said to Gregor, "I hate to ask this of you, sir, but can you lend me—"

"The truck again?" Gregor smiled. "Hell, man ... you still got the keys. Just pay me $100 a month. You miss a payment, I repo the truck and turn off your bilge. You hear me?"

"Yes, I hear you. Thank you," Mallen replied. Glanced down at the papers. "Bury those somewhere that they would have to set fire to the bay in order to find them, yeah?"

"Of course. I'm not going to lose the war in the final firefight, son. Not me."

Mallen and Gato went down the stairs to the door. Opened it. "Let's go to my place," Mallen told his friend, "I need a few things then we'll get the fuck out of here." He had to stay away from the only place he'd felt safe since getting clean. That burned in him. He just wanted to rest and make kites, but the other side of him, the side that wanted to help people, just wouldn't let him.

They got to his place and Mallen pulled out his keys. Opened the door. The two men stepped inside ....

The lights flashed on. Gwen sat in the overstuffed leather chair Mallen always sat in, gun in her hand, pointing right at his chest. Her eyes were crinkled up at the edges in humor; she seemed to enjoy having gotten the drop on him. "I knew you weren't in the goddamned city," she said. Indicated for both of them to come in and close the door.

Mallen and Gato exchanged glances. Mallen looked at Gato's right hand as it inched for his gun, but he shook his head. Gato nodded and went and sat on the couch, hand near the gun in his waistband. Mallen stood, hands in coat pockets.

"I said to sit down, Mallen."

"Go fuck, Gwen. If this is a bullshit session I'll stand, thanks."

Their eyes locked. Then she relaxed. Put the gun down on the chair arm. "Okay. Okay ...." she said. "Stand if that's what you want to do." Got up then. Came over to him, leaving the gun behind. "You can pick that up if you want to, Eduardo," she told Gato. He didn't move, but Mallen could see he was lost in what seemed to be going down. And what *was* going down? Mallen wondered what game Gwen played at. Whatever that game was, it was not what he'd expected, at all.

"Gwen, quit beating about the bush. What's up? If you wanted to bring me in, you would've had backup here. If you'd wanted to kill me, I'd be dead and so would Gato. You called me into this, and I don't know why anymore."

She nodded. "I'm"—she sighed—"there's just no other way to say it. I'm working... I guess you would say, undercover."

Mallen stared at her a long time. A long time. Then he went and sat down in his chair. Picked up her gun and looked at it a moment. Then he held it out to her. She wasn't lying. There was no reason for it to be a lie. None at all that he could figure. She came over and took it from him. Put it in her holster. "Not on the outside like you did, but inside. In the department, Mallen."

"You really think we'd believe that?" Gato said, then looked at Mallen, "I wouldn't believe her, man. She looks like a *mentirosa*."

A smile at the word, then she continued, "No, not lying. Unfortunately, I have no way to prove any of this. Mallen? You'll have to accept this on faith, I guess. You've worked undercover. You know what it was like. How would you have proved it to someone, if you'd had to?"

"How long you been a mole?" Mallen said.

"Three long years." That would just about jibe with how long Oberon had said she'd been fixing cases with Wong.

"Really? So you were fixing cases with your boyfriend as part of your cover?"

Silence. Then she nodded. "Yes. Come on, how many times did you break the law to keep your cover? There was no other choice, right? Just part of the job? To play undercover, you have to be undercover. It's not a game. You have to go to the limit, or you're dead."

"And Wong? I gotta say, Gwen, you have more commitment than I ever did. I wouldn't have slept with someone in order to keep the job going."

"But that's because you were married. I'm not. And wasn't,

and don't plan to be." Did she actually shudder? Mallen had to admit, either it was the truth or she was very good at her part.

"So just what the fuck are you doing undercover in the department? What's your objective? Corruption? Drugs? What?"

She looked from him to Gato and back again. "Not only are cops fixing cases to further their careers, they're actually committing the crime then framing someone and bringing them in. Some…some are even running a shadow business, for lack of a better word."

"Shadow business? What's that supposed to mean?"

Now she went and sat down next to Gato. His friend moved away a bit, like she might be a viper who'd strike at any moment. "When I first came to you about the missing kids, I was being honest. Children are being kidnapped. It's not about abuse, like anyone would assume. It's about making money, Mallen. It's about illegal adoption."

"I'd thought that's what it was. The book I—" Caught himself, but it was too late. Gwen's eyes went sharp.

"Book? What book? What do you know, Mallen?"

To Mallen's surprise it was Gato who spoke. "A codebook listing the buying and selling of the *niños*." Looked then at Mallen, "If we're going to save the ones that can't save themselves, we have to be willing to take some risks, right?"

Mallen smiled. "More of your old man's wisdom?"

Gato shook his head. "No, man. My own."

"Okay." Then to Gwen he said, "Yeah, it's a codebook. I got it off of Karachi."

"So. The rumors are true. You did kill that bag of shit."

He nodded. "Oberon tell you that?"

"No. Oberon took a sudden leave of absence from the department. Very sudden. Word is he came back, covered in dirt, and with a broken jaw. Not very happy. Told the boss he'd earned a vacation, then handed over his cases to the rest of the crew and left." She'd said this entire thing never taking her eyes off of Mallen.

"That all he said?" Mallen replied. "Nothing else?"

"Nothing else that anyone is saying, anyway. You know more?"

"No," he deadpanned. "I haven't seen Obie for some days."

"What do you know about the *niños*?" Gato asked her.

"They're targeting children that belong to drug-addicted mothers... mothers on welfare. All the children taken so far have lived in the lowest income strata in the city. I'm sure they're setting up these children to be abducted, and then sold."

"But why would someone overseas want an American kid?" Gato said to her. "There must be thousands of white kids people could buy instead. Russian. Croatian All over Eastern Europe, right? Just like you see in the movies."

"That's true. But it's children here that are being bought and sold... to American families."

"I don't get it," Mallen said. "Why the bother? These white families could land a kid from any adoption place. They're white. They have money. I don't get it."

"I'm not sure," she admitted. "From what I've been able to find out, there's usually something in the family's background that would make it impossible for them to adopt through regular channels."

"What? Like abuse?" Gato said. His fists clenched as he said it.

A slight nod from Gwen. "It's possible, sure. It could also be that either parent committed some other sort of crime. Something not related to abuse. Any conviction would knock you off the list."

"And you don't have anything more on this?" Mallen said. "More than what you've told me?"

"I was getting close, Mallen. I knew Hendrix was involved. I was getting to him. He was going to crack, I know. I just had to get him high enough."

High enough . . . "You know how he was found," Mallen said. "You know he died of an OD. What did you do? Give him that skag? If we're being upfront here, then lay it on the table, Gwen."

She looked at Mallen like he was crazy. "No! I had been talking with him. He'd heard some things. Tripped to it through his network. Look, he was a total piece of shit, but he didn't want to go back to jail. He told me it was through this network he'd heard something."

"This network of molesters."

Another sigh. "Yes . . . of molesters. But he'd found just a thread about the kidnappings. He wanted to pass that on so he could make some money. Then he died."

"Had to be Wong. I know he was there," Mallen said. "At Hendrix's wagon the day he died."

"That's what IA thinks. And I do, too." She paused then. "We have an idea that Wong has involved himself with this sort of large, underground organization before. But we're not sure. We just think so."

Mallen and Gato glanced at each other for a second. "Yeah . . . " Mallen said quietly. "How do you see this ending, Gwen? What's your side's plan? Do you have one?"

"Of course we have one. I involved you because I needed help and knew that once you'd gotten involved, you'd go pedal to the metal on it. Everyone I'm working with knew it. We knew you'd find out things we'd never be able to find out."

And what the fuck had that been? That there was some sort of group operating in the city that stole kids from the Loin and other poor areas of the city, then sold them to wealthy families not only in the Bay Area, but probably also out of state. And he was still no closer to finding Jesse. He was nowhere. Karachi was dead. Lucas had been killed. Hendrix murdered. Blackmore turned into collateral damage. Wong was involved in it somehow. Maybe just as a contract killer, but if Wong was involved at all, it was bad. And he would take Wong down. No matter what.

"I haven't done shit," he finally said. "Too many black holes out there still. And how far are you, and whoever the fuck is behind you, willing to go in order to stop Wong and whatever he's into?" And what if this organization was directly involved with the group that had kidnapped Chris? The one he'd made the bargain with, that cold night under the dome at the Legion of Honor? Then what?

He paced back and forth as he thought, then stopped to face her. Gato picked up on it. Got to his feet.

"Gwen," Mallen said, "Here's the codebook." He put it in her hand.

"You have a copy," she replied flat. Disappointment there.

"I do. An exact copy. You can play your version anyway you want. Good to know we're working on the same side and all that bullshit, okay? But I'm still trying to find Trina's daughter and make sure these fuckers quit and wave the white flag. You've been on my ass to give you something? Well, there it is. Do something with it. I'm damn sure Wong is involved. Like we know, he was seen at Hendrix's wagon right before the fuck was killed. If you can't go after Wong, I will. I owe him anyway," he said as he flexed his right hand.

Gato moved to the door. Pulled out his car keys. Gwen took the hint. "Okay, Mallen," she said. "I'll do what I can with this. Thank you for giving it to me." Went to the door. Stopped. Almost smiled as she said, "you'd make a good cop. Again." Left without another word.

After the door was closed, Mallen said, "I want to believe her, you know? But her past with Wong still sets off alarms. I mean … you'd have to be a very dedicated cop to sleep with the enemy. Hell, maybe she sees herself as some modern-day Mata Hari. Maybe she's willing to do anything to get up the ladder. Shoulders slumped then. Jesus … and people didn't shoot drugs why?

Gato said to him, "Vato, what do we do now?"

Mallen checked the Marin address that Gregor had found in the book. The only address coded into the book that was not in some poor part of the city or any area otherwise mentioned. "We go to this place, and see what we can see." Mallen then looked at Gato, "G," he said softly. "You want to go on with this? There's still a chance for you to walk away. You can go be with your mother. Look again for your sister."

At the mention of his sister, Gato began to pace back and forth. Rubbed at the crook of his right elbow. Mallen knew that his friend was right handed. He thought then about how Gato had been since he'd come back without his sister. The bruises, though

241

faded, where evident. The man's entire bearing was different. In that one movement, Mallen thought he had a slight idea of what might've happened to his friend. And if he was right, what had gone down was very bad and very dark. "Eduardo," Mallen told him, "I'm here for you, brother. You've been here for me more times than I'll ever be able to count. You brought me from the abyss and set me on the road." Before Gato could say anything Mallen put his hand to stop him, "No, let me say this: you brought me from the dark. It was you that cared and showed me the way. I owe you a thousand times over. I'm here for you, man. I have your back. It doesn't run just one way, okay? All you have to do is ask for help, and I'll give whatever help I can. Okay?"

To all that, Gato had listened patiently. After a moment, he smiled the old smile. "Just like always, I see there's a good heart beating in that chest, my brother. I'll be asking, trust me. Let's finish your business then you can help me finish mine, *si*?"

"You got it." His phone rang. It was 4 a.m., and the number was one he didn't know. "Hello?" he said.

"Mr. Mallen?" A woman's voice. Sympathetic. That set him off. Chris? Anna?

"Yes. Who is this?"

"My name is Nancy Perkins. I'm a nurse at S.F. General. Emergency. We found your number in Trina Marston's pocket."

"You found it … in her pocket?" Took a deep breath. "What's happened to her?"

"There was a call from her building about an hour ago. The paramedics found her on the floor of her apartment. Now, she's going to be all right," she continued over his questions, "but it was close. A little longer, or a little more? It was very close."

Mallen knew immediately what that meant. She tried to take her own life.

"Like I said," she continued, "I'm calling because she had your phone number in her pocket. Along with a small bracelet. A little girl's bracelet."

Jessie…

"I'll be right there," he said, and hung up. "Gato …."

"Just tell me where we're going," his friend said he headed for the door.

# THIRTY-ONE

MALLEN AND GATO WALKED quickly down the dock, heading for Gato's car. Mallen felt a sense of relief inside, now that he knew that he and Gato were going to ride this case to the end, just like they'd done the others. They only stopped long enough to let Gregor in on what had gone down with Gwen. Mallen told Gregor, "Just keep the copy as safe as if it were your granddaughter's virginity, yeah?"

Gregor laughed, "Then I should paste it up on a billboard, but okay … I get your meanin', soldier."

The two men then left, running for Gato's car. The drive over the bridge was done in silence, each man lost in his own thoughts. Mallen wondered just what Gato would ask when the time came. Not that it mattered: he'd help any way he could. Gwen. Gwen had been on the inside all this time? Undercover? Fuck man, crazier things had happened.

His friend wouldn't come in when they arrived at S.F. General. He pulled the car into a nearby handicapped spot and put up the handicapped placard. Mallen gave him a look, then left. "It comes with the car, *vato!*" Gato said after him.

He went in through the main doors and to the front desk. Asked for Trina's room. She was still in emergency, but they gave him a pass and let him inside. He walked through the double doors and past the rows of curtained-off cubicles. He'd spent so much fucking time in emergency rooms ever since he got clean, way more than he did when he was shooting gold honey into his veins, that again he wondered at the "why" of it all. Was life supposed to be this ironic? He was on the right road, though, and he knew it. Life wasn't about shoving your head under a rock and pretending that the world didn't matter. It was about taking that rock and throwing it at the people that did wrong in this world. Maybe that was extreme, sure, but he had to admit that he'd seen some extreme crap since that day Oberon had taken him to the drunk tank downtown to clean out. Well, all he could do was keep on going. And going. And going. He'd go until someone stopped him. And at that moment, as he walked down the aisle of emergency room cases, he knew he'd make it truly fucking painful and hard for someone to stop him.

He reached the bay where Trina was, the curtain closed. He pulled it aside and walked in. Her eyes were closed and she looked even thinner than the last time he'd seen her. If she didn't turn it around, and soon, she wouldn't make it. A nurse came in at that moment. Looked at him. Said, "Are you family?"

"No. Just a friend. Heard she was here. Thought she might need somebody."

The nurse turned to her, saying, "She does."

"How much did she take?"

"Thankfully not all that was on her."

"On her? How much was on her? Do you know?"

"The paramedic's report said there were three grams in a baggie near her hand."

Three more grams? That was impossible: she didn't have that kind of money. "Is that in the police report? The grams?"

The nurse nodded abstractly as she wrote something down in Trina's folder.

"Can I stay here for a while? Just be with her?" he said quietly.

The nurse thought for a moment. "Of course. If she comes to, please make sure she drinks some water."

The nurse then left him to be alone with Trina. He stared down at her thin, emaciated face. She'd gone out and bought that smack. But where did she get the money for it? As far as he could tell, this woman was dirt broke. Checked her track marks. No, nothing there. She'd shot herself up. No doubt. Nobody had done this to her but herself. But how did she get the money?

A whimper came from her lips. He thought she might've called out for Jessie.

"Trina," he said quietly as he put his hand over hers, "It's Mark. Mark Mallen."

Took a moment but then she opened her eyes. There was no light there. None. Her body may go on living for a while, but it seemed her soul had already called it a life and left. "Mark... I...."

"It's okay, you don't have to say anything right now. Just... just try to get well. I'm getting closer to finding your Jesse. I promised you I would, and I meant it."

It took a moment but then her gaze met his. Locked onto it. "You won't." Broke down crying. "God!" she yelled at the ceiling. "What happened? What made me an addict? Why? Why? Why did I do it?"

"Trina, I know day-by-day is hard. I know that for a fact, but—"

"Don't even bother with the speech, Mallen."

"Trina, Jessie will come back to you. You have to be here when that happens. She will be back. You'll need to be here, to hold her ... to love her again."

New tears. Then it was unstoppable and she couldn't catch her breath and she was gasping and the nurse came back and then there was a sedative. Her eyelids fluttered, then closed as she fell into a drugged slumber. But even in sleep, her soul still raged. Her hands flexed like claws, jaw clenched. Even under the influence of whatever it was they'd given her, she still murmured and slurred out Jessie's name.

As he stood there, it seemed like she was aging right before his eyes. He had to find Jessie. And soon. Had to, or this woman for sure wouldn't make it. Fuck man ... she might not make it anyway. The inevitable question then reared up at him, hissing and spitting poison: and if he did bring Jessie back? What was he bringing her back to? If ... no, *when* he found Jessie, wouldn't it better to just bring her to Social Services? Until Trina got off the junk? And what if she never did get off the junk? Too many children continued the downward spiral because they didn't know anyway else but down. Our kids were supposed to have better lives than their parents, right? That's the way it was supposed to work.

Mallen hated these kind of arguments. These were thoughts and perspectives that could be argued until Hell froze over and defrosted again. Well, first things fucking first, as the saying went, and worry about the "after," after. He took Trina's hand in his. Held it firmly. Whispered to her, "Just try to hold on, okay? Don't give up yet. Give me some more time. Okay? Just a little more time."

Trina's lids fluttered, and she seemed to relax a little. He pushed a lock of her dark hair away from her closed eyes, then left.

Gato met him just outside the emergency room doors, and together the two men walked back to the car and got in. The sun had come up over the eastern hills while he'd been with Trina. Mallen was actually surprised the sun came up. Seemed lately like the sun would never come up again. His phone rang then. *Jesus, someone else calling before the cock crowed?* And to top it all off, it was *another* number he didn't recognize. "Hello?"

A pause. "I figured you'd be sleeping and that I could just leave a message. Chris told me you'd answer. I really didn't think you would."

"Daniel?" he said. "What's wrong? Is something wrong with Chris? Anna? Why are you calling me?"

"No, no…" came the answer. "Nothing like that. I was just hoping that… well… that we could meet?"

Gato looked at him. Mallen nodded that everything was okay, and his friend started up the car and rolled it toward the parking garage exit. "You mean now? This morning?"

"Yes. Yes, I do. Breakfast?"

"Why?"

He heard Daniel's soft chuckle through the phone. Two dogs in a junkyard. No, he didn't want it like that. Chris wouldn't want this. She'd want it peaceful as possible. And as long as Mallen could be a part of their lives, that's how it would be. He'd always known there was the possibility that this moment, a boyfriend entering the equation, would happen. Of course it fuckin' would, yeah? "You have a favorite place for breakfast?" Mallen asked.

"I do," came the answer. "Judy's Cafe. That all right?"

"Sure. When?"

"I can be there in thirty."

"I might be ten later than you. See you." He hung up.

Gato looked at him. "What's up?"

He took a deep breath. "Seems my ex-wife's new sleep-over boyfriend has invited me to breakfast right in the middle of all the shit raining down."

"Oh," Gato said as the traffic light turned green, "glad it's not anything serious this time."

# THIRTY-TWO

GATO DROVE HIM OVER to Judy's. Said he would wait as he pulled his ragged Bible from the glove box. Judy's had been an institution in the city for nearly thirty years. Not Mallen's crowd, but he wasn't there to fit-in or feel comfortable. Mallen felt he had a pretty good idea what Daniel would say to him. One of those "clear the decks" sort of talks that two guys have under circumstances like this. One of those, "Man, I'm not here to fuck up your shit" moments. A conversation about how Daniel wasn't there to be the new daddy to Anna. About how Daniel realized that Mallen would still be calling to set up visitations while he, Daniel, now slept in Chris's bed. Sorry Mallen, but there you go: you fucked it all to hell and back again, and I'm here to take your family past you and into a new future and pass the salt, please.

Well… fuck.

Daniel stood out in front of Judy's, dressed like page 39 in a

Lands' End catalog. Shit, don't hold that against him, Mallen thought as he approached. They briefly shook hands, two boxers at the beginning of a match. How else should it be? What else could it be? No matter how much either disavowed all knowledge of their stones and the testosterone that filled them up, they were still two guys who loved the same woman.

Daniel had a table waiting for them, which was good. This joint was always crowded. They went and sat toward the back. There were already two menus there. Mallen ordered coffee straight away, Daniel doing the same. At least the guy didn't drink decaf. That was comforting. It was obvious to Mallen, who had been studying people and their reactions for a long time, both as a cop and a junkie, that this was indeed a guy who had something to say. Something hard and uncomfortable. Would he tell Mallen he was in love with Chris? Well, what else? That he loved how Mallen had decorated the den? Sure as fuck wouldn't be that: Chris had redone the den since he'd left.

They didn't talk much at first except about the Niners. Daniel seemed to be a big fan. Then they moved on to talking about the city until the waitress came and took their order. Mallen got more coffee. Poured some cream into it. "So, what's up?" he said directly as he stirred his cup. "Why the breakfast. I appreciate it, but you have to admit I have a right to be a bit wondered at it all, yeah?"

Daniel smiled. Nodded. "Sure. Of course. I just wanted to have some time with you so we could get comfortable with the way things will be, going forward."

"Oh? And which way will that be?" *Stop being such a dick, dick! You want to be able to see Anna any time you want. Don't fuck that up, asshole!* "Sorry," Mallen said as he reached for the sugar. "You know how it must be."

"Yes, I do." Daniel sipped his coffee as he stared past Mallen to the front door. Almost as if he wanted an escape route. Looked down at his coffee. "Chris told me about what happened. Told me everything. How she's working to move forward." Smiled then. "She's not one to just sit in a corner and cry. Incredible."

Mallen nodded. "Yup."

It was then that Mallen caught a glimpse of himself in the window's reflection. Beat all to shit from the last five years plus of his life. Rumpled coat and clothes. Had an automatic pistol in his pocket. People were after him. To kill him. And he was after those people. He looked like a nightmare from a 1970s cop movie. Actually, he looked worse than he ever had as a junkie. Probably much worse. He'd been shot at too many times to count, been beaten almost as much, and at one point had his hand nailed to a fuckin' table. That shit never happens to a junkie.

Daniel was saying something to him and he pulled himself back to the booth and his coffee. "Sorry," Mallen said, "not enough sleep. What were you saying?"

"I'd heard about the hours you sometimes keep," Daniel replied with a smile. Not smarmy. Not anything but some guy who was meeting another guy from a totally different world than he inhabited, a world he could never imagine wanting to inhabit.

"How is Chris?" Mallen asked, trying to keep it all going. "How's Anna?"

"Anna is great. She's a wonderful girl. Smart as hell. Loves kites, and yes … I know about that. Honestly? She's not happy

252

with me being there." Looked directly at him then. "She loves her father. It's a strong, fierce love, too. Not anything I would want to, or could ever, change."

"Thanks. I love her with everything I have. Everything I ever will have."

"I know. Chris has been very vocal about not doing anything that comes between you and Anna." Daniel stirred his coffee until the waitress came with their meals.

Mallen ate a bit. Not hungry, even with all that had gone on. Never could find room for the food when a case was already on his plate. Finally gave it up, pushing his plate to the side.

"Are you and Chris happy? Well … do you think you'll be happy?"

Daniel looked at him for a moment. Nodded. "Yes, we are. And I know that will grow. Once she's able to come to grips with what happened … with the rape, I think—"

Mallen's world shifted to the left. Felt like he would fall out of the booth and not hit the ground. Like he would land outside somewhere, maybe even across the street. Daniel picked up on it. Hell, it would take a dead man to not pick up on the change in vibe.

"Ra … rape?" Mallen scratched out. "Rape?"

Daniel sat there. Just stared at him. Mallen imagined he could almost smell the man's brain burning, knowing he'd just dropped a fucking bomb that would put Hiroshima to shame. "Well … I mean … ."

"She was raped, man? She never told me that. She *never* told *me* about that."

"I'm … I'm sorry, Mark. I had no idea. She never said … ah, fuck … ."

"She told you who, didn't she? Didn't she???" Now a couple people in the booth across from them looked over. Uncomfortable.

To his credit Daniel didn't even try to run a screen. Nodded.

"Who. Who, motherfucker? Who raped her?" The waitress came over but then turned around and left when she caught the look in Mallen's eyes. "Who?"

"She … she wouldn't want me to tell you. I know she wouldn't. She told me so."

"Look, you blew it. Deal with it, okay? We're men, right? We blow it all the time. Just fucking tell me. Tell me, now."

Daniel looked into his eyes. Obviously didn't like what he saw there. Scared the living fuck out of him. "Never knew his name. All she would say was that it was an Asian man who stank of cigarettes and that he had a—"

"—ponytail." Mallen looked at the back wall as his mind played out every time he'd ever met Winstons Wong. He got to his feet. Pulled out a couple twenties and tossed them on the table.

"I was going to pay," Daniel said softly.

"I'll get this, and you'll do me a favor," Mallen replied. Leaned across the table. His eyes were eyes that Daniel had never seen before, and couldn't look away from. Eyes filled with threat, anger, and enough violence to explode the entire city block. "You'll say nothing about what you just told me. Not to Chris. Not to anyone. Not to your fucking therapist. Not even to your steering wheel. If you do, well … ." and here he caught himself.

Took a deep, very deep breath .... "Well, I can't stop you, Daniel. You love my ex-wife. My child will be in your hands. The child I love more than the world enough. I only hope you at least wait a day, or something, or whatever, before you tell her. I need that time, man. You get me?"

"How can I not tell her, Mark?"

"Just a day, okay? That's all I need." Turned for the door. Stopped. Turned back. "Thanks for the breakfast."

———

Mallen was a block away from Gato's car when his phone rang. Knew it would be Chris. Daniel seemed like a nice guy, but he was a nice guy in a hard place. This was his new lady. No way Daniel would've thrown in with him, but he had to toss the dice anyway. If you don't try, you for sure can't win. Checked the number. Yeah ... Chris.

"You should've told me, damn it," he said the second he answered the phone.

"And how was I to do that? We talked after you brought me home from ... them. You told me about your hand. What they did. And I was suppose to add to *that*? How could I, Mark?"

"Jesus, Chris ... I ... I have to do something."

Silence. "Mark," she said, "you can't risk never seeing Anna again."

He stopped right there on the sidewalk. Overhead was sky. He could smell the ocean. Things that always went on, things that would always go on. "What exactly do you mean, Chris? You're going to hold that over my head? In order to keep me in line? Visitation rights to my daughter?"

"If you're going to become a murderer? Then yes."

"I'm not a murderer. Wong's committed more crimes than you could imagine. That fucker has to be sent to the locker room on a stretcher or in a box and I really don't care how." Took a breath before continuing. "I'm not going to murder him though, Chris. I'll make him draw down on me first."

"Mark," she answered. He could hear the desperation and panic in her voice. "You can't do that. It ruins all you've ever been. Both before you became a junkie, and after. Think of Anna."

He said it, but later regretted it. "And what if I want to think of you?"

"Then think that. If it keeps you from doing what I think you're going to do, then think of me."

"But nothing more than that, yeah?"

"Mark...I've tried...but I can't." Added quietly, "You don't understand. Daniel...he's not in that world. At all. I like that. Need that."

He stood there as her words echoed in his head. Stared at Gato's car for a moment, then up into the sky...at the beautiful sky above. Felt that he was now living at a crossroads. Everything he'd hoped for was now somewhere else. In a trash heap? Shithole? Did it matter? All he could find to say was, "I appreciate you trying. Kiss Anna for me."

There were tears in her voice. "I will."

"I love you, Chris." And he cut the call. And cut off the rest of his life. Put the phone back in his coat pocket. Got in the car and pulled the gun from his other pocket. Checked the clip. All good.

"Mallen?" Gato said. "You okay, bro? What was that call?"

"Nothing man," he answered. "Just Chris being concerned."
Was this what the end of the road felt like? Well if it was then it could go get fucked. And fucked hard. Now he had two tasks that had to, *had* to be finished: Bring Jessie back to Trina, and kill Wong.

He would be happy to reunite a mother with her child. Sublimely happy.

He would also be happy when Wong met a bullet, especially if the man met that bullet with his forehead. Yeah, that would also make him sublimely happy.

# THIRTY-THREE

WINSTONS WONG LEANED BACK in his chair. Smiled at the open file in front of him. Karachi was dead. Lucas was dead. Hendrix was dead. These were all things that were good. Looked down at the briefcase by his leg. Fucking stupid thing, but it served its purpose. Really needed a fucking cigarette. Glanced around the detective bullpen. Only Fat Charlie and that fucker Tommy Toner were in. Fuckin' Tommy. Would never live down that toner cartridge episode. Asshole.

Tommy Toner got up from his desk. Came over. Had a file in his hand. Case file. "Hey, Wong. Got a sec?"

A sigh that would fill a football stadium. "Sure," Wong said. "What's up, man?"

Tommy Toner opened up the file in front of him. "It's this drug dealer guy. Shot in some bathroom stall in some shithole bar in The Loin."

A shrug. "Heard about it. A drug thing. And?"

"Right," Toner said. "Except... there was a witness that didn't run out. Some drunk bastard off in the corner saw a guy dressed all in black like Johnny Cash run out of the bar right after the shooting. I think there's something there."

*And there was a God after all....* Wong smiled. "All in black? Any leads?"

"No. Nothing yet. Checking on all street demons that run that part of the city. But... well, it's a big fucking city and I have a lot on my desk."

Wong shrugged. "You check on the dealer's known customers right?"

A nod. Toner laughed softly. "I guess that guy....What was his name? Mallen? He'll need a new dealer."

"That was Mallen's dealer? Really?"

"Was. Yes."

"Have you talked to that fuck? He sure seemed to throw it all away. Maybe he's the guy in all black?"

Toner considered this. "Could be. He lives nearby."

"Lived. Lived nearby."

"Lived?"

Wong leaned forward. Pulled out the file he'd rigged and brought with him. Always thrilled to do it right under their fucking stupid noses. Handed the file to Toner. "I'd heard that Kane gave him some floating home bullshit pile to live on."

"Kane, huh?" Another laugh. More like a snicker as he glanced through the file.

"No, not like that," Wong said innocently. "Well, not that I'd know, you know?"

Tommy Toner considered all this as he handed back the file. "Thanks. I'll remember you in my will."

"The fuck you will, asshole."

Toner laughed as he walked off back to his desk. Wong smiled as he watched Toner waddle off. Now Wong had everything he needed to rewrite the files. Everything to prove that Mallen had killed Karachi and Lucas. Everything was written out so clearly. So nice and neat. Mallen wouldn't have a leg to stand on. He knew that Mallen had been there at Karachi's. Just knew it. Who else could've gotten the drop on that piece of shit Karachi? Whatever he thought of Mallen, and it wasn't a lot, he knew the guy was good. Even coming back from the dead like he'd done. Wong had to admit a certain amount of admiration. Fucker had escaped from him. Had forced the hand of a lot of powerful people to leave him and his family alone. Shit … if he hadn't fucked Mallen's wife so hard, he would've thought the entire enterprise to be a complete loss.

The remaining evidence papers were inserted into the file. Perfect copies of the originals, but with certain important parts changed. Wong closed the file and leaned back in his chair. Smiled again. Time for a cigarette.

Mallen was toast.

———

Mallen and Gato drove through the city, heading down to Gato's place to crash for a few hours when Mallen's phone went off. Jesus, he thought, he was really beginning to hate cell phones. Checked the number. Chris. He almost didn't answer it, but it was Chris, and so he had to. Might be something up with Anna. Couldn't take the chance. "Hey," he said into the phone.

To his surprise it was Daniel. Mallen instantly resented the manipulation. Daniel had known it was the only way to get him to answer. "Hey, fucker..." he started but Daniel cut him off.

"It's not like that, Mallen. It's not. If you want to think that, you'll be making a huge fucking mistake."

"Nice," Mallen chuckled. The guy had some balls, after all. "You got my attention. What's up?"

"Chris. She's..." lowered his voice here, "she's feeling really bad. Really bad. Because of you."

"Me?" He had to play innocent. "What do you mean?"

Now it was Daniel's turn to chuckle quietly. "You know why. She's worrying herself sick. Seeing you face to face is what she wants, but she feels she can't ask you."

Mallen had to admit... that sounded like Chris. *Shit*... Everything else would have to wait. "I'll be over. But she'll know you had a part in it. You ready for that? She's an Aries, you know?"

"I'm ready. She needs to talk to you. And what she needs is the most important thing to me."

Really? Jesus, but that guy sounded sincere. And he both hated that and had to respect it at the same time. Couldn't tell at that moment which was stronger, the hate or the respect. "Okay. There's a lot coming together fast, but if she needs me I'm there."

A silence. "Thanks. She really wants... needs to see you."

"Okay. And I appreciate how hard this call must've been, man."

Another short silence, then, "Thanks, Mallen."

———

261

Anna answered the door when he rand the bell. Practically leapt into his arms. "Daddy! You're early!"

"Early? Early for what, A?"

"Our visit time Saturday. You're taking me to see where you live."

"That's right. I am. But I'm here to see your mother. I won't miss this Saturday, trust me. Not for all the world." Hugged her tight. Very tight. He'd expected never to hug her again, or maybe not until she was an adult and wanted to find out things on her own.

Daniel came down the stairs. Held out his hand as he approached. "Thank you for coming to fast."

"Don't have to thank me. They're my family, even if things change, right?" Smiled as he said it. And he meant it.

"Chris is upstairs," he added in a quiet voice.

"Thanks for calling," Mallen said to him. He told Anna, "I'll see you later, A. Be ready for me, okay?"

"Well, of course," came the reply. Enough exasperation there to fill a football stadium.

Mallen went upstairs to what had been their bedroom, a long time ago. It'd been so long since he'd been upstairs, it now seemed more a stage set than the bedroom where they'd talked quietly about their hopes and dreams for the future. Had made love over and over again. He knocked, but to his surprise the answer came from the room across the hall, the room they'd always wanted to do something with, but never had. The room they'd ended up using pretty much like a storage unit. As far as he knew, it was still filled with things that belonged to his father. He went across the hall. She'd turned it into a sort of crafts room.

Sewing machine. Lots of fabric. A large, open table. Buckets of beads and things like that.

He smiled at it all. "You're finally getting your art on, yeah?"

She sat at her sewing machine. Looked over her shoulder at him, not surprised at all. Wore her glasses low on her nose. Regarded him over the frames. "This is what getting older holds for us? Glasses and sewing?"

"Could be worse, right?"

"Right." She left the bits of cloth she was working on and rolled her chair around to face him. He knew that move. She had something to say. And she had to say it. There was no alternative. He leaned against the wall.

"How far we've come, yeah, Chris?"

"Far. Far is right, Mark." She reached for a strip of linen. Played with it for a moment, looping it through and through her fingers before she said, "I was angry at Dan when I guessed what he'd done. He never admitted it, but didn't deny it either. I know his heart is in the right place, and that's a lot." Tossed the material onto the table. "I wanted to call you, but couldn't."

"Why?"

She smiled slightly as she told him, "It wouldn't have changed your ... trajectory. It never did before, so why now?"

Silence filled the room. He glanced around. All his father's things were stacked in the corner. Carefully, not carelessly. Thought at that moment that maybe he should just go ahead and take all those boxes out to the beach, dig a pit, and burn it all. That would be what his father would've wanted. Ol' Monster was never a man to look back, only forward.

Mallen turned his gaze from the boxes, not liking the emotions they invoked. Looked instead at all the projects Chris had begun. There were a lot of them. A lot. Can you sew your way through what she'd been through, he wondered? He wasn't sure, but he sure as shit knew she was going to try.

"Mark," she said, her voice very quiet, "you need to be here for your daughter. You can't do that if you're in prison, or dead."

"I know that. And don't blame Daniel for dropping the bomb. He really didn't mean to."

"I realize that. But still . . ."

"Chris . . . I have to finish this up. I'm at a place where I can finish this up." He pushed off the wall and paced up and down the room. Gave off an animal intensity as he went. If Wong had appeared at that instant, he would've shot the fucker in the groin and watched him bleed out.

She got up and came over to him. Put her hand on his shoulder, like she'd always done when he was wound up, or ready to blow apart the world. All it took was her hand on his shoulder and he was back on the ground. She only did it when she was either very serious or worried. "Mark Mallen," she told him, "I need you to not go off the rails over this. Yes, I . . . I was raped. And you know who did it. And just like I know you, you know me. I'll make it through this. I have Anna . . . and well, Daniel."

Took him a moment to find his voice. "You love him?"

"I'm not sure, Mark. But he's safe. He's not a cop, not a recovering junkie. He's safe."

He got that. How could he not get it? "Look, I need to finish this, Chris. There's some network out there selling children who have been abducted from their mothers. I need to finish the guys behind it. Wong is a part of that network." Looked at her, and before he knew what he was doing, he put her face in his hands and kissed her. He hadn't kissed her in more than five years. Her lips were warm, but dry. But they were hers. She was surprised, and pushed away from him, laughing softly.

"I gotta do what I gotta do, Chris. I'm sorry." He went to the doorway. Stopped and looked back over the room. Smiled. "Keep up the art."

———

He didn't say goodbye to Anna. She was in her room. Daniel was down by the front door. All they did was shake hands as Mallen left. But then he stopped and came back. Looked the man right in the eyes. Said, "We need to be clear on something, okay?"

Daniel held Mallen's gaze as he said, "Okay."

"I'm entrusting my child into *your* care. You fuck up? I'll hear about it. If I'm dead and you fuck up after I'm gone? My buddies will hear of it. Don't. Fuck. Up. Okay?"

The man tried to make it strong, but it was all too far out of his world. He must've thought he was dealing with someone who should be in prison. Maybe he was right. Anyway, he nodded. Held out his hand again. Mallen shook it, then quickly went through the door. When he got to the bottom of the stairs, he looked back. Just one last time.

# THIRTY-FOUR

THERE WAS ONLY ONE place to go, and that was the Cornerstone. Everyone knew he went there a lot. Hell, even Lucas had known. He'd figured that he would just set himself on the hook and see what predator he brought out of the jungle.

Mallen and Gato walked in like it was just another day. Bill was behind the bar. The first thing that Mallen noticed was the sadness that seemed etched into the bartender's face. Grief could do that to you and then some, Mallen thought as he went and sat on the stool at the end of the stick. He slipped his hand into his coat pocket and flipped off the safety on the semi-automatic he carried. *You just never knew, with so many pieces in play....*

Bill walked over. "Usual?" he asked.

"Yeah, B. Thanks." Bill looked at Gato, but the man just shook his head in answer. When Bill came back with Mallen's drink, Mallen said, "Hey, anybody been looking for me today?"

"Hell, Mal...who *hasn't* been looking for you. Cops. Plain-clothes cops been after you all fucking day."

"One an Asian-looking dude with a ponytail? Or a woman with red hair?"

"Affirmative, both counts."

"Thanks."

As he sat there and the time passed, he wondered if he'd been wrong. Maybe people weren't as smart as he'd thought. A good amount of people had come in, had a drink or two, then left. None of them seemed to pay any interest at all in Mallen or Gato. At one point, he'd had to piss, so slid off the stool and went down the hall to what had been Dreamo's office. He'd hesitated for a moment, wondering if maybe he should just go outside and piss against the wall, but he didn't consider that for very long. Fuck man, he'd have to go in there at some point. He pushed on the door and entered. First thing he noticed was the fact that all the glass had been swept up. Then he noticed the walls had been painted. He took his piss at the urinal, then went to the stall. Pushed on the door. It was like Dreamo had never been there. Nothing to show his passage. Mallen tried to pull out the tile that covered up Dreamo's little stash hole, but Bill had put some new caulk around it. It really was one more ending. Somebody some-where really wanted to drive home the point that he had approached the end of one very long and important phase of his life. What the next phase would look like, he sure as fuck had no idea.

———

Wong walked in fifteen minutes before closing time. Gwen was with him. He knew instantly he'd been played. She'd just wanted the codebook. The whole undercover story had been bullshit. As she came over to him and Gato, he noticed her expression was more one of resignation than relaxed. In fact, she looked very uptight at the moment. Mallen wondered if that was part of the game, too.

Wong came right over to him. "How's that hand, Hypo Hound?"

Mallen flipped him off with that hand. "Fine, dickwad."

Wong acted fast. Pulled cuffs as he threw Mallen backward off his stool. Gwen pulled her gun and pointed it right at Gato's chest before his friend could even move a muscle. Wong slapped the cuffs on Mallen, pocketing Mallen's gun.

"Hands on the bar," Gwen told Gato. She found his gun and put that in her pocket. Looked over at Wong, who nodded. She clapped the cuffs on Gato and pushed him toward the door.

Wong yanked Mallen to his feet saying, "You're under arrest for the shooting of Jimmy Karachi. Also the premeditated murder of William Lucas."

The few patrons in the bar had cleared out the moment they'd seen Wong and Gwen enter. Only Bill stayed, obviously wanting to do something but wondering if there was anything he could really do. Mallen looked over at Gato who seethed at being cuffed. Mallen smiled at his friend. Winked. Gato relaxed a little, but didn't seem to have any faith on tap at the moment. Mallen got the impression that his friend figured this was the end. Hell, if it really was the end? Well, then he was going to go out with his head held up, fighting until the end, not shaking and weeping like some victim. As Wong pushed him toward the door, Mallen told Wong, "You guys have no proof. None at all. Go fuck yourselves."

Wong answered, "It's all in the file, asshole. You're toast."

He'd figured as much. His file had been fixed. Like all the others. He'd be a feather in Wong's cap. *Fuck that....*

He let Wong lead him outside, Gato and Gwen right behind them. "See you soon, B!" he called out with a smile as they shoved him along. "You know a good lawyer?" was all he had time for before he was outside and shoved into the back of an unmarked car. Gwen's, if he was right.

When they turned right on Van Ness and headed for the bridge, he knew his guess had been right: They'd never planned to take him in at all. It was too risky. No, they'd frame it like he'd tried to escape, with Gato his partner in crime. He wondered where they'd try to pull it off. That might make a difference. He began to think of Anna. Saw her face. That always made him feel better. And it did now. If he got out of this, he'd celebrate that next day with everything he had. Gato stared out the window. Mallen was stone cold sure the man was thinking of his mother and his sister at that moment. Hated the thought of his best friend hurting so much.

"Gwen," he said to her from the backseat. "You can't really be a part of this, right? All that bullshit you laid on us back at my place aside, you're a good cop. Not a pile of shit like Winstons here."

Wong ignored him. Gwen turned to look at him. "No, I'm not a good cop. Not on my own. But with some help? I'm—"

"Shut the fuck up," Wong said. "Just shut up. He doesn't need to know anything. Won't make his death any better or worse."

"What does it matter then?" she said to him.

"Because I say it does. Just be the good partner/fuck buddy and keep your mouth shut. The less he knows the better."

"*Estúpido pedazo de mierda*," Gato muttered.

"Hey and you can shut the fuck up, too, spick."

Gato shifted in his seat, cussing under his breath, never taking his eyes off the rearview reflection of Wong. Mallen knew what his friend would do the moment the cuffs were off. He had to try and head that off.

Mallen didn't try to struggle. What good was struggling against a set of cuffs? This wasn't the movies, where he could pick the fucking things with a hairpin secreted in his mouth. His mind raced over the possibilities, and there weren't a fucking load of them. He had to relax. Not panic. There would be a chance. They'd have to remove the cuffs to make it appear to follow their storyline. His hands, and Gato's, would need to be free for that to be believable. And Mallen knew that if he missed that chance, then his friend would die. He would die, and these people would get away with it all. He needed to get them talking. Keep them talking. Again he thought of Anna. He *had* to live. For her. She needed her father. Even if he wasn't in that house, he was in her life.

They headed over the Golden Gate. Just like he'd thought they would do, they were heading to his floating hovel. They wanted the other copy of the codebook. Good luck with finding it, he thought. No way to tie Gregor to him. No way. The old man was just an old veteran to them. The dock keeper. Mallen just needed to keep them talking once they were there, he told himself.

They pulled into the parking lot at the floating home dock. Parked right in the red zone. Wong looked over his shoulder at him. "We're home, Mallen. You or your *perro* there try anything, and we'll shoot you both right on the spot, get the cuffs off in time and say we were arresting you when you attacked us. We're walking to your place, and you will give us the copy of the book that Karachi had. If you don't, I'll make getting your hand nailed to that table seem like the greatest day of your life."

Wong and Gwen got out. Dragged him and Gato out of the car. The two cops kept a good space between them. Just four people walking. In the dark the fact that two of their party were cuffed was hard to see.

As they passed Gregor's place, Mallen noticed that all the lights were out. Except for the upstairs one. Just like always. Wong reached into Mallen's coat pocket and yanked out his keys. Opened the door and pushed Mallen inside, Gwen following with Gato.

Wong pushed Mallen into the center of the room. Removed the cuffs. Mallen knew he'd be shot now, the moment he handed over the book. "Where is it?" Wong said to him.

Mallen turned to face him. He could swear his right hand was throbbing, just like it'd done after the hammer and nails episode. The moment he hesitated, Wong said over his shoulder to Gwen: "Put the *perro* on his knees."

She kicked Gato's feet out from under him. Put the gun to the back of his friend's head. Gato didn't blink as he said, "Mallen.

You give in to *estos puta*, and I will find you in the next life and kick your ass, bro."

"I said shut up," Wong growled as he struck Gato with his gun. The barrel slashed across the man's face, ripping open a deep, ragged gash that immediately filled with blood, dripping all over his shirt.

Gato didn't take his eyes off of Wong's as he said quietly, "*Morirás aquí, puta. Morirás aquí.*"

Mallen had known Gato for a while now, and knew how brave his friend could be, but he had no conception of how deep that bravery ran. This wasn't bravado. This was stone fucking cold, in your face "no fear."

"If he opens his mouth again," Wong said to Gwen, "you take four steps back and shoot him. That distance will give the impression he attacked me while I was struggling with idiot here." The cop then turned to Mallen. "Where the fuck is the copy of the book, asshole?"

Mallen sighed. Resigned. "In the kitchen." He led Wong over to the kitchen area. *So much for getting them to talk....*

"Can't believe you screwed it all up, Mallen," Wong told him. "That piece of ass you married? That's some tight shit. Perfect ass, too. You just can't win for losing, can you, fucker?"

As Mallen quickly reached up to open the cabinet, Wong stopped him. "Easy now," he said, "Move aside." Mallen did as he was instructed.

And as Wong pulled open the cabinet door, Mallen swung at Wong's gun hand. Swung with everything he had, knowing it might be the last thing he ever did. Wong was good, and had turned just enough at the last moment that even though the gun broke from his hand, he wasn't stunned like Mallen had hoped for. The two men dove for the weapon, and Mallen got his hand around it but then there were two explosions: the sharp blasts of a gun going off. All time stopped as both men looked at each other. Mallen felt warm blood dripping onto his right shoulder. He reached up and realized the bottom part of his right ear had been shot off.

But Wong pushed him away and lay there on the floor, incredulous as he stared at the spreading patch of blood low on his shirt. He tried one last time for the gun, but it was no good.

Mallen got to his feet. Looked down at Wong as the man curled up over the bullet wound in his gut. Chris's words rang in his head. His vision wavered, and his head ached with the battle that roared and raged inside him. He pulled back on the hammer. His right hand ached, like the nails that Wong had ordered hammered into it were still there. He thought of Chris. Chris, the woman he still loved, the mother of his child, victimized by this man. What price was he willing to pay to see the scales balanced again? Wong looked up at him, eyes filled with something the man hadn't probably felt in a very long time: fear.

*Well, sometimes we just have to fuckin' throw ourselves on the grenade....*

The gunshot sounded in the very depths of everything he'd ever known. Wong's body rolled over and crumpled into a heap. What would Ol' Monster Mallen say at this moment? What would his mother say? He knew what Chris would say, and what would happen now, but there was no taking back that little bit of lead. He sighed, wondering again why people quit shooting dope. And this time? This time there was no answer.

Gato looked at Wong, then at Mallen. Smiled a grim smile as he nodded with approval. "Good job, my brother." he said.

Mallen turned to face Gwen, her service weapon now pointed at his chest. She shoved Gato down to the ground and undid his cuffs with one hand. Quickly took a step back, her gun never wavering from Mallen's chest as Gato got to his feet, rubbing at his wrists, staring hate at her.

"You just shot a cop, Mallen," she told him. "Now I'm going to shoot you and your buddy here and either get a medal out of it, or promoted. Depends on how I'm able to fix it. Thank you for this opportunity."

"When did you get involved in all this, Gwen? How could you back a child-selling ring? How could you sign off on fixing cases? You weren't always like this, were you? What happened?"

"I needed to be better than I was, but I wasn't able enough. Internal Affairs recruited me. I was just some no name detective, going nowhere. Perfect for what they needed and I gladly went with it. I'd get a step up, so why the hell not take a chance at the brass ring? They knew Wong was no good. Was up to his neck in a lot of bullshit, some they could only guess at. Told me to get close to him. Work on him. Assigned me to him, which he hated. He was a bastard for so long. Treated me like shit, but I kept at him. In the end, all I had left to use to get to him was me. We started going out together. It went from there. It was after I'd 'won' his affection that he came to me with an offer. He'd been fixing cases for a while at this point. Knew he had to start worrying about patterns. Road signs. I knew he was smart enough to make it work, but I had no idea how brutal and cunning he could be. And it was so easy: all it took was a little doctoring here and there. Committing the crimes wasn't hard. And framing people, the types that live in the Tenderloin? Assholes that already have records?" Shook her head then, "No, Mallen, It really wasn't that hard at all."

"What about Internal Affairs?" asked Mallen. "You were playing both sides, Gwen. What then?"

She shrugged. "I was going to give them Wong, and his killer. Like I said, I'd get a medal out of it, or more. I was originally going to give them Karachi as his killer, but well, you fucked that all up."

Gato took a step forward. "But you helped steal *niños*. You took children away from their families. For money."

"No," she replied, "not for the money. Wong was in it for the money. I was just going to 'find' one of the kidnapped kids. That would've put me out in front of the crowd. I'd be known then, as a good cop. A great cop. No, it wasn't for money. Jesus, think about it, will you? We were helping unite couples that wanted a child with kids that otherwise would have *no* chance at all for a good life. A chance at any life worth living," she added quietly.

"Gwen," Mallen said quietly, "you know it's over now. You know it is. This mess is too big. It's overflowing now in ways you can't stop. There's no way you can make this right."

"All I have to do is silence the both of you. The codebook you gave me I burned. And I think I know where you stashed the other one. Your landlord, right? The man I found here the night you sent Lucas to the hospital?"

"You'll never find it," he replied flatly. As if it were pure truth.

"No," she cried desperately, "I can still make this work."

"No, no you can't."

There was the sharp sound of a knock at the door. "Come in!" Mallen said loudly. But it wasn't Gregor that walked in this time: it was Oberon.

"You hear it all?" Mallen said as he relaxed a little. Gato just stood there, his expression filled with amazement and admiration as he looked at the other two men.

Oberon looked straight at Gwen as he said, "Everything." He held up the tape recorder and mic for evidence. "Officer Essex, you are under arrest for murder, conspiracy to commit murder, and anything else the force can throw at you." He came over and took the gun from her. She was too stunned at first to react, but then grabbed the gun out of Oberon's hand and stood back. Faced them all.

"No," she said, her breath a rasp. "No. Not going to prison. No … " She shoved the gun under her chin.

"Gwen!" Mallen shouted but it was too late. She pulled the trigger and the shot echoed around the room as she fell to the floor.

Mallen and Oberon stared at the body silently. Gato put his hand on Mallen's shoulder, saying, "knew you had a *tarjeta en la manga*."

Oberon went and looked down at Wong's body. Shook his head. "Mark? I'm going to have to ask for a larger security deposit."

"Whatever you say, Mr. Landlord. Thanks for not evicting me."

"Who says I won't?" Came the reply. "You're ruining my personal, and most probably, my professional life."

———

It took a lot of caressing and explaining. It took hours, most of it with Mallen and Gato cuffed and in the backseat of a black and white. The Chief's assistant himself showed up and was closeted with Oberon for over an hour. Mallen's wrists burned. His heart burned. Now that the adrenaline had left, he felt empty and depressed. He had no idea if he would ever see his daughter again. This time around, every last fucking thing had blown up. Well, he figured as he looked out the window and down the dock at the place he'd called home, at least he was still clean. That was something. A huge something.

It was Gregor who again had saved the day. He showed up, copies of the codebook in hand, and turned them right over to Oberon. Mallen knew now that Lucy Redding would be tracked through that codebook. That her mother, Jenny, would get her back. That was also a huge something. The code in the book cracked, coupled with the tape that Oberon had recorded of Gwen's confession, let the police go away happy, showing the world that they'd "police'd their own." Mallen knew better than to say anything. They'd paint it with Wong as the ringleader, and Gwen a cop that desperately wanted to get ahead by creating a kidnapping and then solving the crime. The head office was already on it with the press and the mayor's office to ensure this would never happen again.

Now there was only one last thing to do. And maybe doing it would make it all worth something.

# THIRTY-FIVE

OBERON HAD GONE AWAY with the other police, giving him a last look that said he knew Mallen wasn't finished. Even with that, Oberon still left, asking once more for his rent check.

Mallen paced around the living room, unable to sleep. Beyond exhausted. Gato sat on the couch, watching him with tired eyes ringed in dark. Gato looked like he'd been thrown to the dogs and they'd thrown him back.

Gato spoke first. "Mallen? Where to now?"

Mallen nodded as he pulled out the piece of paper with the address. The address in Mendocino. The one Gregor had found in the codebook. That was all they had left.

Mallen showed it to Gato, who then got to his feet as he dug out his car keys....

———

The rising sun cast a pale light along Highway 128 as they followed their way through wineries and redwood forests. Mallen remembered that Mendocino was the first place he thought he'd end up after he'd gotten clean and had solved Eric's murder, putting it in the "finished business" column. The trees worked on his head, calming him … enveloping him. At the time, two suitcases were all he had with him: one filled with books, the other with clothes. No guns. No more Tenderloin. No more blood. He'd imagined himself showing up at Chris's, picking up Anna, and bringing her back here to some house in the woods he would be renting. Nice and quiet, and mostly safe.

*Well … not quite how it'd worked out, yeah?*

They rode the 128 to where it meets Highway 1 and the Navarro River. Continued north. At Mendocino, they made a right onto Little Lake Road. Headed up into the woods. After about ten minutes they found the gated road mentioned in the codebook. Drove a little past. Parked and got out. Wasn't the first time he'd snuck onto someone's private property and made his way to the door. Mallen wondered what sort of response he would get when these people opened the door. How ugly would it get?

"Hey," he said to Gato, "Let's chill for a sec. Need a down moment."

"Sure," Gato replied, looking up at the trees, at how far they reached into the sky. A sort of wonder was there in his friend's expression. As he watched Gato, Mallen felt he caught a glimpse of the ten-year-old inside the man.

Mallen smoked a cigarette before continuing. Had no goddamned idea at all what he was going to do. If there was no kid up there, he was definitely in the shit. It'd all blown up so fast for him, and so many bridges had come burning down, that he couldn't count on any help from past friends now. Had he been at his best in this? The answer came back no, that he hadn't been. He'd lost his edge. If he lived through this and didn't end up in jail, or worse, he'd have to work to get that edge back. It was the only thing that kept him a step ahead of the fuckers he seemed to be destined to chase through the dark and dirty streets.

Well, it was what it was, he thought as he took one last drag and dropped the cigarette to the ground, putting it out with his boot. Looked up at the sky. It was going to be a beautiful, but grey, day. Turned suddenly to Gato. "Hey G," he said quietly, "no matter how this whole thing falls out, thank you. I owe you more than you'll ever know."

Surprisingly, rather than blowing it off with a wave of his hand, his friend said simply, "It's been my pleasure, dude."

They then moved parallel to the long, winding driveway, keeping along the tree line. Their dark clothes worked well to keep them mostly covered. At the line where the trees stopped and the lawn began they paused. Noticed some children's toys by the sliding door that led onto the porch. Toys for a very young child. Toddler age, or so. The sudden barking of a dog startled them. Shit. *Asshole. Of course they'd have a fucking dog!* More than one, most probably. They stood stock still as a large golden retriever bounded around the far corner of the house and headed straight for them. The dog stopped a few feet away, barking its head off. The sliding door opened and a man was there. 30s. Monied. Wire-rimmed glasses, hair already thinning. Had a revolver in his right hand, but that hand was down by his side. "You're on private land," he said loudly.

"I know," Mallen replied, never taking his eyes off the dog. "I just want to talk with you. I'm Mark Mallen. Karachi is dead. Hendrix is dead. And I'm guessing you have a new addition to your family. I have Karachi's … catalog. You want to talk to me, and I want to talk to you."

"Keith?" a woman's voice came from behind him and then there she was. Younger than her husband and dressed as well as he was. "What's happening? Should I call the police?" she said to her husband.

Keith stood there, undecided. Seemed to know who Mark was. How he knew that, Mallen had no idea. Did he have *that* heavy a rep? Of course not. Someone must've told Keith about what he'd been up to. Wong? Karachi?

Mallen's phone rang then, startling everyone, including the dog. The retriever took another step toward him, growling, ears going back. Keith nodded at Mallen, let him check his phone. It was Oberon. Sent it to voicemail.

Keith called the dog to him and the dog quieted down, going to sit near its master. "The cops?" Keith asked.

"No. Not yet. We need to talk, though."

Keith put the gun in his waistband. Right out of a movie. Waved for Mallen and Gato to come inside. Lovely and rustic interior. Keith took them downstairs to his home office. Indicated for them to sit on the overstuffed leather couch. Keith sat in his office chair. Put the gun on the desk, but within reach. Mallen sat, but Gato stood by the door. He kept his eye on every move that Keith made. That seemed to make the man uncomfortable.

After a moment of silence, Keith was about to say something when a child bounded into the room, full of energy. Mallen couldn't believe it: it was Jessie. She climbed onto Keith's lap. Put her thumb in her mouth as she looked up at him. Jesus fucking Christ … here she was.

Keith had kept his eyes on Mallen the entire time. "You know who this is. I'm correct in that?"

"Yeah," he said quietly, "I know her mother. She's why I started this whole thing. I had to find her."

"And now you have."

"And now I have." He looked at the little girl. She wore overalls and a yellow t-shirt. "Looks like you've taken care of her."

Keith petted Jessie's hair. "Jessie has so much love to give. She's really incredible." His hand slowly moved to the pistol on the desk. Gato made a move for his own but Keith shook his head. He lifted up the gun and held it out to Mallen, butt first. Mallen took it. Put it near him, on the side table.

"I did that," Keith said, "so you'd understand what I'm going to say to you. So you'd know I'm being honest."

"This is where you tell me she's better off with you, rather than her mother, yeah?"

"Is that so hard to see? I've read the background on Ms. Marston. I've even seen photos of her. She's a junkie. She'll either be dead soon, or back on the street. And with a daughter? A little girl, just about preschool age?" He looked Mallen dead in the eyes then. "You know what I'm talking about. "

"That's beside the fucking point, man. Jessie deserves to be with her mother."

"I have to hand it to you, Mallen. The fact that you first noticed how Jessie was doing says a lot about you. You could've started by playing the tough street guy, but you didn't. Thank you for that."

"I care about Jessie. Always have, ever since I got involved. Look, I know what she's facing, but that doesn't make it okay for you to buy her from some bunch of street assholes looking to make a buck." Then he added quietly, "Street assholes that have all suddenly been killed. Someone is shutting it all down. Why? They're scared. If news of your ... purchase ... gets out, you'll lose her anyway."

Keith got out of the chair, putting Jessie on her feet. "Jess?" he said, "go play with mommy, okay?" Jessie smiled at him and jogged out. There was a large picture window in the room that looked out over a lush, expansive back yard. Keith went and gazed out. Kept his back to the two men as he said, "Does it have to get out, Mallen? Can't you just look the other way? I ... I have enough to make you look away. We'll sell the house. Move to another state."

Silence reigned in the room for a moment. Mallen finally said, "I don't get it. What made you do this? Get involved with such a fucked-up group of people? You were that desperate?"

A nod. Keith never stopped looking out the window. "Ginny, my wife," he told them in a quiet voice, "developed cancer. They had to take so much of her. No way we'd ever have kids, and that was all we ever wanted."

"But, man," Gato suddenly broke in, saying as he looked around the room. "You have money. *Usted es blanca y educada.* Why weren't you at the top of a bunch of adoption lists?"

Keith turned then from the window. "I have an arrest record.

White collar. I paid for my crime. Three years in prison." Looked over at his computer screen. The screensaver were rotating pictures of Jessie. Happy Jessie. Laughing Jessie. "That follows you the rest of your life."

Mallen sat there a long time. There was a lot to what Keith said. He looked around the room, remembering how the house looked like from the outside, and the land. Even if these people picked up and moved, they'd be set up just like this somewhere else. That was a given.

That was the way the world worked. But...

... Jessie wasn't their kid. He'd promised Trina.

Got to his feet. "I'm sorry, but she deserves to be with her mother, no matter what that might mean. Trina loves her daughter fiercely. She doesn't abuse her. And she's trying to make a life for the both of them. Trying hard. She needs to be with her mother. End of fucking story."

Gato took a step forward. "Bro... "

"I know," Mallen told him, "but this is right. It is," he added quietly. And suddenly, he wasn't so sure.

Keith sighed. His eyes glanced over at his gun. Probably wished he hadn't handed it over. Went to the doorway. Said loudly, "Ginny? Bring Jessie in here, please?" After a moment, Ginny came in with the little girl. Jessie looked scared now.

Mallen smiled at her. "Hi Jess. Remember me? Probably not, but I'm here to take you back to your mother."

Ginny shot a glance at Keith. He only shook his head, face ashen and sad. "Let him take her."

———

The drive back to the city was one that Mallen would remember up until the day he died. It was so surreal. Like a bad dream. He couldn't begin to reason it all out. The way life turned out sometimes amazed him. He'd found Jessie, and here he was, taking her back to Trina. He should feel on top of the fucking world, but he didn't. He felt empty and on edge. Maybe it was because of all that had gone on, but deep down he didn't believe that. It was something else.

Jessie sat in the front seat between him and Gato. She looked sad, scared, and lost. He wondered what she was sad about. Leaving her new house? Going back to her old one? She was only about five. How much did kids really know at that age? Anna seemed to know everything when she was five, but she was special: an old soul in a young body.

"Jessie?" he said quietly, "I'm just taking you back to your mother. Trina. Your mother, okay?"

Nothing. She just stared at him. No way to make her see it, of course. Fuck, she was only a little kid. Very little. "Just trust me. Okay? Just…trust me." He pulled out his phone then. Dialed the hospital. When the operator answered, he asked for Trina's room.

"I'm sorry, but she's been discharged."

"Discharged," he said.

"Yes, she checked herself out yesterday."

———

They found parking not far from Trina's building. As Mallen got out of the car, he looked up and down the street. People hanging out in doorways, or at the bus stop. People walking up and down the street, selling or buying. Even though it was daylight, they seemed like shadows moving in darkness. He looked up at the façades of the apartment buildings. They seemed like depressed ramparts, a failing wall against a tide that ebbed and flowed, a tide that seemed to climb higher every time it came in.

"Come on, honey," he told Jessie as he scooped her up off the seat and put her on his hip, "your mommy's very close now, waiting for you."

Gato locked the car doors and followed behind as the three of them went down the street to the door of the building that Trina and Jessie called home. Mallen figured that at least, if nothing else, he'd done *this*. He'd gotten Jessie home. He'd done what he'd set out to do.

They entered the building. Mallen put Jessie on her feet and took her hand. Led her up the stairs. Reached their door and knocked.

"Trina?" he said. "It's Mallen. I have a surprise for you." No answer, so he knocked again. Then again. She'd just gotten out of the hospital. Was she already out, buying drugs? That thought made him try the doorknob.

It wasn't locked and the door opened with a slight creak of the hinges. He glanced over at Gato, then down at Jessie. Gato came forward. Smiled at the little girl as he took her hand. "*Tu vida será hermosa. Tan sólo ser fuerte, joven.*"

The main room was dark. Very dark. Mallen saw that the bedroom door was half open. Motioned for Gato to stay where he was. His friend got it. Squatted down on one knee and began to whisper to Jessie about the beautiful things that existed in life. A blue sky. The clouds on a warm day. The wind in the trees. The sound of the ocean.

Mallen felt as he'd entered the apartment that there was someone there. Could just feel it. Made it to the bedroom doorway. Passed through and into the room. The air went out of him when he saw the figure on the bed. Trina. She had vomited it all out in her drugged sleep. Went over to her quietly. No pulse. Cold skin. Noticed a piece of paper and a pen near her hand. The paper was torn and crumpled, like the writer couldn't decide whether to toss it away or not. He took it. Read it . . . .

"Jesus . . . " he said to himself.

*I sold my child. For money. For drugs. She deserves better than me. Sold her to a man named Karachi. A man named Hendrix got me in contact with him. Hendrix has protection. The police protect him. Fuck the police for protecting him. Fuck god for doing this to me. Fuck me, too . . . for selling my little Jessie for money. I didn't know what else to do.*

"Oh . . . oh, Trina . . . ." Mallen spoke in a whisper. Then it came to him. The code by her name. O.U.F.M. Offered Up For Money. *Jesus . . .* He looked around the room, like looking for an answer. Put the note back, knowing immediately what he had to do. There was Trina's cell phone. He picked it up and dialed 911. When the operator came on he said, "A woman's overdosed. She's dead." Gave the address and threw the phone across the room. Hurried out.

The way Gato looked at him let him know his friend got everything. "Mommy?" Jessie said, her voice small and brittle there in the hallway. He got down on one knee, and looked at her.

"Shhhh . . . " he told her softly. "Your mommy's very tired. She's been sick. Look, Jessie . . . " But he couldn't continue. What the hell do you say? He wracked his brain frantically for an answer as he looked at her, into her innocent, uncomprehending eyes. What was the best thing to do now? Only a few minutes ago, he'd thought he knew the answer to that question. But now? Leave Jessie for them to find? That thought made his heart break and the paramedics would be here any fucking minute.

"Mallen?" Gato looked from him to Jessie, and then back at the apartment doorway. "I think moving on would be a good idea, bro."

"Jess?" Mallen said to her quietly. "Where I found you? You like it there?"

Took a moment, but then there was a nod.

"Come on, then."

———

The drive from the city was done in silence. Gato put on some music for Jessie to listen to. Classical music. Didn't make a difference to her, but Mallen had to admit that it helped him.

Made it back to Keith's house. This time they pulled to the gate.

Gato made a move to get out, but Mallen stopped him. "No, man. I'll do this one. I know where your heart lies. Thank you."

Mallen got out with Jessie, picking her up off the seat, carrying her to the intercom by the gate. She seemed totally wiped out by everything that had happened. As he pushed the call button, he realized he was very mad at Trina. Fuck yeah he was. But he could also understand. He knew desperation. Knew need. Knew the horror of not being able to feed that need. He also knew there were some things you just couldn't live with, no matter how hard you tried. They were too big, too heavy, and all you could do was pay off that chit with your life, giving back to God the life he'd given you.

The speaker next to the button filled with ambient noise, and then there was Keith's voice. "Yes?"

"It's Mallen. Get out to your gate. Now."

Silence. "Okay," came the simple reply.

There was the sound of a door opening. Then Keith appeared, coming quickly down the driveway. Stopped when he saw Jessie. Opened the gate. Stood there, looking like a man not sure he was about to experience what he felt was about to happen. Mallen came over to him. Put Jessie in his arms. She barely registered the motion she was so emotionally exhausted. Maybe she'd end up thinking it was all a bad dream. Maybe she would only remember it during a session with her therapist. Who knew? The only thing that Mallen knew at that moment was that whatever Jessie ended up remembering, at least here in this home *she had a chance*. And a chance was all any of us wanted. Knowing there was a chance at something better was what made humans go on. He also knew that putting her into the foster care system was a crapshoot, with lousy odds. And he would never forget how Keith's wife looked when Keith told her to hand Jessie over to him. She loved the kid.

Or, that's what he hoped.

"Listen to me," Mallen said to Keith as the man stood there, holding Jessie tightly, like he'd just been given back the key to the kingdom of heaven. "Her mother's gone. And she won't be back. I think this … you, are her best chance. But," and here he pulled his gun and put the muzzle right in Keith's face, "you do anything wrong to this child, I will hear about it. I'm going to follow the next fifteen years of her life, see? Until she's a legal adult, see? I'll find out everything you try to hide. I'll hear about it if you're arrested. I'll hear about it if she runs away. I'll hear about it if she gets a fuckin' cold. You read me? If you *ever* make me regret this, I will leave you where I find you. I will burn your house down. I will shatter your body and your soul, *then* I'll leave you for the dogs. I'm putting a huge amount of trust in you. More than I've ever given anyone. Ever. For your life, do not make me regret this."

There was a rumble of thunder off in the distance. Keith looked up at the sky, then back at Mallen. "You won't regret this. I swear."

Mallen turned without another word and walked back to the car. The car door closing was the final exclamation point on it all.

# THIRTY-SIX

MALLEN WAS BUSY ON his hands and knees, trying to scrub the blood from the floorboards of his home. He had to admit, even if he couldn't get the stains out, he would never move. It was too beautiful to live on the water in one of the greatest communities left on this planet.

As he scrubbed and scrubbed, he wondered again at how his life had gone ever since he'd gotten clean. Life had been very violent, bloody, and strange. He missed Dreamo, not now as a guy who'd sold him smack, but only as someone he'd known and liked and was now gone. And Bill? Maybe he would call the guy up and take him out for a beer? He smiled, almost laughing at that. *Yeah... sure.*

And how would he ever pay Oberon back? Letting Mallen slam him in the face, the cop working on pure instinct when Mallen quickly proposed the plan to send him off into the darkness so he could shadow every move Mallen made? Oberon had risked everything for him. How can one person ever pay another back for something like that? He had no idea.

The stain from Wong's blood finally began to fade as he worked. He still couldn't work up the nerve to call Chris. He was slated to see Anna in a couple Saturdays, and he had to wonder how that would go down, or if it would go down at all.

There was a knock at his door, and he tensed. Ever since he'd gotten clean, he'd been jumped and surprised at his door too many times. He went and glanced through the break in the window curtains. It was okay: it was Gato.

Mallen opened his front door and his friend entered. It had been a couple days since Mallen had last seen him. Gato looked so careworn, so empty. "What's up, man?" Mallen asked. "Is it your mother? Is she doing worse?"

Gato shook his head, and it took him some time to answer. "I have to go back to Vegas, *vato*."

"Yeah?" He knew what was coming. It was the only thing that would make his friend feel better. And he got that, one hundred percent.

"I have to go back and get Lupe. That Mike cat? I can't let him stop me, you know?"

"I know."

Gato looked down at the ground as he worked to the get the words out. "I … I need … "

" … some help," Mallen said, then went and put the sponge in the sink. Washed his hands. Went upstairs and grabbed the pistol from the office file cabinet. Full clip, with another in his pocket. Hell, Vegas wasn't far. And if anyone needed a vacation, it was this recovering junkie, ex-undercover cop.

He came down the stairs, house keys in hand, and went to the front door. Gato was all smiles and relief.

"Just let me lock the door on our way out, my friend," Mallen said as they left.

**THE END**

Photo © Dawn Vail

## ABOUT THE AUTHOR

Robert K. Lewis has been a painter, printmaker, and a produced screenwriter. He is also a contributor to Macmillan's crime fiction fansite, Criminal Element. Robert is a member of Mystery Writers of America, Sisters in Crime, the International Thriller Writers, and the Crime Writers Association. *Innocent Damage* is his third novel. Visit him online at RobertKLewis.com and at needlecity.wordpress.com. He lives with his wife in the Bay Area.

# www.MidnightInkBooks.com

From the gritty streets of New York City to sacred tombs in the Middle East, it's always midnight somewhere. Join us online at any hour for fresh new voices in mystery fiction.

At midnightinkbooks.com you'll also find our author blog, new and upcoming books, events, book club questions, excerpts, mystery resources, and more.

## MIDNIGHT INK ORDERING INFORMATION

### Order Online:
- Visit our website www.midnightinkbooks.com, select your books, and order them on our secure server.

### Order by Phone:
- Call toll-free within the U.S. and Canada at 1-888-NITE-INK (1-888-648-3465)
- We accept VISA, MasterCard, and American Express

### Order by Mail:
Send the full price of your order (MN residents add 6.5% sales tax) in U.S. funds, plus postage & handling to:

> Midnight Ink
> 2143 Wooddale Drive
> Woodbury, MN 55125-2989

### Postage & Handling:

Standard (U.S. & Canada). If your order is:
> $24.99 and under, add $3.00
> $25.00 and over, FREE STANDARD SHIPPING

AK, HI, PR: $15.00 for one book plus $1.00 for each additional book.

International Orders (airmail only):
> $16.00 for one book plus $3.00 for each additional book

Orders are processed within 12 business days. Please allow for normal shipping time. Postage and handling rates subject to change.

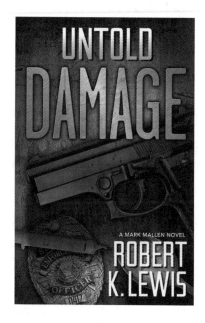

# Untold Damage
### Robert K. Lewis

Estranged from his wife and daughter, former undercover cop Mark Mallen has spent the last four years in a haze of heroin. When his best friend from the academy, Eric Russ, is murdered, an address found in his pocket points to Mallen as the prime suspect.

As the police turn up the heat and Russ's survivors ask him to come up with some answers, Mallen sets out to serve justice to the real killer. But first, he'll have to get clean and face the low-life thugs who want him dead. Surviving drive-by shootings and beat downs, Mallen discovers the motives behind a string of vengeful murders. But turning a life around is hard work for a junkie. Bruised, alone, and written off by nearly everyone, can Mallen keep clean and get back into his daughter's life?

**978-0-7387-3576-4**                                    **$14.99**

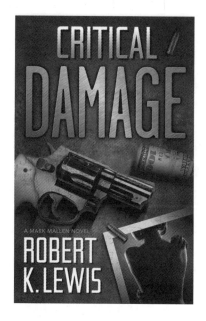

# CRITICAL DAMAGE

A MARK MALLEN NOVEL

## ROBERT K. LEWIS

# Critical Damage
## ROBERT K. LEWIS

When ex-cop and recovering junkie Mark Mallen is asked to track down two very different girls who have gone missing, he doesn't think twice about putting himself in harm's way to find them. Bloodied and bruised, Mallen shakes down the pimps and hustlers who could crack the cases wide open, leaving no stone unturned in San Francisco's criminal underground.

But something isn't right. Somebody's trying to scare Mallen off, and it's no ordinary street thug. With heat coming at him from all angles, Mallen's search for the truth leads him to men who will stop at nothing to make sure their twisted desires never see the light of day.

978-0-7387-3623-5                                    **$14.99**